The Darkness Within

By Alanna Knight

a&b

The Darkness Within

An Inspector Faro and Rose McQuinn Mystery

ALANNA KNIGHT

Allison & Busby Limited
12 Fitzroy Mews
London W1T 6DW
allisonandbusby.com

First published in Great Britain by Allison & Busby in 2017.
This paperback edition published by Allison & Busby in 2017.

A CIP catalogue record for this book is available from
the British Library.

10 9 8 7 6 5 4 3 2 1

ISBN 978-0-7490-2142-9

Typeset in 10.5/15.5 pt Sabon by
Allison & Busby Ltd.

The paper used for this Allison & Busby publication
has been produced from trees that have been legally sourced
from well-managed and credibly certified forests.

Printed and bound by
CPI Group (UK) Ltd, Croydon, CR0 4YY

For Sheena and Allan

CHAPTER ONE

Orkney 1906

Three mourning women, black statues against a heavy grey sky; seagulls screaming above their heads turned them into a monochrome, the prologue to a Greek tragedy.

Faro shuddered as the Stromness ferry touched the landing stage and as he leapt ashore the three statues became alive rushing down to welcome him, led by his two daughters Emily and Rose, followed a little slower by his mother, Mary Faro. The next moment he had gathered his girls into his arms, Emily the bereaved widow, murmuring his condolences suddenly changed into inadequate words.

'My dear, you must forgive me for not getting here in time. We had just got back from France and I'm afraid any kind of news takes a while to reach Carasheen. Ireland is like that,' he ended lamely.

Emily merely shook her head. The funeral was a week past and already seemed a long time ago, unreal, a kind of brutal nightmare from which there was no awakening. 'No need for apologies, Pa. Erland would have understood – always travelling, he knew how difficult it was to get in touch with us.'

'Imogen feels badly about it, too,' Faro added awkwardly and Emily nodded in weary acknowledgement, leaving him more embarrassed than ever, never quite sure about how his family regarded Imogen Crowe, officially recognised as his travelling companion but everyone knew she was much more than that.

He kissed Emily's cold cheek, guiltily aware that he had lost touch with his younger daughter after her marriage in Orkney. Now her husband's untimely death had turned her into more of a stranger than ever. Even her looks had always been at variance with the Faros, with her long, straight black hair, round eyes in a face always pale, now stricken in grief. A throwback, she was, whispers ran, the image of Sibella, that scandalous selkie great-grandmother who had lived to be well past a hundred.

Rose was waiting for him, eagerly holding out her arms. Rose, his firstborn and dearest, so like his beloved long-lost Lizzie, the daughter always close to him who had followed in his footsteps.

'Let me look at you.' The passing years had been kind to Rose. Past forty she still looked young and petite with that cloud of yellow curls. 'You look well.'

She smiled. 'You too, Pa.' He didn't look seventy, this Orcadian-born policeman. The Viking warrior image was undimmed: thick fair hair, now white, the deep blue eyes, which she had once imagined would force the truth out of any criminal, because they seemed to look right through you, deep down into your very soul.

His mother, Mary Faro, watched the tableau, keeping a little distance apart, letting them give rein to their emotions, her main concern as always her only son, her beloved Jeremy, proud of him in his days as chief inspector in the Edinburgh Police Force, hoping and praying that retirement would bring him home again. But that had not happened; Jeremy had spread his wings to wider shores. Long a widower, she had brought up his two girls in Orkney always expecting – and even resenting, she had to admit – that he might remarry. Now he had this Irishwoman, the writer Imogen Crowe, famous they said she was, and him going all over the world with her.

He came to her, smiling sadly, and hugged her. 'So sad, Ma, but you're bearing up well – as always, you can be relied on.'

Her reply was lost in the noise of a shining motor car approaching down the road and braking alongside.

'That's ours, Pa,' said Emily at her father's look of surprise. She sighed. 'Erland was so proud of it. Bought it only last year just when we were getting used to having the new motor bus between Kirkwall and Hopescarth, not that Gran would have anything to do with either.'

The driver was accompanied by a ten-year-old boy, tall for his age, fair, strong-looking. He leapt down and she put an arm around him.

'Magnus, this is your grandfather.' As they shook hands, Mary Faro came forward, beamed approval.

'The very spit of you at his age, Jeremy,' she said proudly. 'The same island stock. He'll make a fine man in a year or two.'

Magnus took his hand, a firm steady grip, a slight bow and a shrewd glance from eyes dark blue like his own.

'Glad to meet you, sir. I have heard so much about you.'

As they walked towards the car, huffing and breathing a quantity of smoke as it waited, Rose came to his side and took his arm.

'So good to see you, Pa,' she sighed. 'Two years is a long time.'

'Too long, far too long.' And guiltily Faro remembered that the last had been a very fleeting visit to Edinburgh, a pattern throughout the years of his retirement and his travels with Imogen, communication interspersed by the new craze for picture postcards, a blessed relief for those like himself who found writing letters burdensome.

'Could have been a happier occasion, lass,' he said. 'Poor Emily.'

Rose nodded sadly. 'Jack and I were shocked, a funeral when we should have all been meeting here to celebrate her fortieth birthday on Lammastide, the birthday she shared with Sibella, the very day it happened. I still can't take it in, that Erland is dead.' Looking up sad-eyed, she shook her head. 'The most beautiful voice I ever heard, stilled for ever.'

'I am sorry I couldn't be here with you. Just couldn't book a passage to Orkney in time.' He sighed. 'I never knew him, never got the chance,' he added, too late now for the son-in-law he had only met when the cruise ship on which he and Imogen were travelling docked overnight in Kirkwall. A hasty meeting had been arranged, dinner at the local hotel, a return journey down to Stromness and Hopescarth impossible.

'Magnus was just a baby, hadn't even started school and just look at him now,' Faro smiled, watching the others heading towards the motor car. 'A fine young fellow. And how is your wee girl?' Meg was Rose's stepdaughter, the child of Jack Macmerry's first brief marriage.

'She's fine, getting along very well with Magnus, her new-found cousin, as she calls him. I'm pleased – and relieved. I was rather anxious about this first meeting, and boys tend to despise girls at his age. But not Magnus, he's very protective and kind. Seems to enjoy her company.'

'Where's Jack?' Faro asked.

Rose giggled and pointed to the driver. Behind helmet and goggles, he recognised Rose's husband, now Chief Inspector Jack Macmerry of the Edinburgh Police.

As they greeted each other with a warm handshake, Jack grinned. 'You're up here, Pa, beside the driver.' Before assisting the women and Magnus into the four seats at the back, there would be a slight delay. Mary Faro, as housekeeper at Yesnaby House, took the opportunity of 'gathering a few things from the shops'. Waiting for her return with Rose, Faro realised that a lot of things had changed in the last decade, progress had overtaken the island as Jack, patting the steering wheel, asked proudly:

'Well, what do you think of her? Hammer Tourer, 24 horse power, 4-cylinder. And virtually brand new. Isn't she just great?'

Faro nodded vaguely. With not the faintest notion about defining the merits of one motor car from another, he gratefully regarded this new species of transport, like the railway trains, an increasingly popular and painless method of travel.

'They only provided horses, for the lucky – or the

unlucky few, depending on how you cared for riding – in my day,' he said.

Jack laughed. 'They only provide motor cars for the lucky few now, provided that they are brave enough to learn to drive. I enjoy being behind the wheel and this was a rare opportunity, albeit a sad one, a chance to visit Orkney and bring Meg with us. She was quite determined, although it meant leaving Thane behind.'

Thane? Faro frowned. Oh yes, he remembered Thane was Rose's deerhound. With her vivid imagination she tried to persuade everyone, himself included, that this mysterious animal had supernatural powers, that a kind of telepathy existed between them.

Nonsense, of course. He'd seen this Thane on an Edinburgh visit to Rose and Jack, and he seemed quite an ordinary likeable, well-behaved but exceedingly large dog, the size of a pony and more fitted to a stable stall than house room.

'Just a short break to attend the funeral,' Jack was saying, watching out for the two women coming back with their purchases. 'You know what it's like, sir.'

'I do indeed.'

'Of course, Rose has her own life in Edinburgh, too. She's a very busy lady. Who would have thought that it ran in the family – must have got it from you.' Jack's laugh sounded slightly disapproving. More than ten years ago, Rose had returned from Arizona, widowed, believing that her husband, once his sergeant, Danny McQuinn, was dead. Against all the odds, she had set up very successfully as a lady investigator in Edinburgh.

Jack went on: 'We have a housekeeper now, needed

someone to look after Meg. Both of us are so actively involved, we haven't much time left for domesticity.' Jumping down, he saw the women with their baskets into the back seats. 'Everyone settled now? Off we go.'

Mary Faro leant over and asked: 'Where's Imogen, Jeremy? Thought she'd be with you.'

Over the noise of the engine starting up, he shouted the delay in communication, apologised for missing the funeral and added, 'She decided to go home to Carasheen.'

Mary frowned, a little disappointed, as he continued: 'But she wouldn't have come anyway. This is a family matter, you know,' he added gently. Imogen Crowe did not regard herself as part of the family, although everyone guessed she was, in Scottish parlance, his wife 'by habit and repute'. Only from choice, as Jeremy Faro would have added hastily in his own words: he would gladly put the wedding ring on her finger before the priest if she'd just name the day.

Once the motor car got somewhat noisily under way, conversation was impossible and he realised he had never travelled far beyond Kirkwall in his young days, when even a trip to Stromness was regarded in awe as a hazardous adventure, not to be undertaken lightly, and spoken of solemnly in the same hushed tones as voyaging across the Atlantic to America.

It was that same Atlantic he now regarded beating its great heart in wild waves breaking on the rocks far below. A new experience after that brief meeting with Erland and Emily from the cruise ship in Kirkwall. Now he saw that memory had painted a false picture of homecoming. He was unprepared for the emptiness, wild and bleak, the glimpses of

13

a harsh seascape, for this was a land whose waiting was not measured in passing centuries but in that darker millennia beyond the ken of God-fearing, worshipping Christians.

This was an inhabited land long before the saints were born in Ireland. 'The isles at the world's end' mariners called them, to be feared as the home of wreckers and the legendary seal people as well as mermaids and trolls. Seeing distant Skailholm had reminded him that here and there man had been bold, and turning a blind eye on the vagaries of an unreliable climate ready to spit in the face of humans' work, they had planted stone houses perched uneasily as summer flies on hillsides and a boulder-strewn terrain, intercepted by death-dealing bogland and stretching away to limitless horizons.

And here he was now, a descendant of those distant settlers, heading towards Emily's home at Yesnaby House in Erland's motor car. In the front seat beside Jack, a noisy engine limited conversation with the three Faro women and young Magnus crowded into the back, giving him plenty of time to enjoy – or perhaps a more apt word was to endure – the passing scenery.

The sea road was rough and dangerously narrow, running in many places close to the cliff edge and requiring care and skilful attention from the driver. It was not for a nervous passenger. Faro was glad that he had no fear of heights, watching the translucent, wild-green Atlantic rollers crash on to the long stretches of pale gold sand. Beyond the violation of the peaceful strand their progress was interrupted by small irregular shapes of islands, like basking whales, impossible to imagine as being large enough for human habitation.

A signpost loomed into view pointing landwards.

Lobster creels and fishing nets, narrow steps cut out of the cliff rock down to the shore, the glimpse of a single street of stone houses huddled together as if to get the most out of the warmth of a rare burst of sunshine.

Oddly it awoke memories of a boyhood visit to Stromness, swimming in the sea and lying afterwards in the sheltering warmth of dunes, eyeing through the swaying tall fronds of marram grass the bluest of summer skies and serenaded by the joyous chorus of unseen skylarks. That shaft of pure joy was his first true happiness. Memory, though distant, threw in a shadowy companion.

He was not alone; there was someone lying at his side. It was Inga, Inga St Ola, his first love, long before his marriage to Lizzie. Sadly brief, she had given him Rose and Emily and died with the birth of their stillborn son.

He sighed. It was all a long time ago; the years moved relentlessly and seventy belonged in a different world to seventeen, with all the joyous rapture of youth gone for ever. His nostalgia vanished with Jack's shout:

'Almost there, sir!'

They were now on the twisting sea road to Hopescarth, followed far below by dark round shapes bobbing up and down in the sea. Seals, and Faro remembered their curiosity, keeping pace with human travellers at a safe distance. He wondered how they saw these new arrivals, having observed through past ages two-legged creatures who walked on land that were now being replaced by huge black monsters who travelled on wheels. What on earth was the planet coming to?

Following Jack's pointing finger he saw Hopescarth for the first time. Not that there was much more than could be taken in with one glance. A dozen grey stone houses, all identical and staring into each other's windows across a long winding street. At one end a stern square block of a building with two entrance lintels carved 'Boys' and 'Girls' indicated the village school, although Faro wondered why they took the trouble to segregate such a small number. The remainder of Hopescarth was hidden behind high walls concealing a couple of better built houses, he guessed for doctor and minister as the steeple of the church rose alongside a railed-in kirkyard where crowded gravestones of vanished generations told of more currently dead than alive in the village.

Jack slowed down respectfully as they drove past, close by the Yesnaby vault where Erland had been laid to rest. A steep hill, the motor car snorting at this effort, and there facing west into the drama of the Atlantic was Yesnaby House.

Jack grinned at him and mouthed, 'Home at last.'

Faro was disappointed. The Yesnabys were an ancient and, from all accounts, a wealthy family. The houses of their equivalent in Edinburgh were fashionably designed to resemble mini Balmoral castles, but this solid-looking square house squatting on a hillside lacked any architectural frills. In Orkney, weather dictated fashion, turning its face firmly against exterior ornamentation, a waste of time and money soon to succumb to fierce winds and winter storms. Here survival was the paramount issue and in that nothing had changed in a thousand years, when it had been enemies such as the Vikings on marauding raids that threatened. Their other enemy, the fierce climate, remained, a constant siege to be faced with solid stone walls, deep-set windows and sturdy strong doors turned away from the sea.

They were crossing a stone bridge leading up to the house and Jack drove carefully, for, below, the ground dropped sharply across a stretch of bright-green grass. Bogland, to remind new generations that once upon a time the building on the skyline had been a fortress against invaders from the sea.

A brisk wind had arisen; the horizons darkened with a flurry of rain. What would it be like in a storm? Faro wondered. The house must have endured many, for even at this distance at first glance it had the air of the ancient pele tower, which had been its origin.

A tower with a sense of waiting, he thought, windows like brooding eyes. Just a mite sinister, a building that had lived through much, shaped and reshaped by the passing centuries, and holding itself in readiness, preparing for the next catastrophe.

Catastrophe? Why catastrophe, why that word?

Jack stopped as close to the front door as he could. Rose, Emily and Magnus went ahead with Faro and his mother at their heels.

A warm day to welcome him; it was summer, after all. But nevertheless, he shivered, wishing he could obliterate that first sight of those three women on the skyline he had first encountered, the seabirds screaming . . . the sense of something bad.

An omen.

CHAPTER TWO

Rose had found the drive frustrating, longing to sit beside her father, to be close to him in that front seat where only the back of his and Jack's heads were visible. Sighing, she realised that she was still a little girl where he was concerned. Afraid that the passing years would take their toll and that an old man might have overtaken her adored strong father, she was delighted that the years were being kind to him. Proud to note that he remained a handsome man of seventy who still walked tall. The Viking image everyone associated with him, the once fair hair was still plentiful, those deep-blue eyes had lost nothing of the piercing quality of youth.

Apart from shouted comments, with conversation impossible as the motor car had noised its way over the hazardous uneven cliff road, Rose's thoughts drifted back to Emily's urgent summons, the sickening news of Erland's unexpected death, the frantic haste of their sailing from Edinburgh to Orkney in time for the funeral. She took her sister's hand exchanging a sad smile, for Emily had resolutely decided that grief must be set aside and that she must find consolation and comfort in the joy of this unexpected family meeting, especially of seeing her father again.

Nearing Hopescarth was already reviving Rose's memories of that visit ten years ago, especially the village of Skailholm, perched so perilously above the shore. Her bicycle had a puncture and she had been given a lift in a motor car. A more settled day than this, the sky blue to the horizon occupied by a few lazy drifting cumulus clouds, that the schoolteacher in Kirkwall reading Bible stories solemnly would tell the children who asked about where heaven was, that these were angels' pillows.

Jack stopped after a particularly sharp bend, stepping down briefly to look at the engine, and in that short silence she heard the skylarks, tiny dots soaring into the blue. And that brought another childhood memory.

Touching Magnus sitting opposite, she pointed and said: 'Skylarks.'

He grinned. 'We all call them Our Lady's hens.'

Rose laughed as the motor car restarted. 'So did we!'

'Almost there!' Jack's shout as they approached the stone bridge to Yesnaby House brought another flood of memories. Her last visit, the archaeologists at work, the mystery of the peat bog burial and its dire solution. Then there was Erland's amazing garden, so lush and fertile in this otherwise barren wilderness with all its secrets.

As Jack helped his passengers to alight, it was a relief for Rose. Travelling by motor car was novel, much speedier than any bicycle, but she still preferred the exhilaration of fresh air and the feeling of well-being rather than sitting still in the back of noisy machines with cramped muscles after a few miles.

The door opened and Meg rushed out, straight into her father's arms, as if they had been parted for years rather than hours, Rose thought wryly, remembering how much Meg had wanted to come on the car journey, disappointed and cross that there wasn't room in the motor car for her to meet her new grandfather off the ferry. That wasn't the only reason. She had a bad head cold and had been off school for a few days in Edinburgh. As she was just recovering, her father had insisted that sitting in the back of an open motor car with the more than likely probability of rain would be bad for her.

Now settled firmly back again on the ground by Jack, Meg shyly turned to Magnus, smiling as he introduced her to Faro: 'This is our grandfather, Meg.'

With handshakes and hugs exchanged, Mary Faro bustled towards the kitchen while Rose and Emily went upstairs to remove their black veils.

Faro was surprised to discover that, viewed from outside, this was a very ordinary house built in the traditional Orkney style, but once inside it was much larger, much grander. Through the front door, he walked across a marble tiled floor and ignoring the grand oak staircase sweeping upwards, he followed his mother down a corridor that emerged into a large kitchen, the domain of Mary Faro, which could have accommodated the whole of her tiny Kirkwall cottage where he had grown up. Indeed, this was a house with authority, stated and confirmed by the portraits of Erland's ancestors staring sternly down from the walls, while outside, far below, were the remains of mysterious crumbling stone walls that went nowhere, hinting that this was not the first habitation to stand on top of the hill, a watchtower to the sea at the ready for invaders.

Upstairs, this was the first chance for Rose to talk about Faro with the sister who had seen him even less frequently in Orkney than she had in Edinburgh.

'He has always looked young for his age,' said Emily, 'and don't you remember we dreaded what it would be like if he married someone else?' They had both been children then, when their mother died in childbirth, with a late baby, the son she had longed to give to Faro but who went into the grave with her.

Rose laughed. 'Too many wicked stepmothers in fairy tales.' Older, they hoped that he would marry again, and had suspicions that such a handsome man must have had many fleeting romances over the years.

'Do you ever hear anything of Inga?' Rose asked. Orkney recalled memories of a visit long ago when there had obviously been something between her father and Inga St Ola.

Emily shook her head. 'No. According to Gran, she left Kirkwall years ago for a job on the mainland.' She didn't add that Mary Faro was thankful to see the back of this woman who she had never liked, fearing that she would ensnare her beloved Jeremy into marrying her. Inga had been his first love, but her name was never mentioned.

'Any news of Imogen?' Emily added.

Rose laughed. 'We all had great hopes there, didn't we?

21

Ten years or more, and Imogen Crowe, the famous lady writer from Ireland as our stepmother!'

'Yes, we were thrilled at the prospect, but no, the impediment to their wedding, I gather, is that Imogen is a dedicated suffragette who doesn't believe in marriage.' Emily leant across the table and nodded. 'Perhaps their relationship is everything except being churched, if you get my meaning.'

'A Scots' marriage by habit and repute, we call it.'

'Oh yes,' said Emily. 'Sounds so simple – just grab a couple of witnesses and say you are man and wife. Then if you get fed up in a year or two, no binding vows, you just say goodbye and go your own ways.' A deep sigh remembered what she had just lost. She shook her head and Rose stretched out a hand, held Emily's firmly as she went on: 'Would never have done for me, Rose. I wanted it all legal, with a home and children – and so did Erland,' she ended sadly.

Rose put an arm about her shoulders as she went on: 'I still can't believe that I will never be with him again, never have his head on the pillow beside me when I wake in the mornings. Oh Rose, he was my husband and like a father too. Now a light has gone out for ever.'

'At least you have Magnus, something of Erland's.'

'Thank God for our dear lad. Poor Erland, we thought we were to be childless and then Magnus came along.' She sighed. 'We wanted more but it never happened. Strange, isn't it, the way the Faro women seem to be doomed to one child only.'

'I didn't even get to keep my wee boy.'

22

'Oh, Rose, I'm so sorry – I didn't mean—'

Rose squeezed her hand. 'Of course you didn't.' And Emily remembered the letter she had when Rose returned to Edinburgh after Danny disappeared and the baby he never saw died of a fever in the Indian reservation, and how Rose, sick almost to dying herself, dug his grave in the Arizona desert.

Rose was silent too, remembering, and Emily said: 'Do you think it's the St Ringan curse put upon us for some long-forgotten misdemeanour?'

'That's what superstitious Orcadians still believe. I hope it's just a coincidence – at least that is what Pa would insist.'

Their solemn moment was interrupted by sounds of childish mirth from the next room.

Emily smiled. 'At least you have Meg now.'

'And she's like the daughter I never had.'

'You have Jack, and he is so good, I do like him – he's solid and reliable. Such a good husband, just like Erland.'

Rose thought for a moment before asking: 'What will you do now, Em?'

Her sister shrugged. 'I haven't had time yet for it to sink in properly. It was all so sudden, so unexpected. We never made plans for the future for ourselves.' Her voice broke and she dabbed her eyes, then straightening her shoulders again, she went on. 'I love this house and living in Hopescarth but I don't think Magnus and I can stay here without him. Magnus is a clever lad, doing so well, and the school in Stromness is reportedly very good, but Erland always intended that he should go to university and that meant Edinburgh, as he did himself. Travelling back and forth to the mainland would have been nothing to Erland. He was always on the move, across to Bergen or to the Continent, mostly taking Sven with him. I don't know what will become of Sven now . . .'

'Tell me about Sven,' Rose said. The tall, fair young man with outstanding good looks she had first seen as a pall-bearer at Erland's funeral was part of the Yesnaby household.

Emily shrugged. 'What do we know about him? Only what we were told. Erland always had close business connections with Norway, trading links and so forth – I was never sure exactly what – but when he met up with Sven, a couple of years ago, he brought him back and proceeded to treat him like one of the family, as he had none of his own in Bergen. He had been adopted. Said having him around was a great business asset, especially as Erland, bless him, who was so good at everything, was hopeless at speaking any other language.'

Rose found that strange, considering his beautiful voice, as Emily went on: 'So having Sven as a fluent speaker with Norwegian his native tongue, was invaluable.' But the way she said it and her frown suggested to Rose that her sister had not always approved of this newcomer.

'Erland had many contacts over there and even took Sven to see the royal coronation at Trondheim earlier this summer.'

'How exciting. Didn't you want to go with them?'

Emily shook her head. 'Not really. It would have been quite a voyage and I didn't want to leave Magnus. He couldn't have come with us,' she added and Rose suspected that she hadn't been happy at being left behind. She said, 'I'm a terrible sailor. So that's where our said selkie connection falls short.'

Rose looked at her. 'Possibly,' she said. 'But as you know, Sibella couldn't swim and hated the water. Strange as it seems, if the story was true, maybe she was scared, going into the water, that the sea would reclaim her, take her back to . . . to that previous life, before she was old and tired and ready to go.'

'Anyway,' said Emily, 'about the coronation. As I expect you know, Queen Maud is the youngest daughter of our king, so there were quite a number of British people there and by all accounts, some very elegant receptions.'

'I wonder how you could have resisted it.'

Emily shook her head, said again, 'No, Rose. I'm a home bird, never like leaving the nest. I'd have had to dress up, buy travelling clothes, a wildly expensive wardrobe that I would never have occasion to wear again.' She groaned. 'And all that corseting! Being tightly laced up every day like an hourglass is an absurd fashion. I'm glad I never have to bother about such things here, I can just wear whatever I like.'

That was something they had in common. Rose had never followed fashion and refused the 'S' shape of bosom and bustle considered de rigueur among Edinburgh ladies.

'And there's always been Gran – she relied on me,' Emily continued and Rose said: 'Now, that's just an excuse, Em. She had a perfectly good life in Kirkwall; a strong healthy woman, she would never have wanted you to waste your life looking after her. For goodness' sake, her ambition was that we should get married, and practically as soon as we left school she was constantly on the lookout for suitable husbands.'

'That may be so, but she was horrified, I can tell you now, when you went off to America to marry Danny McQuinn.'

'I think that was more concern about going to the ends of the earth, as she would call it, to live among savages than an unsuitable husband.' Rose paused. 'How did you persuade her to move to Yesnaby when you married Erland?'

'Oh, he did that. He thought after our early years – you know, the miscarriages before Magnus – that I was a bit frail and that she should come to us, especially when he was away so much, and that I needed help with a baby to look after.'

They were seated by the big window overlooking the sunken garden with its ancient wall, all that remained of the original medieval tower, and Emily looked down at Sven, who was also the gardener, busy, head down, trowel in hand. 'Sven has been such a treasure and I am glad he is happy with us. Not married, he has no other responsibilities, although I did wonder when he enjoyed the coronation experience so much that he might have decided it was time to go back home.' She smiled wryly. 'Especially as Erland said the girls in Norway fell over themselves to meet him.'

'He's quite a stunner,' Rose said. 'I should think he has lots of chances here too. Seems odd to me that he's managed to escape the matrimonial net.'

Emily nodded. 'He's young enough still, of course, but

thirty is considered quite old up here. Most men his age have young families by now. But all he seems to want is the garden here by day and the lobster fishing. He takes the boat out every night and collects the creels, takes them into Stromness and puts them on the motor bus to be delivered to a dealer from Kirkwall to sell. In a good season it makes a reasonable income for him, and Erland always let him keep the proceeds. There was a limit to the lobster we could eat and I hated the business of cooking them.' She thought for a moment. 'He never intrudes on us, you know; when his day's work is done he goes back home to his cottage, rarely ever stays for a meal.'

'Does he cook for himself, then?'

Emily shrugged. 'I imagine so. I gather he has a woman from Hopescarth looks in to clean and do his laundry. Erland gave him the cottage rent-free and a few pounds each month. He has asked me if that arrangement can continue and said that he didn't need much money as he is a man of simple taste.'

And a bit of an enigma, thought Rose, who would have liked to take the top off that handsome head and look inside. What was he really like? she wondered. His hermit-like existence seemed all wrong somehow for this good-looking Norwegian living alone in that cottage on the estate, isolated from the community at Hopescarth and people of his own age.

There was a pause and Rose felt her sister had more to say about Sven but her concern was what was to happen in the immediate future.

'If Magnus and I can't manage here, perhaps it would

be best if we moved to Edinburgh. The idea appeals as it would be quite a novelty after living here most of my life. Ever since Mama died all those years ago and Gran took us on, I've hardly ever set foot on the mainland for years—'

'You could come and live with us in Solomon's Tower, there is plenty of room, Em,' Rose replied eagerly, delighted at the prospect.

'I must stay here for Gran, although I sometimes have a feeling that she misses Kirkwall and would be happy to go back to her cottage. She must be past ninety, although she'll never tell any of us her age. And she's getting frail, too frail to manage a house as big as this with all its stairs and corridors and empty rooms. She wouldn't give in until she had a nasty fall and hurt her leg. Erland insisted then that we should have a younger housekeeper.' She gave a wry smile. 'You could have heard her indignant protests in Stromness.'

Rose said, 'Well, I know one thing. She wouldn't be happy coming to Edinburgh. It has never been her favourite place. She's hated it since all those years ago our policeman grandpa, the one your Magnus is named after, was killed in a traffic accident when Pa was just a wee lad. And now, she doesn't even have the lure of Pa living there. He has always meant more to her than either of us.'

Emily looked at her. 'Do Imogen and he have any permanent home these days?'

'They have a house in Dublin, more convenient for ships and the like than Carasheen tucked away in Kerry.'

'What about London or Edinburgh?'

Rose shook her head 'Alas, no. You know Imogen was

regarded as an Irish terrorist in the United Kingdom police records until fairly recently, when the King granted her a Royal pardon for a miscarriage of justice in his mother's reign.'

'I remember. She was just fifteen when her uncle brought her to London and planned to assassinate the Queen. When he died they kept her in prison, didn't they?'

Rose nodded, 'They couldn't prove anything against her and she was sent home to Ireland. This was thirty years ago, but police records have long memories. There is always trouble in Ireland and it wasn't helped that Imogen never made a secret of being known to the British government as a dangerous Irish nationalist.'

'Nor do they look kindly on suffragettes.'

Rose laughed. 'As are so many women of our generation, myself included. Anyway, Imo is no longer an exile threatened with prison every time she sets foot on British soil.'

'That must be such a relief, especially to Pa, knowing they can both visit us. Whatever folks say about Bertie's morals, I think we have a good king.'

'And I for one am prepared to forgive him everything for clearing Imogen's name.' She was about to tell Emily that she had met him briefly in Edinburgh with their stepbrother, Vince, then junior physician to the Royal household and again on holiday in Balmoral last year, but their conversation was brought to an abrupt end.

Mary Faro bustled in and stood over them. 'I'm needing help with setting the table downstairs if we are ever going to get something to eat. Your husband, Rose, is in need of a good meal, and we have beds to prepare since that Millie didn't

29

come in this morning. Fine housekeeper she is, I must say.'

'What is it this time?' Emily asked.

'Just problems with that daft lad of hers. Goes missing from time to time.'

'Is it serious?' Rose asked.

Mary shrugged. 'I'm just saying he isn't all there, wanders off and sees things. Dr Randall says he has the "doonfa" sickness.' She paused and added darkly, 'There was that business with Sibella.'

'Sibella? What was that?'

Rose was intrigued at the hint of a mystery. But she would have to wait for an answer as Jack came in, wearing an expression she recognised. It meant something vital and urgent.

CHAPTER THREE

'Where's my clean shirt?' Jack demanded. 'Does it need ironing?'

With a sigh of relief that this was just another of Jack's domestic crises, Rose took it down from the rack and handed it to him solemnly.

He kissed her and smiled. 'Have to go, love, as soon as I can get a ship to Aberdeen. Leith would be even better. I wish I could stay.'

Mary said shortly: 'Surely even detectives get a summer holiday. It's a disgrace, that's what it is. No respect for a family funeral, insisting you go back to work.'

Jack shrugged. It was pointless arguing with his grandmother-in-law.

'I'll help you pack,' said Rose. As they left she saw that look of yearning on her sister's face and realised how many times Emily must have said those same words to Erland.

Upstairs in their bedroom, Jack didn't really need help

to pack, but it was one of the housewifely duties Rose enjoyed, making sure shirts were carefully folded and ready to wear as he had a tendency to push things into a case rather haphazardly and then grumble about the creases.

Removing clothes from the wardrobe, with Jack whistling rather tunelessly as he stared out of the window watching the two children playing tennis on the lawn below, he looked happy.

'She's getting along fine with Magnus and without Thane.'

Rose said, 'I have to admit I was dreading it.'

Jack laughed. 'That's a moment I'll never forget. Back home, the kitchen door opening and this enormous dog rushing towards her as if he was ready to swallow the wee girl, in one gulp. I expected tears and screams of terror but she sat there smiling, calm as you like, reached up and put her arms around his neck.'

'She was delighted. He was hers from that moment.'

Jack shook his head. 'Weird it was, almost as if she had been expecting him. And the family was complete. We were all happy.'

Rose kissed him, glad to be past forty, settled and happy, content with a husband and a little girl after the strangeness of her early life: how at twenty, against all advice, she had left a teaching post in Glasgow to follow Danny McQuinn out to Arizona where he was working for Pinkerton's Detective Agency, determined against all odds to marry the man she had loved since she was eleven years old.

Emily, however, had been content to remain with her grandmother in Kirkwall before moving to Hopescarth to be Erland's housekeeper at Yesnaby House, and when his wife died, he asked her to marry him. Emily could hardly believe her good fortune. Although he was some years older, she had never been in love, never had a man in her life and Erland, childless, wanted children. So did she and they were almost desperate after several miscarriages. Then at last Magnus was born, strong and healthy, fated to be their only child.

As for Rose, her second marriage to Jack Macmerry seemed doomed to be childless. Now she was thankful and heartily glad to have Meg, a stepdaughter she loved and could not have treasured more had she brought her into the world.

The bond was shared by Meg, who regarded Rose not only as her mother but as a confidante with whom she could share her joys and her sorrows. And Thane, Thane was hers. From the moment she had set foot in Solomon's Tower as a three-year-old, the great deerhound seemed to recognise her as a kind of soulmate. A strange affinity sprang up between them, the same he and Rose had shared from their first meeting, and utterly devoted to Thane, Meg refused to do anything, go anywhere unless he came too. This devotion had its drawbacks. He could hardly come over to Orkney with them, although Meg was adept at ignoring obvious difficulties of transporting not a small lapdog but one the size of a pony and much larger than herself.

It was a difficult and not infrequent argument and one that Rose was used to. Meg was determined. She would not move without Thane, but Meg loved visiting new places and this time desperately wanted to see Orkney. It sounded quite magical to her and as one without any siblings, or indeed any relations apart from much-loved Macmerry grandparents in Peebles, there was a new cousin to meet – Rose hadn't the heart to tell her that Magnus Yesnaby was not blood kin – and there were fascinating, exciting stories too about a great-great-grandmother who was a selkie.

A compromise was reached: Thane would stay in Edinburgh at home in Solomon's Tower, but he would be well-cared-for by Sadie Brook, part-time housekeeper, who moved in and looked after Meg when the master (Mr Jack) was away on police business and the mistress (Mrs Rose) was heavily involved in her work as lady investigator. By an interesting coincidence, Sadie's Aunty Brook had been Faro's housekeeper in Sheridan Place. Not that Thane needed looking after: he was quite capable of taking care of himself by hunting for rabbits and small animals as did normal dogs on Arthur's Seat, his mysterious home long before he 'adopted' Rose McQuinn.

Voices downstairs. Mary and Emily were laughing about something with the two children. How strange life was, Rose thought. Here she was with Jack, a policeman who faced violence and even death each day of his life chasing evil criminals. And there was Emily, whose husband, when he wasn't travelling, lived a peaceful, tranquil life; an elderly, yet strong, healthy man who, while sitting at home in his own beloved garden and in the warm sunshine of a summer afternoon, closed his eyes and died.

Jack put his arm around her. 'Thanks for your help. Don't know what I would do without you,' he grinned. 'Our Meg's a cheerful little soul and Magnus must be glad of her company just now.' He sighed. 'Thank God someone can get some joy out of this sad business.'

'Erland was such a lovely man. Poor Emily, she'll never get over it. The love of her life. Pity you never met,' Rose added. 'You would have liked him.'

Jack frowned. 'I did meet him once. In Edinburgh.'

'You never told me. When was that?'

Jack thought for a moment, frowned. 'Oh, a few years back. Probably before we were married.'

'Well, I am surprised you never even mentioned it to Emily. Did she know?'

'I have no idea.'

'What was it about?'

He shrugged. 'Police business, to do with contracts, just routine stuff,' he said casually, opening the door. 'Shall we go? I'm hungry.'

As they sat round the kitchen table enjoying a meal so well provided by Mary, an excellent venison stew followed by an apple dumpling, Rose sitting opposite Jack thought about their conversation. She had been taken aback by the revelation that Jack had met Erland before. Just routine stuff he said, and she was well aware that she need not expect any more information as Jack was the soul of discretion and never discussed cases with her.

Police business and contracts could be innocent, of course, nothing criminal in that, but there was something else besides, a feeling that could never be put into words. For some reason, never to be told, Jack Macmerry had not liked her brother-in-law, Erland Yesnaby.

He had promised Meg a ride in the motor car, to

compensate for missing out on the drive to Stromness to collect Grandpa. Yes, of course Magnus could come too. Meg was enjoying Hopescarth, already determined that her cousin should have holidays in Edinburgh, especially to meet Thane and share their walks and explore her places on Arthur's Seat.

After they left, Emily had another chance to spend precious time with her father alone by taking him on a tour of the house with its many rooms, once intended for a Yesnaby dynasty that had failed to materialise.

She had decided that he was to have Erland's study at the top of the house and Faro had his suspicions about the wealth of Yesnaby confirmed by Erland's grandfather's ancient but powerful telescope to observe the stars as well as shipping in the area.

Such instruments intrigued him and in his Edinburgh days he had been the proud owner of a modest telescope. But nothing on the scale of the one he was now looking through, a lacquered brass refractor with an equatorial mount allowing the scope to follow the movement of stars and planets by swinging in one arc and engraved with a twenty-four-hour scale in roman numerals.

Emily laughed and explained that Erland spent hours up here, looking over the sea. 'After his precious garden, it was his most treasured possession, and if the house burnt down, after rescuing Magnus and me, that would be next.'

Faro had only glimpsed the hidden garden far below but had seen enough in the house to appreciate valued antiques, paintings and ornaments acquired from London over the years. Tokens of Erland's own travels added to contributions from past generations of Yesnabys who could not resist beautiful things.

Were they smugglers? Faro wondered. Was that where the fortune had originated?

Downstairs in the great sitting room with its view of the sea, Meg and Magnus had returned from the drive, cut short to Meg's disappointment by a heavy shower of rain. Rose was showing her two mementos of her first visit and said to Magnus: 'Just before you were born.' On one wall, the watercolour she had painted at Erland's request of his sunken garden, with its ancient wall and that distant hint of the sea.

'Did you do that, Mam? It's lovely.' And as Faro followed them, Meg pointed to a pencilled sketch and studied it frowning. 'Is this yours too?'

Rose said yes and again Meg frowned. 'I think you are better at painting than drawing. You should stick to colours.'

'Why do you say that, dear?' Rose was taken aback as she always carried a sketchbook with her and, indeed, was more at ease, more confident and decidedly more skilled, she believed, with portraits than landscapes.

Meg gave a shrug. 'It's just, well, not like her at all. I mean,' she added uncomfortably, 'you've made Aunty Emily look quite old.'

Rose laughed. 'That isn't Aunty Emily, dear. That's Sibella, Magnus's great-great-grandma and she was a very old lady, past a hundred. I even flattered her a bit.'

So this was Sibella. Faro realised why Emily and Rose looked so different and not at all like sisters. One so fair, the other dark, with not a mite of likeness in their bone structure either. He found it slightly alarming that Emily was indeed a throwback.

Did Rose see it too? There were memories of Sibella in exquisite and delicate embroideries they had inherited, as well as a beautiful tapestry on one wall, but Mary Faro had been careful that he should never meet his selkie grandmother, although she lived at that time only a short distance from Kirkwall on one of the other islands. Ashamed that she should have a seal woman in her family, Mary Faro had denied him knowledge of Sibella, the suggestion being that she had passed on long ago.

Walking with Faro later, Emily said, 'I do miss Sibella. We got along so well together. So did Rose, she just wished she hadn't been so old when they met, knowing she would never see her again. I had known her for a long time.' She continued, 'Erland befriended her as he did so many people when she lived alone like a hermit.' She paused. 'Gran made things difficult, you know. She had her reasons. When she lived in Kirkwall, she could ignore the stories about Sibella's existence, but here it was different, and that made us both sad. We had such a close bond.'

'You certainly took after her in many ways,' Faro said delicately.

Emily nodded. 'You remember how Rose and I quarrelled when we were little, I wanted her curls and she wanted my straight dark hair. And I wanted her curves and she wanted to be thin. When I met Sibella, I realised where it all came from.'

It was a revelation to Faro as well. 'I'd like to put flowers on her grave,' he said.

Emily looked at him wide-eyed and shook her head. 'There isn't one,' she whispered.

'You mean she's still alive? Well, that is extraordinary, she must be well into her hundreds,' he said eagerly.

'No, no. It was two years ago, but . . . but no one knows what happened. Just that there wasn't a body to bury.'

'What on earth do you mean? If someone dies there has to be a body.'

Emily linked arms with him, shook her head, unable to find the right words. She looked embarrassed and he said:

'You're surely not trying to tell me this old legend about her being a selkie is true.'

She smiled wryly. 'Yes, she just returned to the sea.'

Faro gasped. 'Well, that must have caused some consternation among the local police, not to mention the procurator fiscal. Surely this would appear to be a missing person believed dead? How did you explain that?'

Emily sighed. 'We don't need a local police, only PC Flett, and he was as bewildered as the rest of us, so the procurator fiscal wasn't informed.'

'Then he neglected his duty,' Faro said sternly.

'They didn't want the local community involved. It was quite awful, really, a mystery that no one wants to look into. There was this lad out shooting seals – they are allowed a cull but it's a nasty business – and he came running home in a terrible state, crying that he'd murdered someone, but didn't mean to. Finally they calmed him down and he said he thought he'd shot a seal, but when he went closer it was an old woman, she must have been lurking about and got hit. He was in a terrible panic, not knowing what to do, but

39

when he reached her, she just slid away into the sea like a seal and vanished.'

Faro had listened, polite and interested, but for him there had to be a logical explanation. He didn't believe in selkies who went back to the sea and already his detective mind was setting to work and he didn't doubt for one moment that human agencies were involved.

Again he asked: 'When did all this happen?'

Emily repeated: 'Two years ago.'

Faro sighed. A pity, as that was more than enough time for every trace of evidence to disappear, especially in an isolated island community with no proper police authority, and doubtless the one man who represented the law would also have accepted Sibella Scarth's strange history.

He had already worked that part out. Even if the local copper couldn't understand it, everyone knew that the old lady, so respected and feared by everyone, had supernatural powers. No one at Skailholm ever went to the only doctor when they could get herbs from Sibella, and any questions regarding her remarkable disappearance after being shot would bring down the whole wrath of the community upon him.

'What about this young lad?'

'Archie Tofts? He seemed to get over it, I suppose,' Emily replied. 'But he's always been a bit odd. He's Millie's lad. You haven't met her yet. They live in Hopescarth and she came to help Gran after her fall. Erland had her stay on as housekeeper.'

'This Archie, is he the one who wanders a bit?'

Emily nodded 'He is a very quiet lad, doesn't say much,

but folk who know him at the local inn say it seems likely he will keep the vision of that dreadful day for ever, still believing that he killed Sibella. That he is a murderer.'

'What does he do now?'

'Odd jobs. And a bit of gardening. He's not very bright and not very reliable, I'm afraid.' Emily frowned. 'But you know, Pa, I feel uncomfortable when he's around, as if he is always listening for something, that there is something there, a shadow that he can never escape.' She shivered. 'A curse. Not that Sibella would ever curse anyone, she had a wonderful potential for loving and forgiving.'

'You remember, I told you how I met her once long ago. I was a young policeman investigating the seal king murders. But I knew her as Baubie Finn.'

Emily smiled sadly. 'She is greatly missed. We could all do with a lot more folk like her.'

The light, rather friendly breeze that had lingered over them was changing into a brisk and somewhat gusty wind. A darkening sky and gathering clouds said that rain wasn't far off.

'There's a storm coming. Better get back, Pa, before we get a soaking.'

Walking briskly along the path towards the house, Faro asked: 'What made you think Sibella wasn't just the victim of an unsolved mystery that has become a legend? That the young local fisherman, Hakon Scarth, had caught a selkie in his nets when she was the sole surviving passenger from the ship that had gone down off the bay.'

'That's what everyone wanted to believe,' Emily replied, 'that this tiny naked wee lass had come from the Norwegian

41

shipwreck. Except that the few sailors who swam ashore insisted that there were no women or children on board.'

Faro said: 'There was a reason for that. It was illegal but skippers turned a blind eye and knew that, on a long voyage, sailors needed their women who could actually be very useful, washing and cooking.'

'It was the folk here who decided she was a selkie. Poor great-grandfather Hakon thought he had caught a mermaid with all that seaweed tangled round her. But when that was removed and his mermaid had no tail, they were scared, horrified, and thought he should have thrown her back into the sea. A selkie, that's what he had caught.'

'And what made them think that she wasn't just an ordinary wee girl?'

'For one thing she had webbed fingers and toes and she hated that. From when she first went to school, she insisted on wearing mittens and she kept that habit all her life.'

She frowned. 'There was something else, the way she walked, she sort of glided along.'

'Did you find this strange?' Faro asked.

'Odd, perhaps, but not scary odd. I loved her and we had a bond from our first meeting because I had taken after her.' She shook back her long dark hair. 'I had eyes like hers too. And when she met Rose, she adored her and said she was the most beautiful girl she had ever seen; she could just sit looking at her for ages. And Rose was past thirty. They had this great bond. I think I was quite jealous because I had always wanted to be Rose, all curves instead of tall and skinny, and I did so want that great mass of yellow curls, like Mama's,' she added sadly. 'Rose was her image.'

It was Faro's turn to remember as Emily linked his arm and said, 'Oh sorry, Pa, to go on like this. It's all past history now but you know what young girls are like. It all changed when I met Sibella, though. She was lovely, I thought, and I was so glad then and proud to have a selkie for a great-grandmother.'

'If that is true, Em,' Faro said soberly.

'But we will never know, will we? It could just be another of our island stories, like the one about the Maid of Norway, way back in history, on her way to marry the young King of England, but dying on the way and her body brought ashore and buried somewhere hereabouts at Hopescarth. Then there was the treasure ship that came with her and disappeared never to be seen again. They are still looking, the archaeologists, hoping to find that treasure. Such a tiny place we inhabit, but with so many mysteries, Erland used to say. He was always intrigued by our origins. The story that a poor crofter, Huw Scarth, had followed a rainbow to its end and found a pot of gold, and how wicked Black Pate, the Earl of Orkney's son had given him in return the land to build Hopescarth.'

They had reached the house and Faro wished that the walls now bracing themselves against the coming storm were able to reveal the truth in some of the stories that Emily had told him.

He was getting to know his two daughters more in a few hours staying at Hopescarth, he decided, than he had ever had the chance to know them as children. Of course, that was his own fault, he thought guiltily, packing them off to Orkney after Lizzie died, a little sorrowful but more relieved that he was not faced with the prospect of bringing up two little girls on his own, consoling himself that there would be school holidays. He would have them in Edinburgh, make them at home in Sheridan Place, but never for him in Orkney, always too busy with the police and that seemed far more important than family commitments, catching criminals rather than taking little lasses on picnics or to the zoo.

He could remember to this day, their eager, smiling little faces, staring up at him as they hugged and kissed him. And then the excuse, the inevitable disappointment, but Mrs Brook was always at hand, his solid reliable housekeeper, devoted to him and the girls, ready to stand in and perform the duties of a parent. But he often recalled, opening the thank-you letter dictated back in Kirkwall by their grandmother Mary, that look of reproach on their small sad faces as he kissed them goodbye at the ship in Leith before hurrying back to the next case awaiting him, the next murderer to bring to justice.

Like Emily's stories his guilt was past history, the selkie legend of Sibella beyond his powers of logic but the story Archie Tofts had told about shooting a seal, well, there was a mystery here, and one which he gave him that familiar itch. He must make the acquaintance of that young man.

CHAPTER FOUR

Jack had returned to the family circle. With warnings of a full blooded storm approaching, there would be no ferries from the island that night.

He wasn't exactly sorry to have to spend another night with them and another day with Meg, who was delighted when he grinned and said: 'It's an ill wind that doesn't blow someone some good.'

As for Emily, Faro and Rose saw that she was determined that they should enjoy the rarity of being together, and her father remarked that he could not recall the last time he had sat around a table with his entire family. If he had one regret it was that Imogen wasn't by his side to share this moment. Skilled at fitting into any social gathering, how she would react to the Scarths was a different matter.

Enjoying the meal and the company of both his daughters, he was relieved to find that those first ominous feelings about Hopescarth had vanished as soon as he stepped across the threshold. He dismissed them as a moment of panic, just imagination, perhaps one of the penalties of increasing age, compensation being the two grandchildren; he fondly remembered when the front door had opened, how a small girl hurtled out to greet them. First her father, Jack, straight into his arms as if he had been gone for years rather than hours, then turning she saw Faro, one glance took him in from head to foot. A happy sigh as if she was not disappointed, she ran to his side, curtseyed prettily and took his hand shyly.

'Grandpa. I've heard a lot about you.'

'All of it good, I hope.'

Eyeing him shrewdly in a grown-up way, she nodded. 'Yes, of course, and you do look like a Viking, like Magnus,' she added with a fond glance in the direction of the boy she now regarded as her cousin and friend.

Faro smiled. She was so much Jack's daughter. His very image, sandy hair, freckles, a typical Scots' peasant face through the ages, but there was a trace of something else, a quality he couldn't define behind the nondescript features of the seven-year-old. Something indefinable whispered that one day she would be a beauty, just a hint of breeding and authority, of dignity.

He was to get the answer to this mystery his senses had recognised from Rose when, ignoring Emily's warning that they would get soaked, they decided to have a stroll before the storm broke.

There was a strange stillness, a prelude as the series of black clouds gathered, waiting for the crescendo, a full orchestra of torrential rain as they walked along the cliff path

46

where a great rock formation sprouted out of the sea below.

Rose pointed down to it. 'That's the Castle of Yesnaby, Pa, it's where Erland's ancestors, the original settlers who came from who knows where, took their name.'

Faro was surprised, having expected at least the word 'castle' to produce ancient ruins and seeing instead an ideal place, with all those secret caves dotted along the coast, for smugglers through the ages.

Voices from far below echoed up to them. Meg and Magnus, two tiny figures racing along the empty strand of glittering sand. 'Shouldn't those two be abed?' he said sternly.

Rose smiled. 'Come along, Pa. It doesn't feel late. Have you forgotten? There is no real darkness in an Orkney summer. Remember the locals playing midnight tennis? Meg is very interested in the seal king legend and is hoping to see him leap out of the water, just like those images of King Neptune with crown and trident, and take a human bride back to his kingdom under the sea.'

When Faro laughed at this absurdity she added solemnly, 'Emily says there are still girls who believe it.' And looking to where the two children were still now, standing close together staring across the sea, 'Meg wants to believe it and she hasn't any Orcadian blood.'

'But a lot of north-east Scotland. What was her mother like?'

'Jack never spoke about her.' And although she had never told anyone, least of all Jack, she felt for the first time the need to share the knowledge of Meg's nativity with the one person closest to her.

There was a seat on the path nearby and they sat down together high above the sea in a world turned silent, waiting for the storm, the great stretch of sand empty now of the two children. The seabirds, too, had disappeared, their shrill cries stilled for the night.

It was a moment as if the cliffs themselves took refuge in the menacing silence, rested uneasily and slept away from the torment of the twice-daily onslaught of the Atlantic's mighty roar. And so Faro heard the story of Meg's Romany heritage from the mother she had never known and how the Faws had tried to reclaim her last year when they had holidayed with Vince at Balmoral.

'She knows nothing of this,' Rose ended.

'Will you tell her?'

'One day, when she is no longer a child, I will tell her what the old woman, her grandmother, the matriarch of the tribe, foretold.' Rose paused. 'The odd thing is that I don't suppose she will be completely surprised as she has always been drawn to gypsies, even the ones who camp out in the Queen's Park below Arthur's Seat in summer and are despised by everyone. I thought it was just the idea of living in a horse-driven caravan – superb in summer, and very romantic.'

'No one else but Jack could have been her father. She's his image.'

Rose sighed. 'And I can't tell you how relieved we all were about that.' And she told him the story of Jack's first marriage. 'No one to blame but myself, my own fault entirely. It was a marriage on the rebound.'

Pausing, she shook her head. 'I knew how much Jack loved me and wanted us to marry, but one day we had a bitter argument, he accused me of putting him off by making excuses.

48

His last words as he stormed out were that he wasn't waiting any more. I thought he would be back the next day but he had gone to Glasgow on a case and still feeling angry went out and got very drunk, took the barmaid back to his hotel.'

Again she stopped and sighed. 'Meg was the result. Or so the girl said, and being an honourable man Jack married her. It wasn't a happy marriage, although it was mercifully brief,' she continued ruefully. 'When he heard that she had died and her sister who was childless would take care of the wee girl, he was relieved; he didn't want to see her, wasn't even sure if she was his child. We had been reconciled, he had told me the whole sad story and that after all, there had only been that one night together. Seeing that she had been so eager, he suspected that he was not the first and she had got him to marry her by the oldest trick in the business.'

'But after we married, I was the one to worry, especially when I miscarried and it seemed that I wouldn't ever give Jack a live bairn.'

She sighed sadly. 'The curse of the Faro women, isn't it, Pa? One bairn and one only.'

Faro merely shook his head, he wasn't expected to reply and the logical reasoning on which he had built his life did not credit the existence of curses as she went on: 'Anyway, four years ago I was on an assignment near where the aunt lived, so I decided to look for Meg. She was three years old and after the aunt died she'd had a pretty rough time with an uncle who was a drunk and a ne'er-do-well, plus his new wife, with bairns of her own, who didn't want her.'

Rose laughed. 'I knew in that first glance that this was Jack's bairn, there was no mistaking that, and his parents are quite ecstatic about her. When I got her to Edinburgh I still had to persuade Jack to meet her. You have never seen any man more reluctant but I wish you could have seen his face at that first meeting. It was like seeing his own childhood face in a mirror and never have I seen such relief.'

She paused for breath and Faro said: 'Happy ending, all round. She loves you too. Mercifully, I expect she was too young to remember those early years and accepts that you are her real mother.'

'Someday I'll tell her and what I learnt when she went missing last year on our Deeside holiday, that she is part-Romany. Her mother married a gorgio and was disinherited by the Faws. I often think of that old matriarch and how she could see into the future and knew that someday Meg would be great and might claim her rightful inheritance as a leader.'

Returning to the house, a family friend had looked in. Introduced as Dr John Randall, he had served as an army doctor abroad and, glad to be home again, when he took over the Hopescarth practice, he and Erland became firm friends.

'They were more than that,' Emily added. 'Cousins several times removed. It happens to most families – all related. Since this is a small island and before travel was as easy as it is today, some folks never moved more than a mile or two in their whole lives.'

Faro had heard this story before and how the inevitable interbreeding had produced lads like Archie Tofts.

A good-looking man, Faro judged Randall to be in his late fifties and Erland's nearest kin. 'No brothers or sisters,' Emily said, 'the last of the Yesnabys until Magnus came along – apart from some woman in Aberdeen. They sent each other Christmas cards. She was very proud of the connection, always planning to visit Orkney.' She sighed. 'Erland was expecting her this summer. John was interested in meeting her too, they were talking about it the week just before – just before—' She stopped and put a hand to her mouth. 'Dear God, how terrible, if she just walked in, coming all that way.'

With an apologetic glance at the assembled family, Randall smiled at Emily, said he had been worried about her not sleeping, and in case she needed something he reached into his pocket and produced a small packet, which he put in her hand with another gentle smile.

For someone prepared to come up to Yesnaby House on foot from Hopescarth – as he explained, just a hurried dash at nearly midnight – in a threatening storm, which had stopped the ferries and had brought Jack back, one thing was obvious to both Faro and Rose, both used to taking in situations at a first glance: Dr John was more than a family doctor, he was a would-be suitor for Emily.

There was an old saying of the Irish that Imogen was fond of quoting that Faro remembered looking at Randall: 'the candles were lit behind his eyes for her'. Of this, he was sure Emily was quite unaware and in casual conversation with her later he learnt that they knew little of his life before he arrived in Hopescarth, and that from Sibella who he had watched over in her last days. He had married young, long a widower, his wife had died of consumption.

Randall was delighted to meet Faro and Jack. He already knew Rose, since he had been called in to examine Meg with reassurances that the head cold she had in Edinburgh was recovering nicely. He made a great fuss of Magnus, and eager to please, had bought him a colouring book. A little too young for this particular ten-year-old, Rose thought, despite his enthusiastic thank you.

Apart from Emily, the person Randall most wanted to impress was Jeremy Faro. He shook his hand warmly and said, 'You are a legend in your own time, sir. Why, everyone has heard of the great Inspector Faro, who was also personal detective to our late Queen, God bless her.'

Faro acknowledged the compliment graciously while feeling certain that 'everyone' was something of an overstatement and that he was being unnecessarily flattered. However, the good doctor doubtless meant well. At one point in their conversation he paused and, looking towards Emily and Magnus, shook his head sadly.

'Erland was a great man, sir, we will not see his like again. A great man,' he repeated with a solemn head shake, 'and a great friend. I was with him at the end, you know,' he added in a confidential whisper although they were unlikely to be overheard. 'I will never forget. We had been playing chess as usual on Thursday, my afternoon off from the surgery, enjoying a pipe together and a dram, laughing about something inconsequential when – suddenly – suddenly he wasn't with me. He had gone, sitting there in the chair in front of me, but quite dead. I know what death looks like, I have seen it too often to be mistaken. But maybe it was something I could deal with this time, I did all I could but it was too late.' He sighed deeply. 'A serious heart condition, but there had never been any indication of such a thing, not in all the time I knew him, I always thought he was in perfect health, the sort of man who bragged that he had never needed a doctor, and I valued our friendship too much to insist.' His voice broke, 'Oh God, I wish I had insisted, perhaps he would still be with us.'

'How are you two getting along?' It was Emily. She had walked over to where they were sitting in a corner of the room, unable to restrain her curiosity.

'Is my father telling you all about Edinburgh police and the most gruesome cases he has solved?'

Randall's quick smile held a warning glance for Faro as Emily continued.

'John has always wanted to be a detective, has he told you that?' She smiled at him. 'Your secret ambition all these years here in Hopescarth.'

Randall seized on the topic with relief. 'Not many crimes to solve in our little community, I am thankful to say. Not only healthy God-fearing folk but also law-abiding too.'

'I imagine he's read too many stories about the great detective Sherlock Holmes. Fiction is very different from real life, isn't it, Pa?' Smiling she said: 'You must have felt very like him, when you had Vince on call to help solve your greatest crimes.' Then to Randall, she added rather proudly: 'Our stepbrother, Dr Vincent Laurie, is now physician to the royal household.'

'Mostly to the servants, he says,' Rose put in, 'but he's on good terms with the King. Even when he was Prince of Wales and came to Edinburgh, he would bring Vince along, the soul of discretion if HRH wanted to sow a few more wild oats, I suspect. We are all so proud of him, but he's another of the family,' she added with a reproachful look at her father, 'we hardly ever see these days. It's a shame, but despite all our progress in travel, trains and motor cars, Edinburgh is still a long way from London.'

'I've only been to London once, with Erland years ago,' Emily said. 'It was the first time I'd been so far south, and I was quite scared. Such a great bustling city. You were offered London once, weren't you, John?'

He nodded. 'Yes, indeed. The share of a practice in Harley Street. I was flattered but that kind of life is not for me. I am an islander born and bred and, quite frankly, I begrudged those years I spent abroad on Her Majesty's service. Now that I'm home, and that's here, I mean to spend the rest of my days . . .' He looked up at Emily and Faro saw fleetingly in his eyes the yearning that added the unspoken words: 'with you'.

And that wouldn't be a bad idea either, Faro thought, his mind racing ahead. It would solve Emily's problem and Magnus's too. If she remarried the local doctor then there was no reason for leaving Yesnaby House.

Later he was to discover that Rose also guessed that Randall was in love with her sister, who treated him with playful affection and seemed the only one unaware of what was staring everyone else in the face.

'Randall would be a good thing, Pa, quite the best that could happen to her and Magnus.'

And so it seemed, a conventional happy ending to suit everyone, but there were darker shadows gathering that no one had expected.

CHAPTER FIVE

All was silent when they awoke the next morning, the storm had not broken over Yesnaby after all, but after a show of torrential rain had moved on, leaving in its wake a heavy mist brooding over the landscape with only the ghostly boom of an unseen sea.

'Worse than ever,' said Jack cheerfully. 'I doubt whether the ferries will negotiate this.' He was rather pleased at the prospect of yet another day with Rose, and Meg was delighted.

Faro didn't share their enthusiasm; thick fog made him claustrophobic, wanting to keep his voice down and walk on tiptoe, a primeval instinct of being trapped like some animal.

'Lammastide,' Emily was saying, 'in the Anglo-Saxon "loaf-mass", the first harvest festival of the year.' In Orkney's dark unforgotten days this festival had acquired its own sinister legend of the seal king and perhaps it was Faro's ancestral link that added to the feeling of unease. However, an early riser unable to sleep after dawn, which never really happened in summer in Orkney, he was first down to breakfast.

In Yesnaby House, others shared his morning vigil.

A tall, blonde young man was working in the walled garden far below his bedroom window, while in the kitchen downstairs a pleasant-faced stout woman was moving briskly about with brush and bucket.

'You must be Mrs Yesnaby's father,' she smiled, 'the policeman from Edinburgh. We've heard a lot about you,' she added darkly, intimating that none of it was beyond speculation. Curious to hear more he said:

'And you must be Millie.'

'That's right. I like to make an early start before Mrs Yesnaby is up and about, gives me a clean sweep, with all these extra folk to take care of. Making up for a bit of lost time, so to say.'

Not quite the image his mother had presented of her assistant housekeeper, but that last remark opened the topic of Archie.

'We gathered you were concerned about your son.' He could hardly ask if he was better and framed the words more diplomatically: 'Is all well now?'

Millie frowned. 'Well as it will ever be. It's this time of year, every year, he gets strange, goes off and spends hours sitting at the shoreline, watching the seals and hoping that . . .' She paused and shook her head in embarrassment, 'I expect you know the story. A whole lot of nonsense but there's no convincing my Archie about that seal cull—'

'So you've come back, Millie.' Mary appeared at the door and said firmly, 'You'll find plenty to do, so I won't delay you.' In a changed tone, she came over to Jeremy, kissed him and said: 'You're up early.' And patting his shoulder, observed, 'A long lie would do you good. You should take the chance of it when you are on holiday.'

Although he had managed over the years to conceal feelings of irritation behind a mask of gentle teasing, he was annoyed at this interruption of a conversation with Millie that was just beginning to interest him. He wanted to know more about Archie, and Sibella's alleged transformation into a seal and when exactly she had disappeared.

The rest of the family drifted in, including the gardener, introduced as Sven, who made short work of bacon, sausages and eggs prepared by Mary, who refused to let Millie lay a hand on the cooking beyond preparing vegetables; their skilful assembly into meals was Mary's province, although Emily was permitted to bake in normal circumstances.

Despite the thick fog, Magnus was always happier out of doors, especially as he had a hoard of secret places to show Meg on the rocks, tiny caves and homes to various marine creatures. This was exactly what she liked most, the sort of adventures she never had at home, with Leith or Portobello the nearest sands, and as she said: 'They're all very well for picnics and bathing but there's nothing there except ice cream.'

Faro and Rose were eager to seize the rare opportunity of being together, while Jack took the motor car with Emily into distant Kirkwall to get advice from a garage owner as she decided on its future.

'I don't drive and I don't want to keep it at Yesnaby,' she said sadly, 'too many memories of Erland, remembering how he loved driving it around. Magnus will be disappointed, he is just longing to be old enough to drive.'

Jack laughed. 'By the time he is ready for that, there will be many new models to choose from.'

'Meanwhile it will just lie for years in the garage and get rusty and out of date. Perhaps it would be best to sell it, if we can get a buyer.'

Mary, too, had a future to be sorted out. The injury to her leg had left her with a permanent limp, an ache that she could not always conceal, and to Faro she was forced to admit, however unwillingly, that she could not always do things as fast as she once did.

'Sometimes I feel my age,' she said.

'We all do, Ma,' he said, putting a sympathetic arm around her thin shoulders. That was true even for him, and his mother at ninety had been trying to run Yesnaby like a woman of fifty.

'And with Erland gone, I don't see how Emily will want to stay – the house was always too big for three of them.' She paused and said wistfully, 'Y'know, Jeremy, what I would like is to go home again.' She added firmly, 'I know my little cottage would be far too small for them, but if Em sold Yesnaby, then we could maybe buy one of those big houses in Kirkwall,' to which Faro only nodded, vaguely aware that his mother's bright idea would never appeal to Emily. Without even discussing it with her, keeping Yesnaby – his family's home for generations – at all costs was what Erland would have wanted, with Magnus to continue the tradition.

Deaths do more than break up homes and break hearts, he thought. They also destroy the foundations the family have built over the years, foundations each generation believe are firm and unshakeable. It just took one man's unexpected and untimely death to make his kin realise the shifting sands of material things.

While they were deciding what to do next, Magnus and Meg rushed in with exciting news.

'There's a ship out there, Grandpa, and it seems to be heading this way.'

A ship heading for Hopescarth seemed unlikely, if not impossible, and Faro decided that it had got off course in the fog and would probably be making its way to Kirkwall.

Magnus shook his head. 'We watched it for ages and it never moved. It seems to be anchored.'

'They are probably waiting for the tide to turn,' Faro replied and thought no more about it until the children returned from their fascinating vigil once more. The ship hadn't moved. It was a mystery.

There was only one way to find out, get a closer look, and they followed him upstairs to Erland's powerful telescope more used to consulting the planets at night, he guessed, than the sea's horizon.

First glimpse revealed a large white yacht just offshore from the Castle of Yesnaby, and far too close inland. What was it doing anchored there? The acknowledged harbour for all sailing vessels, including yachts, was Kirkwall.

Was it in difficulties? Faro wondered.

Emily and Jack had returned from Kirkwall with the car's future undecided and neither seemed greatly interested in an anchored yacht, although Emily stressed the dangers of coming so close inland: the sea around Yesnaby had treacherous undercurrents.

Of greater interest, however, when they had driven through Stromness, there was a festival with a funfair that afternoon, all of which seemed much more exciting now to the children, who greeted the prospect eagerly, all piling into the motor car, insisting that Grandpa came too. Faro enjoyed it more than he expected. The children's delight and enthusiasm was irresistible and a family outing brought home to him with regret how much he had missed through the years.

'Enjoying it, Pa?' Rose said.

He took her hand. 'So much, my dear, so very much,' he added with a wistful sigh.

They didn't return until very late that evening. The fog had descended on the coast road again and it was a long and wearisome drive homeward. Emily had met a couple with whom she shared a friendship dating from schooldays. Amy and her husband, Joe, had ten-year-old twins, and she insisted that they all drive back to her house beyond Kirkwall and have supper there, especially as the twins got on so well with Magnus. Meg might have been afraid of being left out but Betty soon proved to be yet another soulmate, especially as she had an aunty in Edinburgh who she visited in the holidays.

Fortunately Mary retired early. Always gloomy and pessimistic about travel of any kind, and particularly by the newfangled motor car, she was spared the anxiety of their late return.

The house was wreathed in a white shroud creeping up from the garden and they climbed the stairs hoping not to disturb her and be subject to an interrogation of endless questions and speculation.

They had forgotten all about the yacht, and when they awakened to a sky that was endlessly blue, the sea once again innocent of anything to ruffle its calm, Faro, looking out of his bedroom window, saw that the yacht was still there. It had not moved from its original position, remaining anchored in the same place as yesterday.

The children had seen it too and bounded up to the top of the house, followed by Emily.

'I hope we're not intruding,' she said with a sad glance at the powerful telescope. 'This is where Erland spent hours every day, watching the horizon. Almost as if he was continually expecting visitors from abroad,' she laughed, as Faro brought the vessel nearer through the telescope.

Now for the first time, in sharp focus, he could see it clearly.

'Let me see, please, Grandpa,' Magnus demanded. 'It's a yacht, just as we thought,' he said, handing back the instrument reluctantly into Faro's eager hands.

For the vessel was indeed a yacht. And a very special royal one. This was the *Victoria and Albert III*, commissioned by Queen Victoria. The third of its kind and famous as the first to be steam-driven instead of under sail, it had been completed in 1899, and was sensational enough to make headlines in the newspapers. But alas, it had been too late for Her Majesty, who died in 1901 without ever stepping on board. It now belonged to King

Edward, an enthusiastic sailor, who had made several voyages to ports around the British Isles.

According to rumour Faro had heard via Imogen, the King also enjoyed private visits to some of the Irish nobility in County Cork. She had been invited aboard as a well-known writer, as well as an outstanding beauty. She had enjoyed the luxurious surroundings, the palatial stateroom as well as the first moving staircase – or elevator – to be installed on a ship, doubtless for the convenience of the elderly monarch. Imogen had also hinted at the flirtatious overtures made by the King of England and Faro was certain that her royal pardon had dated from that encounter with a monarch always susceptible to the charms of a lovely woman who was also highly intelligent.

Imogen had also told Faro that she had heard from one of her friends in the royal circle a whisper that this style of travel suited their host admirably. He enjoyed privacy from prying eyes and the yacht had soon been established as a suitable venue for many interesting cruises with his mistresses and the upper echelons of Britain's aristocracy. Rumour also had it that the yacht could be discreetly hired for a private cruise by any who were in the millionaire category.

That it had found its way to the islands of Orkney was no big surprise: King Bertie enjoyed being at sea and every chance that took him far away from London gossip. Faro was already penning a letter to Imogen to tell her that she had perhaps missed another chance of a visit to the royal yacht by not coming with him to Orkney.

But there was something else. Screened by the cliffs and caves that had seen a fair amount of smuggling in the past, and probably still did but were ignored by those who benefited by illicit trades, was that why it had remained? Why had it anchored so close offshore from Stromness, when offshore from Kirkwall would have been equally effective?

Over breakfast, their curiosity aroused and with a constant flow upstairs to regard the yacht through Erland's telescope, it was decided that it had only been waiting for better weather, and Emily, who knew about such things, said the afternoon tide would see it under way again. They certainly couldn't waste time staring at it, but there was a frisson of excitement at having royalty so close at hand.

Moving or no, Faro's frisson of excitement contained another factor. He was certain things were not as innocent as they seemed, and that, taking all things into consideration, there was a mystery here. He would keep an eye on the yacht with the excellent telescope at his command, with magnification so great that he could see any activity on the decks quite well. There seemed little more than the movements of smart-looking sailors going about their business, cleaning, polishing and so forth. The royal ensign wasn't flying, although he thought there might be private reasons for that too. When he went down to eat with the family at midday and told his mother, she was quite disappointed.

'Fancy wasting your morning watching like that,' she said as if the King was personally responsible by remaining out of sight.

Faro stayed upstairs on the excuse of writing to Imogen.

Rose joined him, equally intrigued by whatever was going on just a short distance across the water and sharing his vague suspicions.

Late that afternoon, they were rewarded by a flurry of activity. A small boat, rather opulent and grand to fit in the lifeboat category, was lowered from the deck to be seen by Faro carefully circling the anchored yacht. This new activity also included some well-dressed yachtsmen as well as uniformed sailors looking down from the decks and staring at the sea. There was obviously some argument as they anxiously gesticulated to one another, suggesting something more serious than a delay due to engine trouble.

Faro handed the telescope to Rose. 'That's more than a boat out to do a little fishing or take out some keen swimmers.'

Rose frowned. 'Looking for seals or dolphins? Maybe spotted a whale.'

Faro shook his head. The watchers, even seen distantly albeit magnified, conveyed anxiety rather than mere curiosity. 'More like a man overboard they're searching for.'

Footsteps on the stairs. 'Come on, Mam,' said Meg excitedly, 'we're all ready, waiting for you.'

Rose groaned. Jack was boarding the ship for Leith the following day, no more excuses to linger, and he had promised them a picnic.

'You too, Grandpa,' said Meg as he made no move. 'You must come!' That reproachful look struck an unhappy chord from the past, with Rose and Emily promised an outing and, when police activities intervened, handed over to Mrs Brook, substitute for a seldom-seen father.

He saw Rose watching him, her wry smile, and he realised she was remembering too. Following them downstairs with Meg clutching his hand and chatting eagerly, the yacht was temporarily forgotten. Despite that much publicised new steam power they had possibly been delayed by some minor technical problem. The anxious looks he had observed on the deck among the crew undoubtedly due to the fact that delays of any kind, minor problems to ordinary folk, brought forth bouts of extreme irritation and anger to royal personages. In this case, he expected they were merely awaiting the afternoon tide, and would be far away by evening, taking the reason for their mysterious visit with them.

Days were precious here with his family and Faro could not afford to 'waste time', as his mother had called it, building on a mystery that never was, as he and Rose were quite capable of doing. Nevertheless, it would make an interesting bit of news in his letter to Imogen.

When they returned, happy and tired from the sheltered strand, which had included bathing and sandcastles for the children and deckchair dozing in warm sunshine for the adults, the yacht was still anchored with what they had assumed was the lifeboat patrolling round it. As dusk fell and became what passed for darkness, Faro retreated once more to his vigil by the telescope.

While the others played card games and read downstairs, Rose joined him. 'What's happening, Pa?'

'Not a great deal. That lifeboat we saw earlier has just been hauled back on board. They had lanterns this time and whatever they were looking for was of considerable interest, not only to the crew but to a lot of the passengers too. Easy to spot from this telescope – men in evening dress, and a couple of ladies.'

Rose had a look. 'Well, they're not there now. No lights, all in darkness again.'

Faro nodded. 'I've been watching them and those lanterns were extinguished so quickly it suggested that what was happening around the yacht was not for casual observation.'

'Or need of help?' Rose frowned. 'What do you think is going on on board that is so secret? Is HM doing a bit of smuggling, perhaps?'

Faro laughed. 'That is highly unlikely. He has the power of access to anything that takes his fancy. I shouldn't imagine he's awaiting a consignment of silks and rare French brandy.'

'Not smugglers, then?'

Faro shook his head. 'No. And I am beginning to think there is another answer to our little mystery.'

'You mean because the King is not on board.'

'Exactly. Imogen was friendly with some of the higher echelons and although she met the King only once, she was told that occasionally HM lent the yacht to minor royals or to close friends – if they could afford it.'

Perhaps that was the discreet answer, but the business with the lifeboat hinted at something deeper: a mystery and an irresistible itch to them both.

Awakened at dawn by the noise of seabirds nesting nearby, their raucous young demanding food, Faro decided to have a quick look through the telescope.

To his surprise, Jack and Rose were already seated at the great window.

Jack turned and grinned. 'Rose had me awake half the night with her speculations about the mystery yacht. The damned noisy birds did the rest. Anyway, my ship doesn't leave Kirkwall until midday, so I thought I'd have a look and add my contribution.'

Rose said: 'They haven't moved, Pa, but there's been a lot of activity. That lifeboat has been out again, going round the yacht as if it's searching for something.' She paused and Jack looked gravely at him as she added, 'Or someone. Do you know what we think, Pa? Someone's gone overboard and that's why the yacht has been delayed and why that boat was out last night with lanterns and patrolling again this morning.' Jack looked at Faro, smiled and raised his eyes heavenward. He had seen this kind of reaction many times living with Rose. It was the same for both men, although her father was more in sympathy. Rose was always sharp and what she couldn't fill in by logical reasoning, just as Faro employed deduction, she would use imagination or even intuition, most frequently to excellent effect.

Jack said somewhat grudgingly, 'The fact that the yacht is still there, anchored so close to the shore, and with that boat searching round, certainly does suggest a man overboard. But if that was the case, if there had been an accident like that twenty-four hours ago and they couldn't cope with it by getting him safely aboard again . . .' He paused and added thoughtfully, 'If there was any doubt that he had drifted away, surely they would have found means to notify the coastguard and get a rescue boat out as speedily as possible. I imagine they have a good telegraph system, all the very latest equipment installed on a newly built royal yacht.'

He frowned. 'So why all the delay? From what Rose tells me, there hasn't been any activity from the direction of Kirkwall. And that small boat isn't a fishing vessel; there would be a name, district of origin initials and number. No Kirkwall lifeboat either. In fact,' he added triumphantly, 'they are keeping the whole thing very quiet and what we've seen is their lifeboat, useful if some of the crew have to go ashore for supplies and the like.'

'Or if some royal personage has private business in mind,' Rose added significantly, remembering stepbrother Dr Vince's tales of goings-on in the royal household to which Imogen could have doubtless added a few from rumours about the *Victoria and Albert III* during its visit to County Cork.

There was one possible solution to the mystery: find out for themselves.

CHAPTER SIX

Breakfast over, Faro said to Emily, 'It is a decent sort of day and I feel like some strenuous activity. Thought I might row the children out for a closer look at the yacht, if that boat on the beach is seaworthy.'

'It is indeed. Sven and Erland did a bit of fishing and Sven goes out every night since they got ambitious enough to put down some lobster creels. He's a good fisherman and does a nightly inspection. Sells them with a bit of profit to the hotels. Would you like him to go with you?'

Faro had been hoping she might suggest something of the sort, as an additional rower who knew what he was doing would be useful when they got near the yacht.

The two children were delighted at the prospect and regarded a row on the sea with the same enthusiasm and disregard for danger as they would have regarded a rowing boat on a village pond. Magnus was eager to offer his services as a steersman. Faro hoped Rose would come too, but she shuddered away from that idea. A martyr to seasickness she had her own reasons for preferring to remain on dry land.

She did, however, wave them off with warnings to keep an eye on Meg, who was utterly fearless and already had stationed herself on the prow, begging Magnus to let her steer.

Pushing out the well-used boat, Faro asked Sven: 'Did you by any chance notice anything going on aboard the yacht over there last night?'

'I don't get too close to big ships, sir. The swell, you know, can be dangerous if they are moving.' He thought for a moment. 'No, I didn't see anything when I was collecting my creels, but it seemed they were having a party – a lot of loud music and noise drifted over.'

Faro said: 'We are all a little curious. Perhaps we might go and ask them if they need any assistance.'

Sven frowned. He did not seem very keen on that idea and not just for the safety of his boat, but he said politely: 'Very well, sir, if that is what you wish.'

Faro had not even rowed a boat on a pond for many years and was heartily glad of the presence of an accomplished oarsman, as regardless of a slightly choppy sea they made good progress and were soon reasonably close to the yacht. Whatever Faro had hoped for, he was to be disappointed, being met with the tall white sides extending high above them, a blank wall with a few faces from portholes and sailors on the deck peering down. He had a much better vantage point than this from the telescope.

From all those faces, all Faro could observe was that they did not respond to his friendly greeting or to the children waving to them. They were as expressionless as the marble heads of Roman emperors and classical scholars in a museum, and equally as forbidding.

Obviously, their presence was not welcome. Someone, a member of the crew, leant over the rail to shout down a warning: 'These are dangerous waters. I would advise you to steer clear, especially with children aboard.'

'We have heard that you had an accident, someone overboard,' Faro shouted back boldly. 'Is he making good headway?'

The heads hastily withdrew. That remark had been greeted by silence, then one head, wearing an officer's cap, appeared. 'I would advise you again to leave at once, sir.' A voice of authority this time and no mistaking a warning note.

Faro was not to be sent off like a schoolboy in disgrace. 'We will continue our progress,' he shouted back, picking up his oars again and indicating to Sven that they resume.

When they reached the shore again, Faro felt that the main object had not been touched upon, much less achieved. He had learnt nothing to throw any light on the mystery but at least the children had been delighted with the morning's activity.

As they stepped ashore, Sven said: 'There were Norwegians on that yacht, sir.'

'How on earth do you know that?' Faro was taken aback and Sven said: 'I heard some of the sailors. I am from Bergen, sir.'

They were interrupted as the two children rushed to Sven's side, impressed by his abilities as an oarsman. Abilities which, they had observed, were somewhat superior to Grandpa's, and they were now begging him to take them fishing.

Back in Yesnaby, Faro was curious to learn more about the handsome young Norwegian. He said to Emily, 'I presumed he was the gardener, a local lad.'

She seemed surprised. 'Sven isn't an Orcadian name.'

'But it is Viking enough to be misleading. Tell me about him.'

'He's been with us a while now. Erland brought him back from Bergen on one of his trips, must be about two years ago. He had met him through old friends who confided that he was no orphan but the love child of a well-off woman, who had to abandon him when she married a widower who had children of his own. Anyway, he knew nothing of his early days and had been brought up to believe he had been adopted and educated by this nice middle-class couple.

'Having supper with them one evening, Erland talked to Sven and discovered that he was intrigued by the Viking connection with Orkney. He had studied archaeology but was finding life without any kind of interesting dig forthcoming very dull in Bergen. Erland found him very likeable and on the spur of the moment invited him over to join the dig at Hopescarth.'

She paused and said sadly, 'Erland was like that; anyone in need and he was always ready to help. Well, when summer was over it seemed decided that Sven should stay and help with the garden – it was getting a bit too much for Erland – and Sven was to have an independent existence with a little cottage of his own on the estate. I thought that was a mistake and that he should have found him somewhere in Hopescarth.'

She smiled. 'Erland always talked as if he hoped that this nice-looking lad would find a wife easier if he wasn't living with us out here in Yesnaby. It hasn't happened so far – well, not as far as we know – although the Stromness girls run after him. You should have seen them at that fair.'

Mary bustled into the kitchen with a basket of raspberries, and as the rest of the morning passed, the family went about their own activities. Meg and Magnus stayed indoors as there was now another complication: the weather had worsened, pushing summer out of its schedule with heavy grey clouds tumbling across the sky accompanied by a bitter wind and sharp showers of hail.

Emily and Mary were jam-making with fruit from the estate while at the top of the house Faro continued his letter to Imogen, which Jack would post in Kirkwall. Resuming his vigil by the telescope, he thought of Sven, who he had presumed was a good-looking young Orcadian. As Faro prided himself on his excellent hearing detecting the faintest of accents, he wondered if he was perhaps just getting a mite deaf.

Meanwhile, Jack prepared to take his departure, sorry not only to leave Meg and Rose but also a family holiday more than usually exciting, with a lot still to be revealed about that mysterious royal yacht anchored nearby, especially when Faro told him about their aborted 'fishing' trip and how Sven had recognised that some of the sailors were Norwegian.

'That's very interesting, especially as their Queen Maud is our king's youngest daughter.'

Faro remembered having read in the newspapers about the Norwegian coronation that had taken place in Trondheim that summer, when Rose came in asking Jack how he was to get into Kirkwall. He could take the car, of course, but how about getting it back again? There was the motor bus from Stromness, but its timetable was variable.

Emily had the perfect solution. Walking to the great south-facing window she pointed down into Erland's garden where Sven was kneeling down attending to some plants.

'Down there,' she said. 'There's your answer.'

And to Faro, who had reappeared clutching his letter to Imogen, 'Sven will post that for you and gather anything Ma's needing from the shops. Sven is our Mr Do Everything,' she added proudly as they went out and down the steep steps into the sheltered sunken garden, with its blaze of colour so dramatic and exotic behind an ancient stone wall in that barren landscape. Explaining to Jack about Sven being Erland's protégé, she added: 'He's an archaeologist, really. Most of his work with a trowel, however, is done in the garden here, taking care of Erland's rare orchids.'

At their approach, Sven stood up and bowed. As Jack was introduced, he said: 'I apologise for not shaking your hand, sir' – and now Faro detected the merest hint of an accent – 'but please look at mine.' They were covered in soil and he made a face.

'You should wear the gloves I gave you,' Emily said.

He shook his head. 'No, you are kind and I thank you but that is not possible. The orchids are so small and fragile, they need gentle handling – only fingers.' He looked round and added sadly to Emily. 'This whole garden, he loved it so. It will be his memorial. Would they like to see the orchids?' The question was directed at the newcomers to the house. 'They were his most treasured possession.'

'Another time, Sven. I am sure they would love that. But

at this moment, Mr Macmerry here needs you to drive him into Kirkwall to catch his ship.'

Sven immediately sprang to attention. 'I will be delighted. I merely need to clean up a little, wash my hands.' Another bow to Jack. 'If you are ready, come with me, sir. We will leave immediately.'

He followed them into the house, and taking the towel Emily handed him, went through to the kitchen while Jack said his farewells.

'I can hardly believe you are going this time,' Rose said, kissing him.

'I don't want you to go. I want you to stay for ever,' cried Meg with a hug. 'Look after Thane and tell him I miss him and I'll be home soon.'

Jack duly promised and climbed into the car beside Sven, their departure watched sadly by Faro and Emily, both with the same unspoken thought: when might their paths cross again? This sadly unexpected call to Orkney had offered a solitary bonus, brief days for a family reunited – including Meg's delight at having found a cousin – death's consolation for bitter grief and loss. Already hopeful plans were being made, Emily hinting to Rose and Jack that they might see Magnus and herself in Edinburgh.

Faro had no such reassurances.

Life with Imogen Crowe, once persona non grata with no legal right to set foot in Britain, had turned him into a nomad. A pleasant enough existence, since during his long years with the police his greatest ambition had been to travel the world, to have all the romantic cities that were only places read about in books suddenly available at his behest.

He shook his head. He had seen most of Europe with Imogen as well as the east coast of America and small bodily twinges warned him that he could not escape time's relentless march. He was getting older and aware that in a year or two, bearing in mind the years between them, Imogen would still be a relatively young woman with himself unable to conceal that he was finding this life of travelling more difficult, his wearying bones telling him that it was time to settle down in a proper home.

Following Emily into the house, she was saying: 'Erland was very fond of Sven, he felt fortune had smiled on him, so lucky he said, finding a lad who was reliable, could drive and turn his hand to anything, even to be trusted with care of the garden and those precious orchids.'

'Seems like a nice fellow.' Very good-looking, indeed, with the Nordic fair hair and a refining of the Viking warrior image.

'Too good for a gardener,' Emily said to Faro. 'You might have noticed the archaeology site.'

'What were they looking for?' Faro asked. 'Are they still dreaming about making fortunes from Armada ships?' He had observed a boat with divers on their drive up the coast road.

Emily laughed. 'Not this time. It is an even older treasure they have in mind. The ship that went down bringing Princess Margaret, the Maid of Norway to Scotland and carrying her dowry – chests of gold and jewels.'

'Buried treasure, Aunty Emily!' Meg was listening eagerly. 'How exciting!'

'A lot more exciting than a silly royal yacht,' was Magnus's comment.

'Maybe we should be out looking for that treasure,' Meg said to him.

'You would be wasting your time, although you wouldn't be the first – or the last,' said Emily.

'Tell me about it, Aunty,' exclaimed Meg. 'This princess, what happened? Why did she die and where is her grave?'

'She was the granddaughter of King Alexander the Third and when his only son died without any children, this Princess of Norway, born in 1283, was the heiress to the Scottish throne,' said Emily as Magnus sighed and listened politely in the manner of one hearing an oft-told school tale. 'The Scots didn't care for a three-year-old girl as queen and being ruled by a regent. There was always trouble with England, so it was decided that she should marry King Edward's son, a year younger than herself, and unite the two kingdoms. After a lot of negotiations and false starts she set sail in the autumn of 1290.'

Emily paused for breath and went on: 'All history tells us is that they landed and carried her ashore after she died from the effects of a terrible sea crossing, and of course there were the usual rumours that the English didn't want a Scots queen and that she was poisoned.'

'What about the treasure ship?'

'It never returned to Norway. After she died, it vanished without trace.'

Meg had listened wide-eyed and Faro said: 'Of course there is a perfectly logical explanation. It was very easy in those days for ships to do just that and go down with all crew lost in storms in uncharted seas.'

'What about pirates?' Magnus put in eagerly. 'I've

always thought that could be the answer. There would be a few of them about, maybe some had trailed the ship from Bergen.'

Meg frowned. 'They must have buried her somewhere, Aunty? If not at sea, when they carried her ashore. So does anyone know what happened?'

Emily laughed. 'That's the question that's been troubling generations of folk in Orkney. The theory has even been that it might be somewhere near Yesnaby: one reason for the archaeological dig.'

'Have they ever found anything?'

'No. Not a thing.'

Faro was watching Rose as she stood by the window. Although she had contributed no opinion, she must have heard the story before from Erland. She was very silent, thoughtful even. Perhaps she had nothing to contribute, but that was not like her; maybe she was bored, but that wasn't like her either. This was the sort of romantic history she found irresistible.

Conscious of his eyes on her, she turned and her expression was not one of boredom. As the conversation turned to the absent Sven again, he was aware that she knew something she could have added to that conversation.

Rose did know something. But she had given her word, and promises are not changed even when death takes a hand in dealing out the cards.

Emily was saying: 'I don't think Sven is disappointed that they never found anything at the dig. Yes, it would have been a special discovery for him, a link with Norway. He would have been very proud.' She shook her head. 'No,

Meg, he has no family or friends back in Bergen and regards this as his home now.'

Meg looked sad as Emily shook her head. 'When you folk go away, I can't think what it will be like in this great empty house alone. Sven is going to miss Erland too. More than a generation apart, that didn't seem to matter. Erland taught him chess—' she stopped, caught her breath, remembering. 'Sven had been with him before John arrived that afternoon.' Her voice choked on a stifled sigh. 'I think Erland would have wanted that, to have one of those closest to him there.'

They began setting the table. 'Nice lad,' Rose said. 'I'm surprised he's not married.'

Emily said: 'Doesn't seem all that interested. There have been occasional sightings of lady friends. But he keeps himself to himself, never confides anything about his private life. Perhaps he confided in Erland, man to man, that sort of thing.' Smiling, she shrugged. 'Erland never told me everything, either. He said once he only told me the interesting things, that his ordinary business activities, that sort of thing, would be too boring.'

A short silence, then Rose looked at her and said: 'You're lucky to have a treasure like Sven. Useful, too, being able to drive these days, although I could see that Jack wanted to take over that himself.' She sighed. 'Such a lovely car, the Hammer Tourer, compared to the police ones.'

'What we will do with it now, I don't know,' said Emily.

'I do,' said Rose excitedly. 'He can teach me to drive. I've watched him. There's nothing to it, I'm sure I can pick it up.'

Mary and Emily regarded her in astonishment. 'I'm used to traffic in Edinburgh,' she added apologetically. 'After years of riding a bicycle, it will be an exciting new adventure.'

She loved all things modern, eager to move ahead with this new century, to be a woman of the calibre of Imogen Crowe, aware that she had already set her footsteps firmly on that role when she first became a lady investigator, discretion guaranteed, in a horrified male-dominated, middle-class Edinburgh.

Mary paused from stirring the soup and regarded her gravely. 'What a dreadful idea and so dangerous. A woman driving a car, what will they think of next?'

'Why not, Gran?'

Mary shuddered. 'It's so unladylike.'

'Well, no one, not even my best friend, could ever accuse me of being a lady,' laughed Rose, since her grandmother had said exactly the same words about her riding a bicycle on her visit ten years ago. Following her father upstairs to the telescope, she decided that progress was not a word in Mary Faro's vocabulary.

As if rooted to the spot, the yacht remained silent and stationary. The only activity now was the river pilot moving purposefully across from the direction of Kirkwall.

'So they got wind of it at last, Pa. Certainly took their time about making an official report and getting some help.'

Faro shook his head. 'A little too late for that. Not much anyone could do, I'm afraid. If there was a man overboard, he would be at the bottom of the sea by now.'

CHAPTER SEVEN

Later that day, Rose decided to introduce her father to Skailholm, which they had passed briefly on the drive to Hopescarth. She had an idea that the local inn would appeal to him and he laughed. 'You are being tactful, lass. What you mean is that I can enjoy more than one wee dram without your grandmother's eagle eye and reproachful tut-tut indicating that I am taking to the drink.'

Rose took his arm. 'You can include me in that.' She giggled. 'Ladies are only supposed to take whisky for dire medicinal purposes.'

'What a waste.' Faro groaned. 'It's not just usquebaugh. There are many different varieties for many different tastes and I'm looking forward to Orkney's special brand, with its peaty flavour – somewhat different to the one my mother keeps locked up in the cupboard, to be produced, hot water added and diluted with lemon, when someone has a cold.'

'What's Irish whisky like?'

'Different,' was all Faro would say on that topic, but Ireland raised the inevitable subject.

'How long can you stay?'

'As long as I like. Until Imo's next conference in York; I was hoping we might meet in Edinburgh. What about you?'

'Until Meg is due back at school later this month.' Rose sighed. 'I don't think Meg will be in a hurry to go home, so it will all depend on Jack, how he copes without us. Meg's happy here and meeting Magnus has been such a bonus – so unexpected, really. She was a bit rebellious as always at having to leave Thane behind, needed some persuading. The prospect of a boy older than herself wasn't much consolation. They're at the age of intolerance between the sexes.'

'I think we are all very lucky with Magnus and I have a feeling that you will be seeing a lot more of him in Edinburgh.'

They were in for a surprise. After all those farewells and the idea that Jack was on his way home, the car returned, and with Sven driving, there he was in the passenger seat.

They rushed out to meet him. What had happened? He should have been on the ship heading for Leith.

He shook his head. 'I'm afraid you'll have to put up with me a bit longer. I'm staying on for a while. The police in Kirkwall had a message from Lothian. They're investigating a fraud case with a link in Stromness they want me to look into. There was a telegraph waiting.'

While welcoming hugs were exchanged with Meg, delighted to see her father again, Faro studied him intently, certain that there was more than he was telling them, something in his manner, a certain implausibility about that message from Edinburgh no one else seemed to have noticed. And that in Faro's experience all added up to a suppression of facts, some serious business that he didn't want the family to know about.

He felt the usual twitch, the hint of a dark shadow, and glancing across at Rose saw her regarding Jack thoughtfully, her expression confirming that she too was having doubts about her husband's glib statement.

'Haven't the faintest,' Jack was saying to Mary Faro, anxious to know how long he would be staying. 'Might be just a couple of days to sort things out.' He smiled at Rose but there was a thin line between his brows that told another story. Jack was worried about something beyond his control.

Carrying his case upstairs, he said: 'I thought I might just drift over to Skailholm,' adding hastily, 'I've never had a chance to explore it.'

Rose smiled. 'Well, that's a coincidence. Pa and I were just thinking of heading that way. He wants to sample the local whisky.'

'I'm all for that. A splendid idea.' Jack sounded interested and somehow relieved, and this set her wondering if this suddenly invented fraud case had something to do with whisky smuggling, while Faro, remembering the brisk river pilot making for the royal yacht, was thinking much along the same lines.

After they ate, with Mary fearing that there would not be enough to go round and Jack insisting that there was more than enough salmon and that he ate too much, the three got on the road to Skailholm, the children kept at bay. This was for grown-ups, Jack told them, we are going to the local inn and even if children were allowed, they would be bored.

As they walked down the curve of the road that hid them from Hopescarth and the anchored yacht, Faro said: 'Was there any report in the police station about the river pilot's visit this morning?'

Jack frowned, considering. 'Oh, that. Just routine, you know.' A moment's pause. 'One of the crew fell overboard. But they got him back safely. Everything all right again,' he added with a bright smile.

'He was lucky. In that wild sea, he could well have been swept away,' Rose persisted.

Jack nodded vigorously. 'That would have been a tragedy and the King would have been most upset too. He is very conscientious about the well-being of his crew and examines the safety precautions regularly. He takes a great personal interest in anything relating to his yacht.'

'The King definitely isn't with them?'

'Not this time. I gather one of his upper echelons have been given it as a treat for some anniversary or other.' And to Faro, 'What news of Imogen?'

'Nothing so far.'

'That's a pity. We were looking forward to seeing her. God! I'm thirsty. Is it far to go?' Jack added, obviously glad to get away from the subject of the yacht. Rose, taking in his reactions as the conversation switched to the safer ground of her father's travels abroad, decided that her husband might well be a brilliant detective but he was certainly not the world's greatest actor.

'At last! Is that the inn I see down there?'

Jack sighed happily as the two men found the local

84

whisky lived up to its reputation, and so did Rose, although the sight of a young lady imbibing such spirits, even in the company of gentlemen, raised some eyebrows among the locals. A small sherry or port would have been much more ladylike for one related to the big house at Hopescarth, at least in public, since the locals could only speculate, as they did at some length, about what were the goings-on behind closed doors in upper-class houses.

It was soon obvious that Erland Yesnaby was held in high regard, and while they were being served, other customers came over to offer condolences to Rose, who to her amazement, was remembered and recognised by the now ageing barmaid; she had inherited the inn on her husband's death and had now added bed-and-breakfast accommodation.

Rose was also welcomed by the local policeman, PC Flett, who shook her hand and, on being introduced to Jack, beamed down at her: 'Well now, I would have known her anywhere. Ten years, is it?' he whistled under his breath. 'And you haven't changed a bit. It must be good for you, living on the mainland.' The mainland to an Orcadian being anywhere off the island.

Flett was also delighted to meet the retired Chief Inspector Faro, whose exploits and legendary fame had progressed further than Kirkwall, doubtless spread liberally over the years by his proud mother.

Preparing to leave, the policeman declined the parting offer of a dram. 'Thank you, sir, but no. I am on duty, you know,' he added importantly, although what those duties were remained vague to the three visitors.

Standing to attention, and saluting them, he said gravely: 'It has been a great pleasure and, if I may say so, an honour to meet two policemen from Edinburgh. Perhaps we will see you again in Hopescarth.' He smiled. 'Your visit has coincided with the royal yacht, a rare occurrence. Presence of royalty always means we have to smarten up, have the uniforms well pressed and give the peedie buttons a polish.' At the door he turned: 'Seen any activity?' he added hopefully.

Rose looked quickly at Jack, who shook his head and said: 'No.'

He was keeping his own counsel and not sharing information received in Kirkwall with a fellow policeman. Outside, Jack looked at the sky and decided that he was getting far too little exercise these days as well as overeating. He always disliked returning from a long walk the way he came and challenged them to a less direct route inland. It was hardly picturesque as he perhaps had hoped, and although something of a novelty to him, his companions found the bleak landscape depressing.

The sun had retreated behind heavy clouds to reveal a land occupied by stones, the scattered ruins of human habitation now shelters for sheep, the skeletons of ancient crofts with fallen roofs and broken window frames. Like eyes emptied of hope, Faro thought each told its own tale of blighted days gone by, of clearance and the beggary that still stalked the northern isles.

The further inland they walked, the bleak landscape was leavened by peat fields with bog cotton, stretching in every direction, and suddenly they were not alone. There were dogs barking and other humans, crofters still hard at work, straightening up from their back-breaking toil to shout a greeting.

'Are ye lost?'

'We're heading for Hopescarth,' Jack said.

'Ye awa' off the track, laddie. Over yonder, keep going south until ye see a glimpse of the sea and that's yer road.'

Half an hour later on the cliff path again, Jack breathed deeply, smiling and exclaiming that all this fresh air had been an unexpected adventure, while Rose was complaining that, had she known, she would have worn more suitable walking boots. Faro, who still suffered from the sore feet that were his inheritance from early years as a beat policeman, decided he was definitely beginning to feel his age and was heartily glad to see Hopescarth loom into view. Below them the *Victoria and Albert III* lay still unmoving at anchor.

'I wonder how long they are staying.'

'I expect they are enjoying a good spell of weather.'

'Good but unreliable. It never lasts long,' said Rose.

Jack shrugged but in the glance Rose exchanged with her father there was a question: Jack's mysterious behaviour, the prolonged stay at police request, and that man overboard – recovered, Jack said, but then why was their small boat patrolling round the yacht with lanterns the night after they had got him safely aboard again?

It suggested that their activity had nothing to do with an attempted rescue and instead brought to the surface that old story so often discredited. Had the King heard from sources near the palace of a possible treasure trove related to the legendary Armada shipwreck, and did the crew of the royal yacht include archaeologists who were also diving at night?

* * *

87

Over breakfast the next morning, Emily told Rose that Sven was also intrigued by the yacht's mysterious behaviour and as there were Norwegians in the crew he had decided to try to find out what was going on, perhaps by meeting them in the local inn at Skailholm.

When Rose reported this to Faro, he said: 'Good luck to him. I hope he has more success than we have had. I suppose it gives him something to do.'

Rose looked at him. 'I gather Emily keeps him busy as a secretary, dealing with her letters and so forth.'

As they returned from their morning walk, Sven was at work with his trowel, carefully scraping at the soil in the sunken garden far below, down a steep flight of stone stairs, invisible from the drive, with its signs of those earlier habitations marked by broken pieces of crumbling masonry.

He looked up and saw them watching him. Shouting a greeting, he beckoned to them: 'Please come down. I want to show you something . . .'

Emily smiled. 'Let's go.'

Faro followed the others into that vast area of bright flowers and shrubs framed by a desolate landscape stretching mile upon mile beyond its walls, once again so completely unexpected, it took him by surprise, this old walled garden from an ancient painting, carpeted by plants carefully chosen for longevity, resistant to the elements and sheltered by the house towering above.

Emily looked at him and smiled. 'Beautiful, isn't it?'

'I can hardly believe that it's real,' he said.

'When Erland first brought me here, he said that it was a miracle that anything survived, given our climate, but he didn't claim it as his creation. All he ever had to do was maintain it in the pattern that his grandfather had laid down. The rest was easy.'

They had reached Sven's side. 'I can see you are all a little surprised.' And raising his hand, 'See, even on the chilliest day with a wind blowing, there is always some quiet spot where one can sit and admire the flowers.' He sighed. 'There is always colour here, even in darkest winter.'

'Incredible,' said Jack. 'It is well-nigh impossible to maintain any sort of garden outside our house in Edinburgh on the slopes of Arthur's Seat. How do you keep it like this?'

Sven nodded eagerly. 'There is a good reason for our soil's fertility. This land, you see, has been lived on continuously since man settled on this island thousands of years ago.' And tapping his foot on the ground, 'In medieval times this was the kitchen midden. On this exact spot, animal bones, human excrement and waste deposit from countless generations have been poured into the earth to emerge as the garden you see here.'

Faro looked round at this scene of perfect tranquillity. Timeless, indeed, it suggested sunlight and birdsong, flowers eternally radiant in summer glory.

'A haunted garden, if I believed in such things,' he said to Emily. She regarded him solemnly for a moment. 'Strange that you should say that, Pa. Erland had a theory that people were like the flowers that grow and they left an essence of themselves. Every person who has laughed and loved and . . . died here through the passing centuries has left something of themselves. In essence they are still here in spirit.'

Rose and Faro were silent, both remembering how very recently Erland's spirit had taken flight from where they now stood.

Jack, meanwhile, was talking enthusiastically to Sven, keen to learn something of the art of gardening about which he knew nothing.

Sven was saying that it was a pity they could not grow tall trees on Orkney. 'But over there,' he pointed: 'That is a hornbeam.'

'A fine Shakespearean name for a tree,' said Faro.

'But it is our orchids I wanted you to see. They are very rare, indeed. You can only see them properly when the sun is shining, for it is only then they open up those shy petals.'

Bending down, they looked over a tiny patch of green. 'This is our treasure, the *Primula scotica*, which would be just as happy growing on the grassy sea cliff a mile away. It rarely survived cultivation, so perhaps it has always been here, like our wild orchids, and firmly established itself long before man invaded. Here is another. Now what does that tiny face remind you of?'

'A monkey?' Faro suggested.

Sven laughed. 'Indeed, sir, you are right. The *Orchis simia*.' Standing up, he said: 'We do not advertise our rare flowers and, alas, in a few years they will be extinct and there are some collectors who would come all the way from Edinburgh and Glasgow and the great English cities too, to harvest our rare specimens.'

Listening to him struck another chord of memory for Rose, remembering how Erland had asked her to imagine what all this looked like before those first settlers came and put down their roots, taking for granted plants and exotic flowers that are now not even a memory. Or else in that fight for survival they evolved into something tougher and less delicate, like the birds who evolved from their brilliant plumage into the camouflage of dull greys and browns to keep them safe from their chief predator: man.

For a moment, Rose slipped back ten years and closed her eyes, hearing how that beautiful voice now stilled for ever had conjured up visions of greens and yellows and browns transformed into rainbow shades. And how Erland had asked her to imagine the perfume of those long-lost flowers. She sniffed the air.

Jack smiled. 'You were miles away there, when I spoke to you.' He took her hand. 'What a garden. I wish we could do something like this at home.'

Rose took his hand. 'Not a hope; not in a thousand years.' She laughed. 'And neither of us is a gardener. But our Arthur's Seat has its own grandeur.'

He laughed. 'And not everyone can live on the slope of an extinct volcano.'

'Food is on the table.' Mary leant over the wall and shouted down to them.

Climbing back up the steps, Jack chuckled. 'Lad's a keen gardener and I did like the royal "we". I'd better remind him that I have to go into Kirkwall again tomorrow.'

'No progress on the fraud case?'

Jack looked at her vaguely as if he hadn't heard the question or, more likely, she thought, preferred to ignore it. She would have liked some dates; it was unsettling somehow not knowing how long he was staying with them.

Faro followed more slowly, hating to admit that he was finding steep stairs more of a trial these days.

Pausing, he looked back down at the garden, at the walls and small embrasures confirming Sven's suggestion regarding the ruins of a much earlier settlement. He had been aware of an aura of solemnity, the kind he had encountered in ancient churches all over Europe. Had there been a medieval abbey on this spot, whose fallen stones were augmented into the present house? That would be worth further exploration, and to this he added the young man, Sven. He had not quite made up his mind about just where he fitted into the scheme of things in Yesnaby.

Rose had paused and was looking back at him. Did she share the same feeling about this place? He must ask her, were they always looking behind the stage setting, as part of their investigative minds?

As the others talked about the garden, Emily said to Rose, 'It was Erland's favourite place. Whenever he was missing at mealtimes, I would look down over the wall and see him on his favourite seat by the mermaid stone. And that is the vision of him I will hold for the rest of my life.'

She sighed. 'For the moment it is almost too painful, although Sven tells me that a time will come when it will be a comfort to me to go down and sit there and that I will find Erland again.'

In answer, Rose took her hand as she added: 'I wish I could be sure of that. All I feel just now is that my world, my whole life, is suddenly empty. If I didn't have Magnus . . .'

The two children were now clustered round Sven, who

was showing them some coins, one of which he had dug up in the garden.

Magnus came over eagerly to Faro and Rose. 'Look at this one. This is one Sven dug up in the garden.'

Sven nodded gravely. 'That is so.'

Jack looked at it and handed it back, with a shake of his head, only vaguely interested in ancient coins. He had more than enough problems with the present day fraudulent variety.

'And it goes to prove that the story about the Spanish Armada ship sinking off the coast is true, doesn't it?' Magnus continued excitedly.

'May I?' said Faro and Sven hovered proudly. 'From *El Gran Grifón*, undoubtedly,' the Norwegian said.

Faro merely nodded as he examined the worn gold piece and handed it back, turning to Rose and Jack who, patiently explaining some problem to do with swimming off the shore to Meg, had observed the matter of the coin from afar.

He had seen enough on the coin to note one word, 'Hakonus', and later that day, he said to Rose, 'It gave me some food for thought about Sven.'

'It was a Norwegian coin?'

He nodded. 'It was not from the Spanish Armada, unless it had been from a captured ship, and it's definitely not a Spanish coin.'

Rose thought for a moment. 'An odd mistake for an archaeologist, is that what you are thinking?'

Faro nodded. 'I have to confess that I know little about ancient coins – it's in the same field as stamp collecting

93

where I'm concerned – however, I would be prepared to identify this as genuine, since Orkney was part of the Kingdom of Norway until 1468.'

Rose found this extremely exciting for her own reasons as her father went on: 'It is perhaps a little too far-fetched to link a coin with an old legend, which is probably hearsay.'

'You mean the story about Princess Margaret, the Maid of Norway?'

'And legend had her buried somewhere on the Orkney coast.' Rose, who was standing by the window, merely nodded and Faro said: 'Interesting theory but what really fascinates everyone is what happened to the treasure ship that accompanied her, which just vanished into thin air after she died.'

'With her dowry destined for future delivery to her betrothed, the future King Edward of England,' Rose shrugged. 'The story has always intrigued these islands, including generations of schoolchildren. You must have heard it in Kirkwall before Grandpa took you to Edinburgh.'

Faro smiled wryly. 'And there wasn't one of us children who didn't believe that the treasure ship had been wrecked off the shore. It was mainly a question – an argument, rather – off which island it was wrecked, especially to lads whose geography was their best subject.' He laughed. 'I wasn't one of them.'

Rose said: 'Thinking about Sven's coin, though, there are lots of other reasons for coins reappearing, not only from dramatic events like a sinking ship's cargo but from lots of innocent reasons.'

'Exactly. Such as sinking into the earth and working their

way up to the surface to appear centuries later. Dropped by someone out for a walk, and as Orkney belonged to Norway, just an ordinary domestic happening. Only, had it been a foreign coin, such as a Spanish doubloon, that would immediately have brought the Armada legend back to life and set many a crofter's hopes racing.'

'But this is different,' said Rose. 'Why, I wonder, is Sven passing it off as a Spanish one? Surely he knows the difference. Any archaeologist would have a modicum of knowledge about such things.' She frowned. 'He wasn't around at my last visit, and ten years ago was probably still a student.'

Faro thought for a moment and smiled. 'You know what Jack will say: there you two go again, making a mystery where there is a perfectly logical explanation.'

'He knows even less about old coins than we do. But I'll ask him when he gets back from Kirkwall.'

'Any idea how long this fraud case is going to keep him here?'

Rose shrugged. 'None at all. Jack never tells me anything about police business.' She had her suspicions, shared but as yet unspoken with her father, that Jack was being economical with the truth, which both suspected had something to do with the *Victoria and Albert III* still unmoving in the bay.

CHAPTER EIGHT

That was the evening when Faro fell asleep and had a nightmare, a rare occurrence indeed. Unused to any dreams that he remembered on waking, this one was particularly vivid and violent, linked to the visit to the garden outside, and when he thought about it afterwards, doubtless related to conversations about treasure ships and the burial place of a royal princess.

He was in the water, wading in the shallows surrounded by men and women making for the nearby shore. They were not of his time, wearing rich garments from another age, in heavy fur cloaks huddled against the piercing cold wind, for this was no longer summer and a pale autumn moonlight illumined the sea. The group heading to the shore were deeply unhappy, afraid, and the women among them wept and moaned as ahead, stumbling through the water, an elderly man carried aloft a small burden.

A dead child. A small girl, for one of the women ran

forward and, weeping, laid a wreath of wild flowers on her brow, smoothing back her long lint-coloured hair, touched by frail moonlight. Another sound arose above the weeping, the susurrus of the waves, the sound of seabirds crying. Behind the man with his pathetic burden, a younger man stumbled through the waves carrying a wooden box, the hastily made coffin awaiting the girl-child. Ahead of them, as they trudged from the sea towards the shore, the distant shape of a solitary habitation, a crude stone building like a hermit's cell on the skyline.

Aware in the dream that this was an island, he followed them, climbing the steep hill with no path, and although this was a place familiar to him, in that cold dawn light there was nothing to break the barren landscape but their destination on the hilltop. They stumbled towards it, over boulders and rocks behind the man carrying the dead child. Momentarily they paused, as someone spoke loudly, but although this was a language he did not understand, the pointing hands indicated that it was a question: where to lay her to rest.

A man came forward, with the important bearing of a priest, bearing a staff, and indicated the hilltop. As one, the group moved swiftly ahead. Added to the lamentations of the weeping women, another sound, that of a dog barking close at hand. He heard it panting and turning; there was a huge dog at his side. It looked at him, with strange luminous eyes, their brightness heightened by the moonlight and he was afraid, not of the animal but of the warning. It was telling him something.

Suddenly he was awake. The dream, or the nightmare

as it was, had gone. There was no dead child, no dog.

He sat up in bed. He felt cold, shivering, as if the threads of what he had dreamt wrapped him in a shroud. He got up; beyond the window he was greeted by only the chill of predawn, the hour once called between wolf and dog. He went back to the warm bed, mystified with never a nightmare like this since childhood. Dreams were rarely remembered when he opened his eyes. And if he did remember, there was usually a good solid reason.

So what had produced this vivid dream? The garden, perhaps, all that talk of Sven's about what it had been like in the past. That must be it, pure speculation of course, and then there were other elements too, like the popular legend about the Maid of Norway. That accounted for the dead child in his dream. He closed his eyes; he could still see her plainly as if she still existed and moved in the circle of his everyday world here at Yesnaby: the still face, white as the pale tresses of her hair. He would never erase that sad image.

Then there was the dog. The huge dog. In his early days, he had never liked large dogs, they were every beat policeman's dislike, rushing out, barking at you. Later, he learnt sympathy for all cruelly treated animals, particularly horses. Edinburgh Zoo made him feel uncomfortable and he had never wished to own a pet, tolerating Mrs Brook's devotion to a tabby cat in Sheridan Place, to be mildly stroked on occasion.

How extraordinary, then, that this huge dog should have entered his weird dream, especially one that he vaguely remembered looked like Rose's wonder dog, Thane – to him just an ordinary dog, but larger than normal. So what possible connection could there be? Perhaps some link with an unseen dog barking when he, Rose and Jack got lost in the peat bog area?

He was quite upset, priding himself that all his life and experience in a police career had been ruled by logic, to find himself trapped in a fanciful nightmare. No doubt his mother would have blamed all this electric lighting and women driving motor cars, not to mention railway trains hurtling along tracks at speeds that God never meant men to travel.

Yet Rose and his Imogen belonged to this new breed of women. They would listen patiently with perhaps a few words of consolation or a logical explanation to offer. He sighed. As Imogen was far away, he would tell Rose. Indeed, he had high hopes of Rose, especially as he suspected but never wanted to believe that this daughter was psychic. She saw other things, trawled other worlds, and had done so since childhood days.

Had she been living in Orkney a century ago, he once told her, she would have burnt as a witch. Although he tried to keep her on the track of logic from her earliest days, she appeared to be instinctively good at observation and deduction. Yes, this dream was certainly something he must discuss with Rose. He was to wait some while for that opportunity.

There were, however, dramatic events on the immediate horizon, which threw out of the limelight the idea of whether or not Sven was a questionable archaeologist or Rose's possible interpretation of his weird dream.

Mentally exhausted, he slept longer than usual. The ancient clock on the stair landing was wheezing out nine o'clock and Emily, placing the bacon and eggs on a plate before him, explained that Rose was concerned about the two children, whose great delight was playing in the sea caves, made by coastal erosion through the centuries. They held enormous fascination, especially for these two who were not lacking in imagination. But there was danger, too, from an incoming tide, a terrifying experience of which Rose had personal knowledge from her earlier visit to Orkney.

They had awoken early and set off an hour ago. Seizing her shawl, Rose had gone out to look for them. Had she mentioned the reason, then Gran, who was always ready to see disaster looming on the horizon, would have panicked. Mary had failed to convince Rose that Magnus, having had drilled into him as soon as he could wander alone the perils of sea caves, would proceed cautiously and take care of Meg, who tended to be headstrong on occasions.

Rose had just reached the path through the sand dunes leading down to the shore when she heard voices, and with a sigh of relief saw the two figures heading homeward. They were not alone.

There was a dog at their heels. Not a mere dog, but the shadow of a large hound. Unmistakeably a deerhound.

Thane! Rose's heart missed a beat. No, that was impossible, and then she remembered how Thane had warned her of danger in the past and how Meg now shared that strange telepathy between dog and human.

But before she had more than a moment to reflect, the

terror passed. The children were just yards away, racing towards her and the dog was real. And he certainly was not Thane.

Its owner had just appeared along the length of the shore, calling a greeting. An elderly gentleman in tweeds waved a stick as the children raced past her up to the house, shouting gleefully, 'We've found a new cave,' followed by the inevitable, 'We're starving.'

Rose waited politely for the newcomers. The dog reached her first, sat down to wait patiently for its master puffing up the slope. She recognised Theo Garth, the family lawyer whom she had met at Erland's funeral.

'Took the shortcut, along the shore,' he panted. 'Vestra needed the exercise and so do I,' he added, patting his waistline. 'She was away after those two peedie bairns like a shot. Wouldn't harm them, just loves bairns to play with, though some get scared, start screaming when such a big lass rushes up to them,' he added following Rose towards the house.

She smiled. 'I have one like her at home in Edinburgh. A male.'

'Really?' They were still talking enthusiastically about the merits of the breed and would have gone on for some considerable time had Mary and Emily not appeared in the kitchen, by which time Vestra had made herself at home stretched out in an attitude of complete boredom.

Garth greeted the two women affectionately, in the manner of an old and trusted friend. 'Just one or two things to clear up,' he said to Emily, 'if this informal visit is convenient,' he added, and went on about his morning walk with Vestra, who continued to ignore everyone, a disappointment to Rose on closer acquaintance. She was not like Thane; a female, she was smaller. And she certainly lacked his remarkable head, and Rose suspected, his hyper-intelligence.

However, she glanced anxiously towards Meg, wondering if this meeting would remind her how much she missed him. Seated at Magnus's side at the kitchen table, she was being scolded by Gran for eating too quickly. Leaving Emily to depart into the sitting room with Garth, Rose sat down beside them.

'Tell me about the sea cave.'

'We decided people had lived there long ago—'

Mary hovered with more toast as eager hands reached out, and glancing at the sleeping dog, at home on the rug and quite unconcerned by his owner's departure, Rose regarded Meg nervously. 'Were you surprised to see Vestra, Mr Garth's dog?'

Meg frowned between mouthfuls as Rose swallowed and put into words the question she dreaded: 'Like Thane, I mean? Didn't she remind you of him?'

Glancing briefly at Vestra, she shook her head. 'Not a bit like Thane, besides, she's a female.'

On the way back to the house, she told Rose, Mr Garth had talked to her about Edinburgh and Arthur's Seat, and although he was interested in Thane, Meg was more interested in whether he often saw dolphins and whales, and what about the sea caves and all those selkie legends?

Rose was relieved that the encounter with Vestra had not made Meg suddenly long for home again. And, watching

102

her with Magnus, she had reasons for optimism that perhaps when inevitably Thane was no longer part of their lives, Meg would be ready to move on without heartbreak and endless lamentations.

Completing his business with Emily, Mr Garth declined the offer of being driven home in the motor car. 'The walk will do us both good and it is downhill all the way,' he added cheerfully. Watching him leave, Emily looked sad and said to Rose, 'He is such a good friend. Erland and he were very close. He is going to miss him terribly. He was quite upset. One of the last to see him that . . . that morning. Brought him a bottle of special liqueur every time. I wonder who will want to drink it now.'

Reporting their talk, Emily sighed. Yesnaby House was left to her in her lifetime, then to Magnus or his issue, or the nearest descendant of the Yesnabys. 'There was Sven's pension to be agreed and the issue of the Yesnaby Jewel, our family heirloom. Was I keeping it safe and making sure it was insured? Apart from all this, alas, it seems there is little in actual money, not nearly as much as I imagined, although Erland kept his business ventures to himself.' She shrugged. 'My fault, I'm afraid, as I was never particularly interested in how or where our money came from as long as I had enough to deal with the housekeeping. I suppose many wives are like that and don't realise until it is too late to ask questions about things they should have been more attentive to.'

Rose could sympathise, for although Jack was not forthcoming on his dealings with the Edinburgh Police, he kept her well informed on their domestic financial matters.

She realised how serious this situation was for Emily as she continued bleakly, 'I am quite shocked by Theo's revelations that there is not enough for us to survive indefinitely in Yesnaby. Erland's main bequest was Sven's pension. Not a great lot, but enough to keep him out of the workhouse, should we have to move. A very generous bequest to Gran, should buy her that cottage in Kirkwall.'

The contents of the will were a surprise to Rose. 'I thought Erland was a man of means.'

'So did I, but what he has left will not last long. Yesnaby is costly to run. The estate, what's left of it, only produces a small yearly income now. I think he always hoped and believed that I would marry again, being so much younger, and I guessed that he had John Randall very much in mind. He was away so often, perhaps there were dangers or rather uncertainties that I knew nothing about, and he always said very earnestly: if anything ever happened to me, I know that John would take care of you and Magnus.'

A man of mystery, indeed. A much more complex character with many more layers than the gentle brother-in-law Rose had thought she had got to know so well from that first visit to Yesnaby. 'How did you feel about that?' she asked.

Emily sighed. 'I loved Erland but our life together had changed in recent years, ever since Magnus was born.' She looked embarrassed. 'As a sister you will understand what I am getting at. It seemed as if by creating a son, he had done his duty – and God knows it had been a struggle to get him conceived and delivered safely. Perhaps that had taken the gloss off lovemaking, when it became a nightly duty rather than a spontaneous delight.' She shook her head. 'It did not worry me, he was so often away abroad and maybe I am not a very physical person, and once I had the baby, Magnus became the focus of my existence; besides, I never expected to meet anyone—'

She stopped and looked down from the window to where Sven was working in the garden. There was something in her expression, a sudden tenderness that prompted Rose to ask: 'What happened?'

Emily swung round to face her: 'Nothing, until Sven arrived. He seemed so young but in actual fact he is only ten years younger than me, Rose.' She sighed. 'Of course, such things do not matter and do not raise one eyebrow if the man is a generation older than the woman, like Erland and me. But the other way round, even a few years older, and it is a talking point, a matter for serious consideration. "She's older than him" – you must have heard whispers like that in your time. Right from the beginning, I felt attracted to him sexually. I had always loved Erland but I realised that it was a kind of hero-worship in those far-off days when I was looking after his wife. This was different, this was something at the root of my being and I knew he felt the same attraction for me.' She paused. 'Have I shocked you?'

Rose shook her head. 'No. Go on. Did you—?'

'No, never,' Emily said firmly. 'It never even occurred to me or to Sven, who owed so much to Erland, that we should betray him.'

Rose sighed. This was something very unexpected and she realised she would have been vastly more comfortable if she had seen Dr Randall in the role of Emily's secret lover. 'What about John, surely you realise that he is in love with you?'

Emily smiled. 'I try to ignore that. A nice man but I am not attracted to him. I suppose he has too long been the family doctor, the great friend.'

Rose had no idea how Gran, who had a hawk-like eye on situations that held a breath of romance, illicit or otherwise, would view her beloved Emily and Sven. She decided to try her out when next they were alone in the kitchen. Moving the conversation away from what they were preparing for lunch, she said: 'I was just thinking, it would be a good idea if Em met someone and got married again. It would certainly straighten out a few problems about the house's future.'

'She should marry John,' was the prompt reply. 'He would be right for her and for Magnus.'

For a moment Rose pretended to be giving that careful thought. 'What about Sven?'

'What about him?' Mary turned sharply. Trying to appear casual, Rose shrugged and said: 'He's a very attractive young man, friend of the family, trusted retainer for the last two years or so. And they seem to get along so well together. He helps her with everything, been invaluable since she lost Erland.'

Mary snorted and applied herself vigorously to rolling pastry. 'Far too young for her.'

'That's what everyone says when the woman is younger,' Rose insisted, and she repeated Em's words. 'No one said that Erland was old enough to be her father and yet she married him. Did you think they would make an ideal pair?'

'Don't you be saying a word against Erland. He was the perfect man for her,' Mary said sharply. 'As for that Sven,

106

well, he's foreign to start with, and not the right man to move into Yesnaby.'

'He seems to be here already, Gran, and by Erland's wish. He brought him.' Rose reminded her.

'That was maybe a mistake, maybe not. Erland usually knew what he was doing.'

'Well, from what Em tells me, he thought the world of Sven, so surely he would be pleased to see the two people he loved most spending the rest of their lives together?'

Mary shook her head. 'I doubt that. Far too full of himself that young man, for a start. And he likes the girls, from what I hear, and they like him.'

Rose smiled. 'Emily likes him too, Gran.'

'And that's a long way from bed and board and happy ever after,' Mary snapped.

Rose gave her a shrewd look. 'You don't like him much, do you, Gran?'

Mary shrugged. 'Whether I like him or not is of no importance. He is part of this household, a good servant, I grant you that, and a great help to our Em with all that correspondence. But that doesn't mean I want to see him as head of the house. What does he do with his time all day when he isn't in that garden?'

'He's been trying to find out what's happening on the yacht out there.'

Mary sniffed. Since the King was not on board, she wasn't interested. 'He's a leaner, that's what.' And that was her final word on Sven.

Their plan was to visit the Broch of Birsay that day. Magnus, who had inherited his father's love of history,

107

wanted to stop on the way and show Meg the Neolithic village, a link with Orkney's first inhabitants.

'It's just a few miles away, no distance really, we could practically walk there – and you must see it. Father took me there quite often. Grandfather wasn't around when it was discovered.'

Faro had never seen Skara Brae but accounts of its remarkable preservation made interesting reading. In 1850 a wild storm swept away all the dunes that it had lain hidden under for past centuries.

Rose, too, was intrigued, she had been promised a visit ten years ago, but the emergence of the peat bog woman and its dramatic and terrifying consequences put visiting ancient ruins out of everyone's thoughts.

Now was the perfect opportunity: a clear sky, warm sun, and no wind had arisen. Faro, Rose and the children would go with Sven driving the car, while Mary, busily packing a picnic hamper, decided to remain at Yesnaby with Emily.

There were still letters to write, thanking the friends and acquaintances who had come from far and wide over the islands and beyond Orkney for the funeral. Erland had travelled widely abroad and had been a very popular man, Emily told them, and she had received condolences from a circle of acquaintances – friends even – who she had never heard of, names that he had never mentioned.

'Thank goodness for Sven. Without his help I'd be completely lost. He can deal with the letters from Norway and help with folk he knew Erland had met. He's an absolute gem. I was so shocked – I still am – and he immediately stepped in, took over everything. I don't know what I would do without him. It's like having a personal secretary and I feel very privileged that he is willing to continue—'

Pausing, she put her hand to her mouth. 'Oh dear, there's something else I'd forgotten. We were to expect a visit any day now from this fourth cousin twice removed, or something of the sort. This woman, Alice, lives in Aberdeen. Erland mentioned her father, William Yesnaby, occasionally, there were even some family photos taken on beaches, that sort of thing, if I can lay hands on them.' Emily sighed. 'I thought I'd written to her. I hope she got my letter before she left. Awful if she just walked in!'

Rose could see the problem. None of the Faros shone at letter writing, although her father was doing his best with Imogen. It was all rather bewildering as each day the postman still brought letters from shocked colleagues and people who had given Erland hospitality or still remembered a brief meeting. All had to have replies and Mary insisted that she could at least address the envelopes.

If she had been truthful, her main reason was that this was a good excuse not to go on a picnic, which she never enjoyed, sitting on a rug, mostly feeling the cold.

Rose also offered to stay. In the light of her sister's recent revelations, she was regarding Sven from a somewhat different angle and had her own ideas about the eulogistic tone of those condolences. So many people who had known and cared for Erland, this quite ordinary-seeming man, was it his beautiful voice that had left them enchanted by his presence?

As for this unseen stranger cousin about to descend on Yesnaby, never could have a longed-for visit have been so inopportune or embarrassing: to have made the journey all the way from Aberdeen to be met with such dire news.

Emily was saying: 'No, you go with Pa and the children. You have never been there and,' she added sadly, 'meeting so rarely over the years, I do want you and Pa to take back some pleasant memories.'

They were about to leave when PC Flett arrived at the door. One look at his harassed expression indicated bad news. And they were right about that.

'Is Inspector Macmerry here? There's been an accident.'

CHAPTER NINE

'I had a message from Millie, to tell you she can't come today.' Flett shook his head gravely. 'Her lad, Archie, has been attacked – last night. Down on the shore.'

'How dreadful,' Emily exclaimed. 'Is he seriously hurt?'

'We don't know yet. Dr Randall is still with him. Hit over the head, he was. Knocked unconscious when they found him.'

'Does he know who attacked him?'

Again, the policeman shook his head. 'Can't get a word of sense out of him at the best of times, so you can imagine what he's like now. I tried my best and so did Millie. But all he does is keep mumbling something about selkies and looking round wildly, trying to escape. I had to hold him down for the doctor to examine him.'

Rose and Emily exchanged glances. Had this attack revived his terror and guilt about believing he had shot a seal who had turned into an old woman, Sibella, who had slid away like that animal and vanished into the sea before his eyes.

'I must go to Millie,' Emily said. 'You go on to Birsay.'

'I think not, Em,' said Faro, who was also associating this talk of selkies with Archie's extraordinary shooting incident. 'I would like a word with this young man. Perhaps I can help him,' he added, without much hope of that.

Magnus and Meg exchanged glances and accepted this change of plans with suppressed sighs of disappointment but quite philosophically; Meg could have warned her cousin that this was the way of grown-ups, especially if you had the misfortune to have a father who was also a police inspector. The wry look at her mam confirmed without any words that it was always to be expected, a family failing. Rose's reaction had been to go with Faro, but on reflection, the presence of two strangers, particularly that of a woman, would probably merely increase his confusion.

'I'll go to Birsay with the children, Pa,' she said. 'Sven can take us in the car. It's only a short distance to Hopescarth, and you can walk there, you know the way.'

Faro agreed with a sense of relief. Emily would be taken up with Millie and he would have the chance he had been waiting for to talk to Archie alone. Originally, it had been curiosity about the seal-shooting incident, now there was an added more urgent reason, and as he and Emily headed towards Millie's croft, he wondered if there might be some sinister connection.

They had learnt from PC Flett that the lad's injuries had not been bad enough to put him in hospital. 'Aye, just one or two bruises where he fell and the doctor thought it better to keep him at home with his bandaged head. Places where people are confined to bed just terrify him, scare the wits out of the poor lad. Make him a thousand times more confused.'

Millie opened the door to them, distraught and tearful.

'It was terrible, terrible. He didn't come home and he's been spending hours every night by the shore down there, hoping to get a selkie. He's done it for – for a couple of years now.' She paused and the horrified look at Emily confirmed Faro's suspicions that this was since the seal shooting. 'We just have to humour him. Sometimes he stays out all night but when I got home yesterday, he hadn't been home. I waited, stayed awake, and in the early hours I got scared. I knew something was wrong and I ran down to the shore. There he was lying in the dunes, with his poor head bleeding. Two nights ago he said he'd seen a selkie among the seals but before he could reach her, she'd disappeared. He was sure she was meant for him and she'd come back if he would just go and wait every night. That was when the man hit him.'

She gave a shuddering sigh. 'Thought at first he was killed, lying there not moving, but when I touched him, he just groaned and said someone had crept upon him and hit him, trying to steal his selkie. I didn't want to leave him, but he's a big lad and so I ran to Flett's house, got him up and he came and helped me to get Archie on his feet. Once we were back home, Flett said although there didn't seem much damage – he could still walk – he'd get the doctor to have a look at him. Dr Randall came quick, like, and said there was no cause for alarm, a great bump on his head, but you'd never see it, he has such a head of hair. He said keep him quiet for a day or two, there might be a bit of concussion and that would make him more confused than ever.' She began wringing her hands and looked up at Emily. 'What am I going to do, Mrs Yesnaby? Who would want to harm my poor peedie bairn?'

Who indeed? was Faro's immediate thought. Did he have any enemies? Millie laughed at the idea. Her lad was everyone's friend, far and wide. It was the wide bit that particularly interested Faro.

'What about beyond home?' Faro asked. 'In Stromness or even Kirkwall?'

Again that scornful laugh from Millie. She looked at Faro as if he had gone mad. Such an incredible idea. 'He never stirred beyond Hopescarth. If he ever went into Stromness, it was with me. He was scared of strangers and would never go alone, especially after . . . after that other business.'

Pausing, she shook her head: 'That left a terrible scar on him. He was always a bit different from other folk, not like me or his poor father, who died before Archie was born, but he seemed to manage and we always understood each other. We were that close and he told me everything. He trusted me.'

Following her into the tiny bedroom where Archie was propped up in bed surrounded by pillows, Faro received a shrill scream and a look of wild terror at this appearance of a stranger.

'That's him – that's him that hit me!' he yelled and tried to leap out of the bed, forcibly restrained by his mother and Emily, their repeated explanation that this gentleman was here to help at last calming him, but he continued to stare fearfully at Faro.

At last, they settled Archie down with sympathy offered and assurance that he was mistaken and that this gentleman was Mr Faro, Mrs Yesnaby's father. The wicked man who attacked him would be found and punished by the police.

Faro guessed from the groans and indistinct murmurings that there was little more to be gained from the interview than he had learnt from Millie, apart from the part oft-repeated about a stolen selkie that was rightfully his.

'The poor lad,' Emily said as they walked home, 'has never been quite right in the head, a lifetime obsession with selkies and Lammastide legends.'

The Birsay visit had been postponed. It was raining and Sven had driven into Kirkwall.

'He must have forgotten to remind me,' said Emily apologetically. 'This is market day and he was hoping to meet a prospective buyer.'

'What happened? How's Archie?'

Rose and Mary were receiving her abridged account of the bewildering meeting with Archie when footsteps outside had Meg leaping to her. 'It's Pa! He's back.'

Jack came in, exchanged kisses and hugs, and then, looking over Meg's head, he said: 'I'm really going back to Edinburgh this time, just here to collect my case.'

'Didn't you see Sven in Kirkwall with the car?'

Jack shook his head. 'Didn't know he was there; that would have saved me a trip on the bus. There's a ship for Leith, we leave at five in the morning, so I'll stay the night at the hotel.' He grinned. 'Don't want to disturb everyone, or wake you from your beauty sleep, Rose. Of course, you don't need it,' he added hastily as her hand reached up to slap him. 'Maybe Sven needs his; I don't think he'd relish the prospect of driving into Kirkwall at dawn.'

'Oh, we'll miss you,' groaned Meg, clinging to him, 'I want you to stay for ever.'

Jack laughed. 'If I did, pet, we would all starve. No money or anything. Besides you have school very soon and your mam and I have work to do every day.'

'You were needed here earlier on,' Meg replied. 'Guess what! Millie's son had an accident. He was attacked by a man while he was watching the seals.'

Jack darted a questioning look at Rose, who said: 'Pa and Emily went to see him, nothing serious,' she added hastily. Not wishing the children to be alarmed by a lurking attacker in the neighbourhood, which at the least might encourage nightmares, she was to discover that her fears were groundless, such dangers being treated merely as additional excitement.

Emily said, 'I suspect he just fell and hit his head and imagined the rest. Hardly an incident needing an investigation by a police inspector from Edinburgh.'

'That's a relief, anyway,' Jack said. 'Can't imagine there's much in the way of crime in Hopescarth.' He paused. 'By the way, Rose, I'm taking your father back to Kirkwall with me. There's someone who has always wanted to meet him, just a social visit,' he added at her expression, 'an admirer.'

As he finished speaking, Sven arrived back with the motor car and Rose went in search of Faro, who was enjoying a pipe and wondering if he had missed something essential in Millie's account and Archie's inarticulate version of the accident.

He put out his pipe and said yes, he would enjoy a visit to Kirkwall. 'What is it all about, this man who wants to meet me?'

Rose shrugged. 'Jack told me nothing, just some fellow he'd met.' They both knew what that meant. Over the decades, Chief Inspector Faro's reputation had followed him. She had learnt from experience that such reputations soon build up. In eleven years, she had made a name for herself as a lady investigator and now often encountered strangers in Edinburgh who had heard of her and took the opportunity of asking for advice.

Family farewells repeated once more, Jack's eyebrows raised in mock despair. 'This is getting to be a habit,' he said. Disentangling Meg's arms from around his neck and setting her feet firmly on the ground, he leant over and kissed Rose.

Seated in the motor car, Faro related the details of Archie's accident. Sven was shocked and said that he hoped this dreadful man would be caught and sent to prison. Since having any meaningful conversation travelling the rough cliff roads was impossible, there was no hope of Faro getting answers for the many questions he wished to put to Jack seated behind. However, in an uneven stretch of road, the ever-alert Sven detected a tremble in the accelerator unnoticed by his passengers, but meticulous about such things he apologised for the slight delay while he groped about knowledgeably inside the engine.

Faro and Jack disembarked, taking this chance to stretch their legs.

'What did you conclude about this attack on Archie?' Faro asked.

Jack shrugged. 'Same as everyone else. Looking for selkies every night and this Lammastide legend just threw him over the edge. He stumbled and fell, hit his head, knocked himself out and imagined the rest.'

'So you don't believe anyone attacked him?'

'No, I do not.'

However, Faro had a more important question unrelated to Archie's so-called accident. 'You haven't been quite straight with me, Jack.'

Jack looked puzzled. 'In what way?'

'To start with, about the fraud case.'

Jack frowned. 'I can't tell you any more than I know. I had a telegraph, direct instructions from Edinburgh that I was to remain here on the pretext of a fraud case. That I might be needed.'

'And that was all?'

'Just as I told you. I have been in communication with Central Office and I gathered that their instructions came from a higher authority: His Majesty's government, no less.'

Faro thought for a moment. 'What about this man I am going to meet? Has he some connection? What do you know about him?'

Jack shook his head. 'Nothing, except another message from Edinburgh saying there was someone who wanted to meet Inspector Faro and that he was to regard this as of the utmost importance.' Frowning, he turned to his father-in-law. 'May have something to do with your past police activities, but they certainly were not willing to share that information with me.' He sounded slightly offended, considering his seniority in the Force.

'We are ready to leave now, gentlemen.' Sven was wiping his hands and donned his goggles.

With no opportunity for more speculation they reached Kirkwall, and Sven set them down outside the local hotel where a tall man, formally attired in what Faro guessed was from the regions of London's Savile Row tailors, stood before a blazing fire in the cosily furnished parlour. Even in summer a fire was one of their attractions for mainland visitors who might find the wind or the unreliable weather troublesome.

Guessing ages was not one of Faro's attributes and this man, immaculately attired from expensively shining boots to smoothly pomaded hair, could have been anywhere between fifty and a well-preserved sixty-five. A gentleman of substance, Faro decided, confirmed by the antique French watch with an elegant gold chain, consulted and held in a well-manicured right hand with a signet ring bearing the coat of arms of some noble house. And the final touch: as soon as he opened his mouth there issued forth the voice of authority. Clearly not a retired policeman wishing to shake the legendary inspector by the hand or a local resident with some minor or major problem and some confidence to be shared.

Jack gave a smart bow to the gentleman, who had introduced himself as Mr Smith, and his presence no longer required, he excused himself. He had some business, a few minor details to attend to before returning to Edinburgh. As he and Mr Smith were both staying overnight in the hotel, Jack suggested that they might have supper together. Mr Smith bowed. He would be delighted. And Jack turned to Faro. 'Perhaps you would care to join us?'

Much as he enjoyed Jack's company, Faro did not relish

the prospects of supper shared with this stranger. With no idea of what the man had in mind, he wanted to get this interview over as quickly as possible and declined the invitation on the grounds that Sven would be waiting to take him back to Yesnaby. On the assumption that this meeting would be brief, giving his father-in-law a parting hug Jack departed, telling him to take care of himself, and to pass on warmest greetings to Imogen.

Faro took a seat. His observation having already taken in all the details, his mind was racing ahead. He would not be surprised to be told that the man sitting opposite was not really called Mr Smith, and taking in his immaculate appearance that it was neither Kirkwall nor Orkney matters, nor the desire to make the acquaintance of a once famous policeman, that had brought about this meeting.

The stranger spoke first: 'You may be surprised to know that I am from the King's yacht.'

That suspicion had already entered Faro's mind as Mr Smith continued, 'You may have observed the *Victoria and Albert III* anchored near Stromness.' A slight pause and Faro observed the merest suggestion of a nervous twitch. Whatever this was about, whatever urgency had driven him to seek out the retired chief inspector, Mr Smith was not a happy man, and Faro decided to help him out.

'The yacht is visible from our house at Yesnaby and we might have had our meeting there. You would have been most welcome and, of course, if there was anything you required . . .' Faro added, thinking of the yacht's small boat being rowed across the short distance, but Mr Smith shook his head and continued.

120

'It was more convenient and would attract less attention from the local community to arrange this meeting in Kirkwall. I trust it has not put you to any unnecessary trouble. I gather you came by motor car.'

While Faro was mulling over the significance of attracting less attention, Mr Smith said: 'I will not beat about the bush, Chief Inspector—'

'It's just Mr Faro now, I am retired, so if this is police business, I am afraid that I can no longer be of any assistance.'

Mr Smith shook his head vigorously. 'This is a matter for private investigation. You have, I expect, already realised that it relates to HM's yacht.' He paused, breathed deeply before continuing. 'Our cruise took us over to Norway, visiting personal friends, and on our return voyage when the approaching storm threatened, we were in sight of Orkney and decided to take refuge.'

Faro remembered Sven's account of a party in progress and loud music. Hardly a refuge, as Mr Smith, biting his lip, said: 'There was a most unfortunate accident, a member . . . of the company fell overboard.'

Most probably drank too much, Faro had already decided as Mr Smith went on, 'Of course, we set to work immediately to try to rescue this . . . this person but despite all our efforts soon realised that it was beyond us.'

'Did you not consider calling for the assistance of the lifeboat? They are always at the ready, on the alert and adept at dealing with such matters in all weathers.'

Imagination supplied the negative reasoning to that suggestion as Mr Smith made an impatient gesture. 'Of course, of course. It was suggested, but the idea was speedily abandoned, I'm afraid. Such a decision would have led to the inevitable publicity raised in newspapers, and so forth.' He paused and regarded Faro solemnly. 'I am sure you understand, sir, that bringing such an unfortunate incident before the public eye would be very intensely displeasing should it reach His Majesty's ears.'

Not so distressing or displeasing as the loss of a man's life, thought Faro, who was beginning to like Mr Smith less and less as he continued: 'So we have remained at anchor, taking shelter unobtrusively, hoping to sort it out with a happy conclusion before proceeding on our way.' Pausing to sigh and shake his head, he went on, 'Sadly nothing, no evidence of any sort came to light despite intensive searching and diving by members of the crew.' He made a despairing gesture. 'We can delay no longer: the yacht is scheduled for another cruise so we must return to London and face the consequences of a disastrous voyage.'

Again, he paused regarding Faro hopefully, whose mind was already confronting the next question. Who had commissioned this cruise to Norway without the King himself? Who was so important in royal circles? Although he knew that Imogen could have answered that: some minor royal, someone high in government circles, or a person of considerable wealth wishing to impress and willing to pay dearly for it. Which of these categories, he wondered, fitted Mr Smith, whose intense gaze continued? But Faro shook his head; without further information there was no suitable or helpful comment he could think of, although listening closely to Mr Smith had revealed other facts.

Besides being fearful, Mr Smith was not English. The very

slightest of accents had given him away and by his expression he had waited long enough to guess the once brilliant chief inspector – his last resort – was not going to be of the slightest help with his mysterious reason for this meeting.

He said, 'I am sure you understand, sir, that it would be tragic, but quite necessary for us to return with some evidence.' He coughed, paused a moment and asked: 'Tell me, Mr Faro, what is the estimated time for a drowned body to be washed ashore?'

Faro regarded him wide-eyed. That was a question to which no one could give a reliable or comforting answer. He said: 'The curious tides and any number of factors make its probable destination unpredictable. It could be washed up, drifted by the vagaries of the tide on to any of the islands. Some bodies remain for weeks; some are never recovered.' He did not add, many beyond recognition, broken up, made limbless by savage waves beating a corpse upon the rocks.

Mr Smith nodded. 'I understand. And I realise from this information that there is little reason to hope that by delaying our return voyage south' – he frowned – 'we might be in possession of a body.'

There was a slight pause before Faro asked the question that had been troubling him. 'How did you think I might be able to help you?'

Mr Smith looked vague and uncomfortable as Faro added: 'I am puzzled to know who suggested that you should contact me in this matter, especially as my visit had been arranged at short notice. It was for a family funeral.'

Mr Smith shook his head. 'I can say only that information reached me by way of reliable sources, so I took the liberty of getting in touch with you. Of course, I had heard of your remarkable career and we met once at an embassy reception in Edinburgh. It was a long time ago, back in the '80s so I don't expect you remember.' A slight smile. 'However, I have a good memory for faces and thought I recognised you in a rowing boat near the yacht with some young people. A passing remark and all things seemed in my favour, particularly with the remarkable coincidence that you happened to be staying in the vicinity.'

Remarkable, indeed, Faro thought, as one who did not believe in coincidences. Words, he realised from his long experience, often used to veil very sinister plots. Furthermore, he had not the slightest recollection, even with his own excellent memory, of any earlier meeting with Mr Smith, or whatever his real name had been.

He said: 'Whilst I accept what you have told me and the difficulties involved, I fail to see how I can be of any assistance, especially if I am to be kept in ignorance of the identity of the person involved: the man overboard?'

Mr Smith rose to his feet, he seemed considerably agitated. 'Then we must leave the matter where it stands. My only hope was that you might have some helpful advice. I see that I was wrong and that I made a mistake.' He gave a slight, rather foreign bow as he added: 'I will delay you no longer, Mr Faro, and can only offer apologies for taking up your valuable time.'

Sven was hovering, seated near the door, intently reading a newspaper. Faro wondered if his curiosity had been aroused and how much of their conversation he had overheard as he asked Mr Smith: 'How do you get back?'

'The river pilot will return me to the yacht. He has been instructed to collect me in the morning. We sail on the afternoon tide.'

As they shook hands, Faro was aware of the man's despair and desperation, frustrated and a little angry that he had learnt nothing of Mr Smith's motives behind a meeting that had been for both of them a waste of time – time now so precious to him, that he might have spent with his family, and Rose in particular. They never seemed to get enough hours together, with so much missing, so much information to be gathered and gaps to be filled from the years they had spent apart.

He wondered if Rose with her intuition might hazard a guess at Mr Smith's motives for the meeting. If only she could have been present she would no doubt have contributed vital questions that had not occurred to him, and he would now be brooding on more than a wasted few hours.

Sven was waiting. 'Sir, there is a problem with the motor car. There was something wrong with the engine on our way here, as you may remember. The garage will sort it out but have warned me that it might take some hours to correct. I must wait, but they are providing you with transport.' Pointing to the waiting motor car he said, 'I am so sorry for all this inconvenience, sir. Please convey my apologies to Mrs Yesnaby.'

CHAPTER TEN

The hired car, with a driver as silent as any in Edinburgh, put him down at Yesnaby. Still brooding angrily over his wasted evening with Mr Smith, he expected Rose to be sympathetic and suggest some reasons for what seemed an extraordinary interview. But all she contributed was, 'Poor Pa. That's the price of fame!' and went on to tell him that, in his absence, she had been trying to get some sensible facts about Archie's mysterious attack.

Millie had arrived shortly after Jack and Faro departed. Her neighbour next door had promised to keep an eye on Archie while she went to apologise to Mrs Yesnaby, knowing how greatly she was needed, and ignoring Mary Faro's sniff of disapproval or disbelief, when there were so many people to cook and clean for as well as this Aberdeen cousin, who Emily had warned her might walk in unannounced any minute.

'There has to be a room ready for her. We must do our best to make her welcome.'

There would be no help from Millie now, the shocking accident to poor Archie was the last straw. Emily tried to be comforting, assuring her of everyone's concern about Archie and that they would do their best to manage without her for the present.

Rose decided she would walk back to Hopescarth with Millie, an offer that was received gratefully but from Rose's point of view for entirely the wrong reason. She wasn't sure, as certain as the others, nor as ready to accept that Archie had fallen and had an attack of imagination. She wanted to walk along the shore and ask Millie to show her where she had found him.

Millie was more than willing to lead her to the exact spot. 'There, among the sand dunes, Mrs Macmerry.' The place where he had lain all night was flattened and a closer look revealed nothing sharp to indicate that was where he struck his head when he fell. As they moved on, away from the bruised grasses, while Millie chattered on tearfully reliving the drama once again, Rose stooped, picked up a stone. A smudge that could have been a bloodstain: was this the weapon? she wondered, putting it in her pocket.

Someone needed to talk to Archie, hear his story again, especially as he was much recovered from the head injury but still very confused. Where her father had failed earlier in the day, a sympathetic woman used to consoling words for distressed clients might succeed. She needed only to convince Millie.

'Of course you can see him, Mrs Rose. He is much better now and I am sure just longing to tell someone else about it all. He is weary of telling me and I am weary of listening to the same story. Poor peedie bairn,' she added with a deep sigh.

It was what Rose had hoped for. Archie was no longer in bed but sitting up in an Orkney chair by the window.

Millie said: 'This is Mrs Yesnaby's sister come to see you.'

Turning, he greeted her with a smile, held out his hand. In that handshake Rose felt she was seeing a perfectly normal young lad, whose good looks might have set the Orkney lasses hearts a-fluttering. Under that bandaged head, curling fair hair and bright hazel eyes. In that first moment of meeting there seemed little to connect him with the wild-eyed creature Faro had encountered.

She sat down in the chair opposite. 'I am glad to see that you have recovered. We were all sorry to hear about your nasty accident.'

He regarded her solemnly for a moment. 'It was not an accident, Mrs Macmerry. A man hit me, tried to kill me.' His voice was firm and steady.

'How dreadful.' Rose said the words expected of her. 'What was he like, this man? Can you describe him?'

'I can that. I thought he'd come back for me this morning,' he said with a frenzied glance at his mother. His voice raised petulantly: 'I was seeing him again, like I told you—'

'Archie, please . . .' his mother interrupted. Laying a restraining hand on his arm, she turned to Rose. 'I do apologise, Mrs Macmerry, the poor lad wasn't in his right mind,' she added in a whisper. 'Just confused. The man he thought hit him must have looked like Mr Faro.'

'He was a gentleman; I know a gentleman when I see one,' Archie shouted and Rose interrupted what she guessed was going to be a long story. 'Just tell me about him.'

Archie sighed, closed his eyes for a moment as if in the effort of remembering. 'I will tell you all about it, if you will listen.' A sharp glance in his mother's direction, who was standing by the window, looking apprehensively at him. 'She's been told and doesn't want to hear any more. She doesn't believe me.' And looking at Rose, obviously consoled by this pretty woman with her gentle smile, he stretched out his hand and touched hers. 'But you are different from the others, I think you will believe that I am telling the truth, that a man tried to kill me. He wanted to steal my selkie, and she was coming, I knew, any minute.' His eyes darkened, 'I looked round. There was this man who had been walking on the shore; I couldn't see him now but the next moment, I felt a thud on my head.' His hand reached up and touched the bandage, trembling. 'I saw stars. Then everything went black. Next thing I knew, it was day, Ma was bending over me crying, there was a policeman and my head was bleeding.'

Suddenly the calm young man had vanished, his eyes were wild, his hands thumped the arms of the chair. He groaned, covering his eyes, sobbing, the tears flowing. 'Now, I might never see her again,' he wailed.

Rose leant over, touched his shoulder, said: 'It may not be as bad as you think,' knowing they were empty words. There was no comfort or even truth in them, but they had the right effect.

He looked up. 'You think so?'

Rose smiled, reached out for his hand. 'But we have to find this man who you think attacked you.'

She asked: 'Had you ever seen him before?' Ignoring the fact that he had resembled her father.

Archie shook his head, thought for a moment. 'He wasn't close enough for me to see his face, but I would know him again.' He paused. 'You've all asked what he looked like. Well, all I can tell you is that he was smartly dressed, not casual like our folk. Not from the island. He was a gentleman.' He sighed again. 'You are a lady, missus. You will know where to look for him.' And looking over to where his mother still stood watching them, he shouted, 'I'm hungry. Get me some food now, please.'

Rose stood up, ready to take her leave. The interview was over; there was no more information to be gained. Refusing Millie's offer of refreshment, of bannocks and cheese, and heading back to Yesnaby, she was alerted to the approach of a horse and trap. The driver waved to her.

Dr Randall. Coming to a halt with a friendly greeting, Rose realised this was exactly the opportunity she wanted. 'I have just visited one of your patients, Doctor. Archie Tofts.'

The doctor sighed. 'Ah, yes, young Archie. Look, can I offer you a lift to Yesnaby?'

The house was almost visible, but Rose guessed that the doctor had thought fast and this was another chance to see Emily again. Thanking him, she stepped up and he moved alongside for her. 'Young Archie,' he repeated. 'Did he tell you his story, of the attack?' When she said so, he shook his head. 'I am afraid we are all victims of his imagination.'

'You mean none of it was true?'

'Alas, no. I've looked after the lad since I first came here. He was just into his teens and the first thing I spotted was that he suffered from what is all too frequent on the island, commonly known in Orkney as the "doonfa" sickness.'

Rose frowned. She had heard of it, of course, in her young days with Gran in Kirkwall. Randall continued, 'In other words he has epilepsy, although his mother refuses to accept it. He takes fits and has done so since childhood. She ignores that, especially as they are less frequent these days. She has the forlorn hope that he has recovered from what was just a childhood disorder.' He shook his head. 'That is unlikely, and I am afraid what happened last night might be an all too frequent recurrence, not helped by the Lammastide mythology and his obsession with selkies.'

He paused. 'My diagnosis, which of course his mother rejected, is that he had an epileptic seizure, fell and hit his head on a rock, was knocked unconscious and believed that some man, an innocent walker he had observed nearby out for an evening stroll, had hit him on the head. His mother not unnaturally wishes to believe his story, since she completely rejects the "doonfa" sickness diagnosis.'

They had reached the house where Emily immediately invited John in for a cup of tea. Both seemed pleased by this unexpected meeting, which cheered Rose, who could not help but feel that her sister's infatuation for Sven would end in heartbreak.

She had no intention of revealing Emily's confidences to their father – such matters were sacred between sisters – however, as he had seen her arrive with John Randall and observed his warm reception, Faro said that the doctor was a fine fellow and it would be excellent, as well as solving the problem of staying on at Yesnaby, if Emily could come to regard him less through the eyes of a long and trusted friend and more as a life partner.

Rose was pleased but shook an admonishing finger at him. 'Well, Pa, this is a surprise. Since the time has come that you no longer have crimes to solve and criminals to put behind bars in the interests of public safety, you might well go into the business of matchmaking.'

He chuckled and shook his head. 'My dear, it is merely my lifelong observation and deduction at work, the desire to restore order out of chaos. Anyone with half an eye can see that the good doctor is devoted to our Emily.'

Ignoring what she regarded as her father's regrettable tendency towards clichés, and remembering her talk with Archie, she asked, 'What did he look like, this Mr Smith? Describe him.'

Faro did so and she laughed. 'Now there's a coincidence. When you said Archie was terrified of you and thought you were his attacker, I think we have the answer. This tall gentleman from the yacht seen at a distance also fitted your description. Don't you see, Pa? From what we now know, there is every reason to consider that despite Dr Randall's diagnosis, perhaps Archie was telling the truth and from what you have told me, Mr Smith might well have been his attacker.'

Faro smiled. 'As always, my dear, our thoughts run along the same track. It would seem that our royal yacht is implicated, but as yet I can't see any obvious link with a lad who had to be hit on the head, except that he was in the vicinity, innocently waiting for a selkie to appear.'

Selkies meant Sibella Scarth to Rose. 'I loved Sibella. When we met, I realised that Emily might, if she lived to be very, very old, be her image. Remember the portrait I did of her?'

He smiled. 'Yes, and quite extraordinary, Meg's mistake thinking it was Emily. At least I know now that I've solved one mystery, why my two daughters looked so unlike sisters. Emily didn't look like any of us. But you, my dear, were the image of your mother, my beloved Lizzie.' Was this, he wondered, why Rose had always been his closest bairn?

Rose was saying, 'I couldn't understand it either, I only knew that I wanted to be like Em, envying her looks, and then when I met Sibella, I guessed the seal woman story was right.' She looked at him intently. 'Especially those mittened hands, and even the rather . . . slithering way she walked. It was very odd, a bit scary, but she was such a wonderful person and she was very proud of you.'

There was a slight pause and as Faro made no comment, Rose said: 'You don't really believe that story about Sibella and Hakon Scarth rescuing her from the sea, do you, Pa?'

He sighed. 'I prefer the more rational and logical explanation that regardless of the denials of the sailors from the wrecked ship – and they may have had good reason for that – I think she was undoubtedly a survivor, a tiny child too young to remember her parents, who went down with the Norwegian merchantman.'

'What about Archie's story, then, about shooting a seal, which turned out to be an old woman, our Sibella. Don't you believe that?'

The story made Faro uncomfortable. He did not like to face the fact that there was no grave for his grandmother, that she had drowned and her body was never recovered or, as Rose would prefer to believe, the seal woman had gone back to the sea. Faro was a man who liked tidy ends to stories and this one upset him.

'We have to remember that by all accounts she was more than just an elderly woman. She was incredibly old, well over a hundred. Although I gather from you and Em that she was still independent and went walking each day by the shore, she must have been very fragile, frail enough to fall into the sea and drown.'

Rose said: 'Always looking out for Hakon, I remember her telling me. That someday he would come for her, and as he had always loved the sea she would go back there to be with him.' She smiled at her father. 'She once pointed out the particular rock where he would be waiting.'

'A nice romantic tale, Rose,' Faro replied, determined to have the last word. 'Let's pretend, for the sake of argument, that since her eyesight was no longer good, and quite incapable of seeing through the island's frequent mists, she imagined one day that he was there waiting for her, so she tried to reach him and, well, that was the end. She disappeared into the sea, but not out of some magical impulse.' He shrugged. 'As for Archie's tale, he is obsessed with selkies, and he was out shooting illegally, I understand, and everyone knows that seals' heads can look like humans. Like old men, mostly.'

They looked at each other, each the same thought.

Or the head of the passenger who had gone overboard and drowned off the royal yacht.

There was an interesting epilogue to their earlier speculation regarding Mr Smith and the royal yacht that neither could know at that time. In Kirkwall, Jack had returned to the hotel awaiting Mr Smith in the dining room. The hour appointed passed, and still he did not appear. Jack ate alone, and although annoyed that some message might have been sent in the interests of politeness, he dismissed the incident and after an excellent meal finished off by equally excellent Orkney whisky, he retired to bed to be wakened as requested by the alarm.

He declined breakfast and paying his bill to the all-night reception clerk, his curiosity was suddenly aroused by the register lying open, and scanning the signatures, he asked: 'I had a supper engagement with Mr Smith, but he failed to appear. I wonder did he leave a message for me?'

'A moment, sir,' the clerk consulted the rack. 'Nothing here.' He frowned. 'Mr Smith did not occupy his room last night. He did not pick up his key, said he was going for a walk before dining. So he obviously intended to return. But he seems to have left, and I regret to say, without paying his bill for yesterday's luncheon and his drinks' bill.'

Heading towards the ferry, Jack was still sleepy and wished he had not applied himself quite so enthusiastically to the whisky; it always had this effect on him. As for Mr Smith, he would have liked to have had a word with his father-in-law about the outcome of that interview, but that would have to wait. Curiosity was not one of his failings, he was a practical man and used to interpreting what was in front of him rather than making speculations often based on intuition, which he regarded as women's business and fitted often quite successfully in with Rose's role as a lady investigator. He smiled. Her intuitions were commendable and doubtless when she returned home he would hear all about her father and the man who had so wanted to meet him.

Although the mysterious Mr Smith had looked like a gentleman, good manners as well as honesty regarding a hotel bill were in dispute, but what most occupied Jack's thoughts was returning to the Central Office and hoping that someone could throw some light on the reason why there had been a message from what the police headed under 'higher authorities', a vague term disguising HM's government, that he had been told to remain in Orkney on a fabricated reason of a fraud case and warned off any matters relating to the presence of the royal yacht.

However, he did not associate Mr Smith or his subsequent disappearance with those orders from Edinburgh. Those revelations were to remain hidden for the present.

CHAPTER ELEVEN

While Rose and Faro had accepted Dr Randall's verdict that Archie's so-called attack had been an accident caused by his epilepsy, PC Flett was called to a similar incident in Skailholm. A local lad of Archie's age was leaving the inn when he was brutally attacked and, even worse than Archie, left for dead. Dr Randall, who served both communities, was called and the young man rushed to the local hospital where PC Flett sat patiently by his bedside, notebook at the ready, awaiting his return to consciousness, to reveal details of the attack.

On hearing of this new crime, Faro sighed. It was becoming evident that here were some doubtful areas in the local police administration.

Emily said defensively, 'This is new to us, Pa. We hardly need a policeman at all. We are very law-abiding citizens. The only things Flett ever has to sort out are occasional drunken brawls, mostly at Hogmanay, or poachers.'

'What about smuggling?'

She laughed. 'Only whisky, perhaps. And for obvious reasons, that is completely ignored.'

'By "obvious reasons", I presume you mean bribes.'

She shrugged. 'If you want to put it that way, but it is hardly corruption on a large scale, all fairly innocent, no one gets hurt except the revenue of the mainland excise.' And with a smile, 'You are too law-abiding for us, Pa.'

Later, as they watched the *Victoria and Albert III* disappear over the horizon on the afternoon tide, the reason for its continued presence to remain a mystery, Rose was eager to hear more about her father's meeting with the man in Kirkwall, and although she was intrigued by his connection with the royal yacht, she was disappointed that her father had learnt so little.

'I wish you could have been present, my dear. You are so much better at probing questions.'

'I doubt that, Pa. I will never have anything like the number of criminals you have successfully caught in your career.'

But bearing in mind her success with Archie, Faro recalled his interview with Mr Smith and the explanations he was doubtless inventing for the drowning accident as well as the captain's unhappy duty of informing the man's relatives. Perhaps Rose would have been more successful in making sense of it all.

There were problems at home now as Mary had seized upon the similarity of that poor young man now in the hospital to the attack on Archie. In her opinion, Hopescarth was in the grip of what she called a wave of terror, a term that summoned up thoughts more appropriate to the French Revolution and heads dropping into baskets at the guillotine than a one-man street attack in a small Orkney hamlet.

Faro sighed, it was obvious to him from whom Rose had inherited that remarkable imagination, although hers was under firm control most of the time. His mother's so-called 'new wave of terror' was set to engulf Yesnaby in a relentless grip as she extended her anxieties to encompass their two innocent children, and with a murderer at large she was insisting that Sven should accompany them everywhere.

A suggestion that Emily and Rose dismissed as nonsense. Rose knew of her sister's secret regarding Sven, whose virtues she sang at every opportunity, but she was also aware of a disquieting factor that had escaped Emily. It had become obvious to Rose, always sensitive to the emotions of those around her, that although Sven seemed fond of Magnus, treating him in a playful, good-humoured manner, the boy winced from his teasing and certainly did not share his mother's fondness and admiration for this member of their household. She wondered if Faro had noticed it too, especially after his own early problems with an eleven-year-old Vince.

Thankfully she had no such problems with Meg, to whom she had never seemed other than her real mother. They reacted to the same things and so she was not greatly surprised when Meg said: 'I don't think Magnus likes Sven.'

'Indeed. Has he said why?'

Meg shrugged. 'Not really. But I just know somehow. He doesn't like being teased such a lot. Sven should leave him alone, you know, Mam. Magnus is really quite grown-up.'

Rose laughed at that. Ten years old and already grown up, but there was something very mature about the boy, she could see that, and if Emily was a throwback to Sibella then Magnus had inherited much of his grandfather. He had the same eyes, that piercing-blue direct look and a maturity that struck her as what Faro must have been like at the same age, and she felt entirely happy leaving Meg in his care, aware from that first meeting that he would take good care of their wee girl.

Mary's constant warnings about the surge of a local crime wave were placated by Emily. She agreed that until the Skailholm attacker was apprehended, if the children were to venture far from the house, then Sven should go with them, a suggestion to which Sven was in instant agreement. Indeed, he said, the same idea had occurred to him.

Meanwhile, beyond the long drive up to Yesnaby House, gossip that spread quicker than wildfire or the telegraph system had put residents as far as Stromness and Kirkwall in full possession of every detail of the murderous attacks on Archie Tofts in Hopescarth followed by that on Jimmy Wells outside the Skailholm inn, the latter incident rare enough to make front-page news in bold lettering in the weekly newspaper, *The Orcadian*.

Sensational and reader-grabbing as those headlines were, sweeping aside avid interest in farming matters and fat stock prices, as well as births, weddings and deaths (known locally as hatches, matches and despatches), the reporter would have benefited greatly from a seat at the table where three of the local ladies, a better dressed and more civilised edition of Macbeth's three weird sisters, including Millie Tofts when available, met regularly each Wednesday afternoon in the parlour of the hotel. There, the owner's wife, Bessie, away from her husband's eagle eye, provided bere bannocks and cheese and a less inflammatory brew than those famous witches, in small ales guaranteed to loosen tongues and give more import and shrill exclamations to what had been happening since their last weekly meeting.

The royal yacht, the *Victoria and Albert III*, was high on the opening agenda, but summarily dismissed as of little interest since neither the King nor any of the royal family were aboard. Local pregnancies came next, babies imminent with discussion about whether the prospective parents could afford them and whether they were happy or no, which led inevitably to illicit love affairs, lodgers (known as 'bidey-ins') – a keen topic – and about whose lad was seeing whose lass and late-night assignations down by the shore.

This led not unnaturally to Archie Tofts, Millie's poor laddie who saw things and had the 'doonfa' sickness. Heads were shaken over all that business about selkies, which none of them believed, but in years gone by as lasses themselves they had taken care not to walk alone by the shore at Lammastide, when the seal king arose rampant from the waves and took a young lassie back to his kingdom under the sea for a year and a day.

Heads were shaken again and the glasses solemnly refreshed for there had been incidents. Aye, one lass, innocent no longer, came back after twa' years and was seen walking along the shore as if she had just been out for an evening stroll. A sensation that was and, although the centre of attraction, she couldn't remember a thing about such a remarkable experience. Later information leaked out and it transpired that they had all been cheated. The lass had never been awa' in that kingdom under the sea but had in fact skipped off to the mainland wi' a fancy man her parents didna' like. They had been right about him and she had come home again, wiser, stouter and with a wee bairn in tow.

Next on the list was Yesnaby and yon ex-policeman Jeremy Faro, whose mother never let anyone forget that he had been personal detective to the Queen at Balmoral. Then there was his daughter, over forty she must be, but still girl-like and bonny, with not a grey hair yet in that wild, untameable yellow hair. They shook their heads conscious that not many island women these days, themselves included, stayed young-looking after thirty and a bairn a year.

She didna' look much like her sister, Mrs Emily Yesnaby, that was for sure, the poor widow lady with her peedie lad, Magnus, left without a father. They had been at his funeral, great man that he was, folk from all over the island and far beyond the mainland. Aye, and a great do it was, grand food and drink for everyone. A reminder to Bessie that their glasses were empty and a short silence and clearing of throats indicated the need for refills.

Then Bessie asked: what would happen to the big house now? No one had an answer to that and Bessie said quickly: 'Yon foreign lad, Sven. What do you think of him?' Young and unmarried, they always hoped for some scandalous goings-on, especially as the novelty of having such a handsome foreigner in their midst had raised hopes in the hearts of many a local lass.

A pause. 'Is he all right?' Heads swivelled towards Annie, who always had the latest news from that direction since she went to clean his wee cottage and do his laundry. But Annie said quickly, 'I think he's a bit queer.' Asked how so, she came out with what she had been dying to tell them. 'I think he likes dressing up in women's clothes.' More than any suggestion about fancying other men, often hinted and not completely unknown, although the well-off folk dismissed such matters under the heading of 'confirmed bachelors', this piece of news really shocked them.

Eagerly, they awaited more details, but at that moment Bessie's husband appeared in flourishing a dish towel: 'Better get moving. Some customers have just arrived off the ferry. There's ladies with them.' As they all knew, real ladies were not to be seen in the common bar; they needed the parlour. Bessie hustled her two friends off the premises and prepared to return to her duties, ushering the newcomers into a saloon set aside for important visitors and indicating a room set aside for ladies, for the purpose of freshening up after a long journey, with toilet and washing facilities.

One of the ladies, very upset, was being comforted by her companions.

'What's amiss wi' her? Is she seasick?' Bessie asked her husband.

'No. Seems there was an incident on the ferry, there was a man in the sea as they were about to land.'

'Close to the landing, that's dangerous. He could have been drowned.'

Frank nodded. 'Aye, drowned he was. They thought at first he was just a swimmer. The passengers who spotted him crowded over, some shouting warnings that he was to get away, that he was too close. He took no notice and suddenly they were ushered away from the side. When they asked what was wrong, someone said one of the crew had realised that this was no swimmer. This was the corpse of a drowned man.'

At the same time as Bessie and Frank were busy in the kitchen preparing a meal for the new arrivals and speculating on the dead man's identity, the news was about to reach Yesnaby House, where Faro and Rose had decided to take the two children into Kirkwall. Meg wanted to buy some presents to take back to Edinburgh, and in particular one for Pa, while Magnus had some birthday money he had been unable to spend, since his birthday was the same as his mother's but he had been too saddened by losing his beloved father to even consider such things.

The main excitement today, however, was for them to travel on the Stromness to Kirkwall motor bus, still such a rare novelty in Hopescarth. Their departure coincided with the postman's arrival. Sven was waiting to collect the letters from him and take them upstairs to Emily, who was making sure Magnus had everything for the Kirkwall journey and telling him to take care of Meg and show her the right shop to buy more notepaper and envelopes, their supply exhausted by condolences which continued to arrive from abroad.

The two children had rushed downstairs and away along the road to be in plenty of time in case they missed the bus, whose times were somewhat erratic.

Dave's daily delivery was greeted by the usual question: 'Any news?' to which his usual reply 'Not a lot', was today somewhat more dramatic.

'I have awfa' news the day.' He shook his head. 'A man's body's just been washed ashore.'

Faro and Rose looked at each other, the same thought in both their minds. This must be the man who fell overboard a few days ago from the yacht, whose identity Mr Smith had been so vague about, and they both looked towards the sea aware that the yacht would be well under way on its voyage south, with the unenviable task of reporting a missing passenger, drowned off the coast of Orkney.

Faro's frustration regarding Mr Smith returned once more. If only the man had been more forthcoming with him. He said so to Rose, who realised that her father was still angry with this mystery man with the false identity who had wasted his time, still pondering on the purpose behind it, some urgent private reason, which Mr Smith had declined to reveal.

Such were his thoughts as the bus rolled across the miles towards Kirkwall. The two children seated behind were enjoying this new experience with occasional shouts of: 'Look, Grandpa, see over there.' And 'Mam, did you see that porpoise?'

At last, the rose-red spire of St Magnus Cathedral appeared on the horizon and minutes later they were set down in the main street. Faro had decided to call in at the police station and ask Sergeant Hatton whether there was any information regarding the identity of the body washed ashore, curious to learn how the police here would deal with sending the remains down to England, and particularly how they would communicate the dire news to the royal yacht.

Faro said: 'In fatal accidents we call in the procurator fiscal. I imagine that is not easy in the islands with long distances to travel and subsequent delays.'

The sergeant agreed, and recognising his visitor's one-time importance wondered why he was showing such an interest in a dead body washed ashore.

Hatton was not a happy man; he felt instinctively that there was trouble ahead, especially after he had received official instructions earlier that week that Chief Inspector Jack Macmerry of the Edinburgh City Police, and this retired policeman's son-in-law, was to steer clear of the *Victoria and Albert III* and to remain in Hopescarth awaiting further instructions.

The sergeant enjoyed an easy life, a tranquil existence with set hours in his office, every day untroubled by subversive activities, like riots and no domestic crimes worthy of the name. He had a sudden awful feeling that there was something seriously amiss, something to do with the reason why the royal yacht had anchored near the Castle of Yesnaby instead of coming into Kirkwall; if, as had been hinted to the river pilot, they had merely been taking shelter from bad weather, their later delays vaguely described as minor repairs.

The river pilot had shaken his head, considered it an unlikely story and immediately suspected smuggling activities of some sort. But he didn't care to dig deeper, sharing with the sergeant the desire for a quiet life with as little disruption as possible. The hint of anything to do with royalty filled him with considerable unease, especially on those occasions, mercifully rare, when the yacht came into Orkney or Shetland and all island systems went immediately on to high alert, although it was usually no more than the ladies in the royal party wishing to step ashore to purchase local knitwear, and for the men, Orkney whisky.

Now sitting opposite Faro, the sergeant wondered again why such an important ex-policeman should take this sudden interest in a local affair, although he hoped it was not a serious matter, having been told by Faro that he had just looked in for a chat while his daughter took the Yesnaby boy and her peedie lass shopping in Kirkwall.

Now, Faro was being sympathetic, shaking his head over what he called such an unfortunate occurrence as a man being washed overboard from the royal yacht. Had the body been long in the water, he asked, as they both knew that even a few days' immersion was enough to cause considerable damage to a corpse given such wildly manic seas beating against such cruel rock-strewn cliffs.

The sergeant shook his head. He had seen the body, and considering the few days' submersion, its state of preservation was remarkable, with no more than the normal bloating of human flesh after a few hours in the sea. Nevertheless, he told Faro, the local doctor, who was also the police pathologist, was greatly relieved that the man's family, wherever they were, would be saved such a distress.

Obviously an accident, he said. Probably had too much

to drink at one of those wild parties since the body was still in a good suit, with a wallet and papers in his pocket. A fine watch, although it would never tell the time again. His only other jewellery, a signet ring, had fared better.

'What age was he?'

'Oh, in the prime of life. Middle-aged, perhaps early sixties, and well preserved. About six foot tall, a good head of greying hair and obviously a gentleman,' Hatton concluded. 'Although that was only to be expected being a passenger on the royal yacht.'

'Any idea of his identity?'

'Oh, yes.' The sergeant opened a drawer in his desk and produced a paper. 'This is from the ferry office. A list of the passengers on the *Victoria and Albert III*.'

He pushed it across to Faro, who scanned through the names, some of which he recognised. Names he had read in the newspapers or had encountered at embassies or on state occasions in Edinburgh or Balmoral, guests when he had been the Queen's personal detective in Scotland. There were also ones on the outer fringe of the royal circle: viscounts, honourables, a couple of barons. Mr Smith, whatever his real name, could have fitted any one of them. A man of substance, a voice of authority.

'What about the name of the man who fell overboard?'

The sergeant leant over. 'That's him, sir.' He pointed to a cross against L. Minton. 'Sounds English.'

Minton sounded British all right, but not one from the higher echelon and no name on that list stood out to confirm Mr Smith's claim that he and Faro had met on some embassy occasion. He sighed, laying aside the list.

When the royal yacht reached London, he did not envy the captain having to account for the drowned passenger, Minton, whose corpse was lying here in Kirkwall waiting to be formally identified and sent home for interment.

Something else was bothering Faro. Although there had been no means of identification on the body, neither passport nor, more significantly, money in the wallet, its miraculous condition after several days' immersion was causing alarm bells to ring, a deadly suspicion at the mention of that watch chain and signet ring as well as the condition of the body.

He said to Hatton, 'I might be able to help you. Is the mortuary nearby?'

'Just across the road, sir.' The sergeant thought this rather curious but a bit of help with an unidentified corpse was not to be dismissed. He scribbled a note and Faro said: 'This should not take long but if my daughter comes, please keep her here. I'll be back as soon as I can. Give her a cup of tea, she will probably need it after all her shopping with the two children.'

His mission grimly accomplished, he arrived back at the police station just as the door opened and Rose entered. Hatton sprang to his feet to greet the new arrival.

He was delighted to meet Chief Inspector Macmerry's very attractive wife, especially with her connections to the island and the Yesnaby family, who had lived here for generations, as far back as anyone on the island could remember. They were almost legendary, he told her.

Scribbling a note regarding his findings at the mortuary, Faro was suddenly aware of two small faces at the door. Realising that Hatton's animated conversation with Rose could continue for some time, he said: 'Read this when you have a moment,' and shook hands with the sergeant, who said it had been a delight to meet Faro and his family; such interesting and exciting mainland people rarely came his way these days and regrettably few women as attractive as Rose Macmerry, though he failed to put that into words. He added wistfully to Faro the hope that they might share a dram one evening, perhaps the next time he was in the vicinity.

'That might be sooner than we intended,' Faro replied.

Hatton was clearly disappointed that the short interview must end and Faro wished he could see his face when he read the contents of the brief note.

Rose smiled and said to Hatton: 'It has been a pleasure to meet you, but the children are waiting. There is a motor bus to catch for Hopescarth, the last today.'

The sergeant bowed over her hand. The pleasure had been mutual.

Closing the door, Faro crossed the road with Rose to join the children. Eager as they had been for Kirkwall, they were now keen to be home again to show all their purchases to Emily and Mary.

As they boarded the bus and took their seats, Rose said, 'Well, Pa, was your visit worthwhile?' He was silent and she added: 'I know you too well; I realise this was more than a social call. You must have learnt something and I'm dying to hear all the details.'

Faro was looking out of the window, his expression grave. 'Come along, Pa,' she said eagerly, 'who was that passenger who fell overboard? Do we know that now? Was he someone important?'

He turned to her, shook his head. 'The man who fell overboard according to the list of passengers was a Mr L. Minton. The body that was washed ashore was also a passenger, Rose. According to his description and his jewellery, I had my suspicions, so I went to the mortuary and identified him as Smith.'

Her eyes widened in astonishment. '*Your* Mr Smith? The man you met in Kirkwall?'

'The same. And after I left him last night to have supper with Jack, that's when it must have happened.'

'You think he was murdered,' she whispered.

Faro said grimly, 'Whoever pushed him into the water first carefully removed from his wallet, passport and money. They didn't want him to be recognised. But they weren't clever enough. This was no accident; Smith was a frightened man and this, I fear, was murder.'

'You're sure?'

'I am, indeed. And the corpse of that other drowned fellow, Minton, is still to turn up.'

'Poor Mr Minton,' said Rose, 'he could be drifting anywhere between the Scottish mainland coast and Scandinavia.'

CHAPTER TWELVE

Back at the police station, Hatton had just read Faro's note that the body just recovered and in such good shape was not in fact the body of Mr L. Minton washed overboard several days ago from the royal yacht. Faro had identified the corpse in the mortuary as a Mr Smith whom he had met the previous evening.

Mr Smith had also claimed acquaintance with the royal yacht but there the coincidence ended.

PC Flett was called in and together they went over the report from the mortuary. There had been nothing on the body or in the wallet to provide an identity. Indeed, in view of Mr Faro's revelations there was only one conclusion.

Flett looked across at Hatton. 'The fact that the wallet was empty suggests that any contents had been removed.'

Hatton nodded. 'It does, indeed. But if this was a simple act of robbery, then the presence of that gold watch and chain and a valuable signet ring does not quite fit murder with intent, does it now?'

Similar dismal thoughts regarding murder had been going through Flett's mind, while waiting by Jimmy's bedside in the hospital. As there were hopeful signs that he might be recovering from the murderous blow, it seemed to him that the injured man's revelations might also point to the grim possibility that there was now a killer lurking on the island.

Flett tut-tutted silently, this was something new on the island; a murderer at large was something he had never encountered in his twenty years' service and he sighed. Were his hopes of awaiting peaceful retirement doomed, with nothing disturbing his sleep at night and sitting at his desk by day reading books of fictional crime?

The sergeant had informed him that this was now a matter for the mainland police and he would get on to it straight away. A letter to this effect was immediately delivered to Faro, thanking him for his assistance and adding that having made a statement, he was not likely to be required any further.

When it arrived, showing it to Rose, she said: 'What do we do now?'

Faro sighed. 'Nothing. We go back to Edinburgh at the end of this week, sad visit over, leaving mysteries yet to be unravelled, which we are made to understand are none of our business. I am out of it, anyway, but as you know I hate unsolved crimes.'

Rose sighed. 'I wonder if they will solve it and if we will ever hear who Mr Smith really was and if they will catch whoever tried to kill Jimmy.' She paused. 'If he is caught, then there is a strong possibility that he might confess to attacking Archie as well.'

Faro shook his head. 'I have an odd feeling that these two incidents are quite unconnected, but somehow I am certain that the royal yacht is at the bottom of it all.'

'In which case,' Rose added solemnly, 'knowing how tight they are about publicity, we can be certain of one thing: we will never know the truth.'

There was much to do with the end of Faro and Rose's visit to Yesnaby as well as the cheerier possibility of Emily and Magnus returning to Edinburgh with them. With a great deal of activity scheduled, the two children felt left out of everything, especially as Magnus had been hoping for that visit to Birsay to show Meg Skara Brae, which had to be postponed by the grown-ups too.

Meg had a better idea. Living in Edinburgh gave her little chance of exploring the sea coast, beyond school trips, but with nothing really more exciting to do than eat ice cream, she told Magnus.

Sven, who had overheard them, had an idea. 'I could take them somewhere in the car, get them out from under your feet,' he told Emily.

'Oh, would you? I'm sure they would love a picnic and Meg would be delighted to explore Skara Brae.'

'That's an excellent idea.'

'Then I'll leave it to you and you can consult with Meg where she would most like to go.'

Mary entered into the discussion. Brooding over the

recent criminal attacks and nervous that the taste for violence might be catching, she was fearful for the two children. However, Emily assured her that Sven was completely reliable and would not let them out of his sight, as he had promised, and he assured her that they would be quite safe at Skara Brae, now so famous that even Americans came to wonder at it.

'Hardly surprising,' said Mary acidly, 'since they haven't any ancient history of their own.'

'Only the white incomers to North America,' said Faro. 'The South is rich; there was a civilisation in Peru when we were still living in our caves.'

Meg was duly consulted. Delighted at the prospect of another adventure in the motor car with Sven, she was less eager for Skara Brae than the sea caves, entranced by her introduction to those near at hand, while Magnus said there were still some that he had never had a chance to explore up the coast further away than Hopescarth and Skailholm. Yes, still in walking distance, but much easier to get there by motor car.

And so they set off on a calm, sunny morning accompanied by a large picnic basket. The grown-ups, they felt, were glad to get on with their preparations for departure and quite pleased at the prospect of Sven taking them off their hands for a day.

Once out of sight of the house, the children seated in the front seat with Sven, Meg said: 'We have a change of plan, Sven.'

'And what is that?'

Magnus said: 'Meg would like to see some of the sea

caves we haven't explored yet. There is one not too far away, just a mile or two further down the coast road and we can scramble down the cliff face.'

Sven frowned. 'You are disobeying your mother and I have promised to watch over you.'

'We don't need that,' said Magnus, aware that Sven did not share his delight in getting close to the sea, and although Sven had not said so, he disliked enclosed spaces and had a definite phobia about them. Once he told Emily that he thought it dated back from being accidentally locked in a cupboard when he was a small boy in Bergen. He had never discovered whether that was by accident or design to terrify or punish him, but it had had its required and lasting effect.

As well as a fear of confined spaces, he also suffered from vertigo, and although he felt safe enough in a motor car on narrow cliff roads, nothing would make him venture to scramble down a steep cliff. He shuddered, but he could hardly admit this to two children. Magnus was one thing but the girl in particular was utterly fearless. Presumably, she had inherited that from her policeman grandfather. 'You had better let me know when we approach the area and I'll let you off.'

'You are not coming with us?'

'No, I am no good with heights.'

They looked a little disdainful. Grown-ups were supposed to be good at everything, at least they did not readily admit otherwise, afraid children would think them cowards. Or take advantage of their failings.

For reasons of his own, Sven was happy with this

unexpected change of plan. He insisted they eat before they made the descent. Magnus, he knew, could climb like a mountain goat, he was used to the area, however he had promised to take care of Meg and told Sven he would take her hand over the hard bits.

The day was no longer quite so sunny. It was past midday and cumulus clouds were gathering on the horizon, but the two children were indifferent to changes in the weather.

'Don't be too long,' Sven said. 'I'll wait here for you.'

'Have you got a book to read, or something?'

Sven laughed. 'I have things to do. Now, off you go. Remember, Magnus, you have to be out of the cave before the tide turns.'

Magnus said shortly, 'I know all about tides, Sven.'

Watching them disappear, Sven decided this plan suited his purposes very well indeed.

Halfway down the cliff, Magnus paused to fasten his bootlace while Meg inspected some interesting fissures like deep dark wells nearby.

'What are these?'

'Chimneys.'

'Chimneys?' Meg repeated and Magnus laughed. 'Not for smoke from fires. These are for water. You'll have heard about the roost. When the tide is high the waves flood the caves and rush out here.'

'How fascinating. Can we watch for them? I'd love to see that.'

'Maybe, if we look sharp. Hush! Listen. That's a motor car on the road. That must be Sven. I recognise ours as it's the only one hereabouts. Wait.' He scrambled forward and climbed on to a boulder from which the road was just visible far above.

'I can just see it. He's heading back towards Yesnaby.'

Meg shrugged. 'Let's get on, then.' Frowning, she looked up at the sky. A wind had arisen and there were big clouds approaching from the west. 'I felt a spot of rain. Let's get to the cave before it starts.'

Five minutes later and they had reached the largest cave Meg had seen and she was quite entranced by the way light from the outside flickered over the steep walls.

'I think it goes a long way back,' she whispered. 'This is different, let's explore.'

Whispering wasn't necessary but the cave had a temple-like structure, an atmosphere that somehow made Meg think of a chapel in the convent.

'It's very exciting. I've never been here before, either,' said Magnus. 'But we had better be careful, there are quite a few paths, leading in different directions. We don't want to get lost.'

'Let's take this one,' Meg said, 'see where it leads.'

On they went, still with that eerie light from the sea lighting the high steep walls ahead and behind them the soft susurrus of the sea. Suddenly they were faced with a high ledge. They had reached the back of the cave.

'We can't go any further. We'd better go back now,' said Magnus.

'Why?'

'We've been here a long time, Meg.'

'But there's so much more to explore. Let's stay a little longer.'

'No,' was the firm reply, 'I think we should head back, now. Listen.'

Halting in their tracks, there was a difference in the sound they had been hearing. That gentle susurrus of the sea had been replaced by a mightier, more ominous sound.

The crescendo roar of wave on rock.

Even before they reached the mouth of the cave, the tide had turned, the rushing waters had reached their knees and were getting steadily higher. Higher.

They were trapped.

Back in Yesnaby House, Emily and Rose had set aside their preparations to have a cup of tea, Mary having gone to her usual women's guild meeting, so they had been rather enjoying the kind of chat sisters enjoy, quite trivial but rather stifled by the presence of another female, particularly one's grandmother.

Suddenly they observed the change in the weather, how the sunny morning had disappeared into heavy mist, which in turn had become a steady rainfall.

'The children should be back any time now,' said Rose, looking at the clock that she had never liked with its unnerving staccato tick. Strange how in moments of tension clocks' ticking gets louder and louder, as if they are perfectly aware of what is going on in humans' minds.

Emily smiled and poured a second cup of tea. 'No need to worry, Rose. Sven will be looking after them.'

'They're going to get very wet,' said Rose anxiously, remembering Meg's recent heavy cold.

Emily shook her head. 'They won't melt. Children like

Magnus are used to it, and so should you be after all the years we both spent here at his age. It was always raining.'

Footsteps, and Faro appeared from upstairs where he had been studying the weather with the telescope, one thing he would be very sorry to leave behind in Yesnaby. He had nothing like it in Edinburgh and he was already planning, if Emily ever offered him anything from the house, what he would choose.

'Getting rough out there,' he pointed to the window, already streaming with rain and looked around. 'Where are the children? Shouldn't they be back by now?'

Emily said: 'They'll be here shortly. Sven will be taking care of them. I hope Meg managed to get a glimpse of Skara Brae before the rain.'

Rose was suddenly scared. She felt as if ice-cold water had been poured down her spine. Despite her sister's words, she was certain something was wrong. She knew it; she knew these feelings were not to be ignored, her intuition like a voice whispering inside her skull told her that the children were in deadly danger.

She ran into the hall, pulled her rain cape off the peg.

'Where are you going?' Emily demanded.

'I'm going to look for them.'

'Rose, you can't do that. Be sensible, Skara Brae's miles away. And I keep telling you, they are all right.'

'How do you know that? Aren't you worried about Magnus?'

'Magnus can take care of himself. He's used to this weather.'

'Maybe he can take care of himself. But my Meg is out there too—'

Certain that she was going to scream if Emily kept on nagging at her, all she wanted to do was go out and search for them, she didn't care where or how. But she had to be outside this house looking down the road, waiting to see the motor car with Sven and the children.

Faro knew his Rose. He could see and feel her anxiety striking into his bones. He knew it was useless to be like Emily and to try to reassure her.

He dragged his coat from the peg. 'I'm coming with you.'

She gave him a bleak smile of thanks. As they opened the door, with Emily behind them murmuring about them being silly and getting wet, they could barely see through the mist, but they heard it above the storm: the sound of the motor car.

Emily pointed to its gleaming shape approaching up the long drive. 'There they are, didn't I tell you Sven was taking care of them?'

The car had reached the front door. They could hardly see inside for the rain on its windows.

But they could see enough. Enough to know as he staggered out that he was alone. Magnus and Meg were not with him.

Rose rushed forward, seized his arm. 'Where are they? Where are they?' she yelled.

He stared at her, speechless. He stammered, 'Are they not back yet?'

'You were taking them to Skara Brae.'

'They changed their minds, wanted to go to the sea cave. It's quite near,' he added as if to console them.

'Oh my God,' said Emily, suddenly white-faced. 'Not that

161

one, not the one with the roost.' And Rose remembered ten years ago how she had been trapped and almost drowned.

In the cave, Meg said: 'What can we do? Shall we swim for it?'

'We can't swim, not in that sea, Meg, we'd be dashed to pieces.'

'There is maybe a way out,' said Meg. 'Remember that chimney on the way down?'

'Let's try for it.' But he thought it was a forlorn hope. There was no certainty it connected with this particular cave and as they plunged through the rising water, he remembered that the cave branched off in several directions.

As they reached the junction, Meg said: 'Which one?'

Magnus had no idea. He pointed towards the left. 'This one?'

Meg shook her head. 'No, I think it's over there, where the rock slopes down.'

There was not time for argument, the water rising steadily and stronger in intensity. Soon it would reach their waists and if it got any higher and fiercer, then even a tall man would succumb.

Magnus was taller and stronger than Meg. She was already a bit off balance and he reached out and took her arm as they fought their way through the waves. Was this the right branch? If he allowed Meg to choose and she chose the wrong one, then they would drown.

The waters were now too strong and noisy for them to speak to each other. All he could shout was: 'Are you sure?'

She wasn't. She was certain as she tried to stay standing and the water was past her waist that it would swallow them both. There was nothing they could do now. Only pray, as the nuns had taught her. But would anyone hear her?

'Oh, Magnus, I am sorry,' she sobbed. And suddenly there was a gleam of light in the darkness ahead. 'That's it, oh, Magnus, that's the chimney! Please God—' she gasped as the relentless flood engulfed her, knocking her feet from under her.

Magnus was now half-swimming, holding her head above the water As they reached the wall where the cave ended, he saw that someone had answered her prayer. There was a high ledge of rock. He could save Meg.

'Up you go,' he shouted, and with all his bodily strength heaved her upward on to the rock. At first she slipped back and then with his weight behind her she got a foothold. There was another smaller rock, nearer the light from the chimney.

'Stand up and I'll push you through.'

She turned, her face panic-stricken. 'What about you? I can't leave you.'

'Yes, you can. You have to go, you're smaller than me.'

'No,' she screamed. 'No!'

'Do as I say, Meg. Go on!'

She was halfway up the chimney. She wasn't sure that she could make it, and when she turned and looked back, it was in time to see the final wave reach over his head.

CHAPTER THIRTEEN

Outside the house, Sven could not get the motor car started. Water had got into the engine. He gave a helpless shrug.

Faro, followed by Rose and Emily, leapt out. 'Come on!'

They began running down the long empty road in the direction of the sea cave; something had happened to the children and Sven was to blame. As they needed all their breath against the high wind and the rain, there was no time to put into words the questions and dreadful thoughts going through their heads.

'He was taking care of them,' Rose yelled, trying to keep up with the two who had longer legs than hers, but Faro was conscious of his seventy years, sadly lacking the energy of his younger days. His two little girls disappeared on a family picnic once long ago and got stranded on rocks while the sea piled in. Did either of them remember?

God only knew what had happened to Meg and Magnus. Where were they? The tide was now a roaring, massive angry white foam smashing against the rocks far below, in a steady, relentless boom, rendering mere mortals helpless against its onslaught.

Rose knew what that meant. The sea cave would now be flooded and unless Magnus had found a way out, they were both lost, drowned. Dead. Oh, dear God, how would she tell Jack that she'd lost his beloved child.

As they reached the cliffs they saw the dreaded roost, the sea, like some submerged monster, gushing out of the chimney.

They stopped, huddled together, Emily sobbing 'Magnus, Magnus', and clinging to Faro.

Then through the rain and mist, the sight of two tiny shapes on the road, huddled together and stumbling along the road.

'Magnus!'

'Meg!' The yards between them disappeared and the children were held close by two mothers, sobbing with relief.

Faro swept Meg up in his arms but Magnus insisted that he was fine and quite capable of walking. 'I'm too big for anyone to carry me,' he said proudly to Emily. Meg leant over to Rose, and seizing her hand, she cried: 'Magnus saved me, Mam. He pushed me up through the chimney. But I hung on to him.'

Keeping pace with them, Magnus said: 'I didn't think I could make it through the chimney, it was too narrow, but she wouldn't let go. It was awful,' he said to Emily, who had her arm tight about him.

Meg gasped out, 'I held on to him and yelled for help. My arm was just about breaking but I wasn't going to let

165

him go. Then an old shepherd with his collie dog, coming back from the fields, must have heard me and he got Magnus out.'

'It was a very tight squeeze,' he smiled at her. 'I felt bruised all over. I could never have managed, even with Meg's help.'

'Where is this shepherd now?' Emily asked. 'Was he from Hopescarth?'

'I didn't know him, never seen him before,' Magnus said. 'When I thanked him all he said was "You're both safe now. Go home".'

Meg looked at him and whispered: 'When we turned round he had gone, remember?'

Magnus laughed. 'Just seemed to vanish into the mist,' and Meg added in a solemn whisper, 'I think he was sent, Mam.'

Faro ignored that. 'Whoever he was, we must find him and thank him for saving your lives.' To which Emily added: 'If he's a local shepherd, everyone hereabouts will know him.'

At that moment, Sven and the motor car appeared. Wordlessly, they piled in. Furious questions surfaced but they could wait. They were almost home, the tall house visible beyond the drive.

An hour later, warmed, well wrapped in dry clothes and seated before a good fire, in Emily's handsome bedroom, the two children were happily consuming scones and already their adventure was just that. A great adventure with all the terrifying bits now relegated into an exciting memory for those years long after childhood was past.

In the kitchen their parents were consuming cups of tea, and something a little stronger for Faro, still suffering from shock. Anger erupted in a tide against Sven. They turned to him, explanations were required.

'If it hadn't been for Magnus's quick-thinking and his knowledge of the sea caves, a few minutes more and they would have both drowned,' Emily said.

'The children are safe,' he said lamely. 'Thank God.'

'Indeed, but no thanks to you,' Rose replied acidly. 'Why did you leave them?'

'What happened to you, Sven?' Emily asked. 'You were looking after them.'

Now that the panic was over, he said calmly, 'I had something to do with the motor car in Kirkwall and as I was returning, one of the Stromness fishermen was in difficulties so I went to help him. I went to the sea cave by the shore route but it took longer than I expected. I didn't realise the storm would overtake us so completely and by the time I raced into the cave . . .' He paused. 'I looked inside, shouted, but they weren't there. I was relieved. I guessed they had left without waiting for me.'

He looked up at them. 'I didn't know what to do.' He was troubled, staring at his fingernails as if they might provide an answer. 'I am so sorry to have put you through all this anxiety. I realise it was all my fault.'

Emily smiled at him. 'You tried to do someone a good deed and let's be thankful it all worked out right in the end and Magnus found a way out.'

She was anxious not to extend Sven's misery and guilt more than was absolutely necessary; his white face told them that he fully realised that the children might have drowned. Because of her emotional feelings towards him she tried to remain calm, but Rose had no reason for sparing him.

'You were supposed to be taking care of them, not letting them out of your sight. You were to take them to Skara Brae,' she repeated.

He regarded her coldly and gave Emily an appealing glance. 'I have already told you. They were determined to go to the sea cave. There was nothing I could do about that.'

Rose laughed harshly. 'You are a man; they are children.'

Emily said: 'You can't blame Sven. I know Magnus can be very determined.'

Rose swung round on her, 'So it is your son's fault that my wee girl nearly drowned.'

Faro put a restraining hand on her arm. Sven might have looked upset but she looked as if she had not yet emerged from the nightmare of the past hours, and he wondered if it would haunt her for ever. He had been making his own assessment, angry and scared, and although more in control than his two daughters, he felt that there was much in Sven's conduct needing a fuller explanation.

So did Rose. She was angry, she had questions and wanted answers. 'What were you doing in Kirkwall that was so important?'

'As I have already told you, I am always aware that safety must be taken with the motor car. As Mr Faro knows only too well, there have been problems lately and if you remember I couldn't get it started just now.'

'More safety for the car than the two children,' Rose interrupted angrily.

Emily was watching him, the closed-in expression. She felt somehow that he was lying and whatever had led him not to wait and to head so urgently into Kirkwall had something to do with a girl who, according to local gossip, he might be courting. Was her dream of a happy ending with Sven to be a mere infatuation? She was too old for him, and according to Millie's whisper only this morning, this rival was a young and pretty girl. He was probably wildly in love and had seized the opportunity of an hour together. She felt suddenly sickened by what she was imagining.

Her father, the most reasonable one of the three, was regarding the faces of his two daughters: Rose angry and tearful, Emily staring at Sven, bewildered, sad.

'I think we have gone far enough with this.'

He stood up, put both hands on the table. 'I am hungry; we seem to have missed a meal somewhere. As for you, Sven, whatever your excuse, you are still guilty of abandoning two young children whose safety was your responsibility.'

They had forgotten about Mary Faro, who would be back from Hopescarth any time now and he added to Rose and Emily: 'I think it would be advisable to keep this from your grandmother as much as possible.'

'Agreed,' said Emily with a shudder. 'I'll tell Magnus that they are not to tell her about this adventure in the sea cave and if he asks why, I'll tell him that grown-ups sometimes don't see things in the same light as people of his age, and that she would get very upset.'

Of course, it was impossible to keep it secret. The children were so eager to tell her the story, although being Mary, she suspected that Magnus was exaggerating the details. It was however serious enough for her to say to Emily, 'That young fellow was to blame. He should never have let them out of his sight and we should be grateful to the Lord that we didn't have two peedie bairns' drowned bodies brought home.'

Emily shuddered. 'Oh, don't say such things, Gran.' Her own thoughts of what might have been and of Rose having to tell Jack about his beloved wee girl were too dreadful to contemplate.

Although she didn't sleep much that night, Rose's terrors were not apparently shared by Meg, who climbed in beside her the next morning as usual for their pre-breakfast cuddle, the way they started the day at home in Edinburgh.

Rose stroked her hair and asked: 'No ill effects from yesterday?'

'Yesterday?' Meg sounded surprised, as if the terror of the sea cave had never existed. But that was childhood's reactions to what were the big deals in the grown-up world. 'Oh, you mean in the cave. Oh, well, we knew Sven had gone off in the motor car and left us to it and when he didn't appear and the sea was coming in at such a rate it was up to our waists, we knew we were cut off so we had to find a place to climb out.' She smiled. 'Magnus was wonderful, Mam, he found this ledge and there was just a gleam of daylight far above our heads, so he dragged me over, through the water and pushed me up. I was to go first because I'm smaller than him.' She shuddered. 'I've never been so scared in my life. It was so slippery I was sure I'd lose my footing and fall back into the water on top of him and we would both drown. He kept shouting to me to hold on. He made me cling on for dear life.'

She paused. 'So I did just that and I prayed, Mam, just like the nuns tell us at school. It worked cos I managed to wriggle through, but he was stuck there. I started screaming for help then – then this old shepherd came along and we got him out.'

She was silent, frowning. 'He saved Magnus's life, no doubt about that. Although he seemed very old and frail with his shepherd's crook, he was very strong. I suppose they have to be, rescuing sheep from the snow and so forth.'

'We'd like to thank him, your aunty and me. I hope we can find him.'

Rose had a strange feeling that proved right. He would not be found. No one in the area would have heard of him.

Meg continued: 'He had one of those sheepdogs and it just sat there, watching and waiting. Anyway, once he made sure that Magnus wasn't hurt they just vanished.' She shrugged. There was a moment's silence as if she was searching for the right words then she took Rose's hand and held it tightly.

'Mam, I think he . . . he was sent.'

Stillness seemed to have entered the room. A tap at the door and Magnus came in, smiling. Rose held out her arms and he ran over to the bed and put his arms around both of them. For Magnus, always ready for the next adventure, the perils of the sea cave were forgotten. He wanted to know all about Edinburgh.

Mary, however, was still curious about yesterday's drama that she had missed. After breakfast, she got Rose aside and wanted more details, and Rose realised that Emily, perhaps for Sven's sake, had made it sound a lot lighter than it was in reality.

Mary sniffed and repeated what she had said to Emily. 'It was all the fault of that Sven. He should never have let those two bairns out of his sight.'

With their return to Edinburgh imminent, Rose was looking forward to being home again, missing Jack and Thane and wondering what, if any, cases were waiting for her, prospective clients with problems to solve.

As for Faro, seated in his favourite spot at Erland's telescope in the study window, he would be sorry to leave Orkney with mysteries unsolved: the unfinished story of Mr Minton washed overboard from the royal yacht; the real identity of Mr Smith; then there was the Yesnaby garden with all its ancient secrets; he wasn't sure that Erland himself hadn't been a bit of a mystery. There seemed a lot of missing threads there, and during this visit it had occurred to him that his daughter knew surprisingly little of the man she had married or his activities abroad.

CHAPTER FOURTEEN

Later that day one truth emerged with one less mystery left unsolved for Faro and Rose as well as for Sergeant Hatton. A solution that was in everyone's best interests, including ending Mary Faro's imagined wave of terror.

Flett's daily vigil in the hospital had been rewarded. The victim, Jimmy, had sat up, groaned and was more than ready to answer questions to reveal his attacker's identity.

'There was no murderous intent. It's all what you might call a storm in a teacup,' Flett came to tell them.

They gave a sigh of relief as he added: 'This was what we call a domestic incident. Two young chaps after the same lass and her leading them both on. Finally, when they were at the inn, the two lads came to harsh words. Jimmy went out and Dave, still angry and having far too much drink taken, hit him harder than he meant to.' Flett sighed. 'Dave is a big, strong lad, a bit of a bruiser, and Jimmy insisted that I did not arrest him, that he had provoked the fight. He and Dave had always been great chums, he had thought about it and now realised too late that it was the lass's fault. She was to blame and she wasn't worth causing trouble between two pals.'

And that was the end of it as far as the police were concerned, and the sergeant would now be able to cross off the supposed attacks on the two young men by virtue of Dr Randall's assessment of Archie Toft's medical condition.

Flett went on, 'There's still this other business about Mr Smith, of course.' And turning to Faro, 'Your suggestion of a connection with the royal yacht, sir. Well, that puts the matter right out of the island police's hands. Sergeant has passed your comments on and we expect to hear no more; it will all be dealt with by them tightly sealed forces of government security.'

Faro and Rose exchanged a glance with Emily. At least they wouldn't be leaving with Mary in a constant state of anxiety about a murderer on the loose, looking for more victims and prowling around outside the downstairs windows.

As they gathered round the kitchen table that evening, Emily asked Faro and Rose whether they had made a booking at the shipping office to take them to Leith, adding that she had been thinking.

'Thinking? What about?' Rose asked.

Emily smiled at them excitedly. 'I've decided, if you are agreeable, Rose, that I would like to come back with you to Edinburgh. I feel like a change of scene.'

Rose gave a shout of delight, got up and hugged her. 'That is a marvellous idea. I've been hoping you and Magnus would come with us and there's masses of room in Solomon's Tower.'

'Are you sure it wouldn't be too much?'

Rose gave a passing thought to those dark rooms up the worn stone spiral staircase. Empty, dusty rooms that hadn't been slept in, she guessed, since the previous tenant Sir Hedley's long occupancy and that would account for almost a century.

'Dear Em, you are welcome to stay as long as you like. What about Magnus?'

Emily smiled. 'No need to worry about him, he has always had a tutor, and he is not due until September. Erland thought that was best until next year, when he is eleven, then he intended he should go to public school in Scotland, probably Fettes in Edinburgh. I can perhaps make enquiries and arrange it while we are with you.'

Magnus had greeted his mother's suggestion with delight.

He wanted to know all about Edinburgh. He loved history and they could assure him that there was plenty of that around. Solomon's Tower was in the very heart of it, close to Holyrood Palace and the many places associated not only with Mary Queen of Scots (his heroine) but also with Bonnie Prince Charlie. When plans for their departure were being finalised, he was constantly waylaying Faro and Rose – what about this, or that?

'He treats us like an encyclopaedia,' she laughed.

'At least we should be flattered as the source of all knowledge,' Faro replied.

Rose was sure Jack would be delighted at the prospect of having Emily and Magnus to stay. Meg's school term was looming on the horizon and, of course, there was Thane waiting to welcome them.

Faro, too, was enjoying the unexpected chance of spending more time with his seldom seen Emily and this new grandson, with whom he had already forged a special bond, and he had written to Imogen hoping that she would join them in Edinburgh, at Solomon's Tower.

Rose sighed happily. How would Magnus take to Thane? As for Emily, she would certainly enjoy Edinburgh's famous Princes Street.

But for Emily, there was only one problem. She sighed gloomily.

'What about Alice?'

Heads turned in her direction. 'Alice?' They had all forgotten Alice Yesnaby, the remote umpteenth cousin from Aberdeen whose longed-for visit was to have been around the same week as Erland's funeral. Shocked and grief-stricken, Emily had written to her and was daily awaiting a reply, vaguely aware of Alice's possible arrival at the back of her mind, and among more vital and urgent matters needing attention now that she and Magnus would be leaving for Edinburgh, the calamity as well as the embarrassment should she just walk in.

Explaining this dire situation to the family, before they could make any obvious comments or suggestions, she added: 'I know what you are all thinking but there is worse to come.' She shook her head.

'I decided to send a telegram but I seem to have mislaid Erland's address book. Sven said he was sure he saw it on my desk but it isn't there.' She groaned. 'There are so many papers all stacked up. I found her last card to Erland but her address isn't on it. Afterwards, she wrote to him about her plans. I remember, he was pleased at the thought of meeting another Yesnaby. He passed her letter over for me to read. I scanned it but I wasn't all that interested.' She sighed. 'Now I've searched but I can't find it anywhere. I'm hopeless about losing things. I vaguely remember the address, some strange-sounding place on the outskirts of Aberdeen, and as Yesnaby is such an unusual name, maybe I should send that telegram anyway and tell her that we are leaving.'

She regarded them anxiously. 'You know, that I haven't had any reply makes me suspect that she has already left. It's such a long way to come and maybe she has friends in the Highlands where she might break her journey.' Pausing for a moment, she went on, 'I asked Sven for his advice; he thinks a telegram would be a good idea. Sven has been quite wonderful, dealing with this enormous correspondence from abroad, mostly business acquaintances. He's been keeping a lookout for one with an Aberdeen postmark from Alice and every day all he has to report is: "Nothing yet".'

It was a serious problem that Emily had put to them. 'What are we going to do? What if she didn't get my letter and intends to just arrive, walk in without warning and finds that we have left and Gran tells her we have all gone to Edinburgh for a holiday. What will she think of Erland's wife then?' she groaned.

Rose thought for a moment. 'There is one solution: let's presume she is still in Aberdeen and hasn't got your letter, write to her again and tell her that as you are coming to Edinburgh with the family, we'll be delighted to see her there.'

Emily frowned. 'There are a lot of "ifs" but that might

possibly work. Thanks, Rose, but if she accepts, isn't that putting a bit much on you?'

Rose shrugged. 'Not at all, and better than having her come all the tortuous way to Orkney and finding no Yesnabys at home.'

Emily's frown deepened. 'But will you have room for her?'

Rose smiled. 'Solomon's Tower is vast, so many rooms that are never used.' And cutting short Emily's murmurs about inconvenience and so forth, she went on: 'How old is she, anyway?'

Emily shook her head. 'I have not the slightest idea. I know absolutely nothing about her. I suppose Erland must have told me at some time, but I can't remember. I probably wasn't listening, but I imagine she might be middle-aged because William was quite a bit older.'

'If that is so, then she'll probably be delighted to be spared the long journey to Orkney, especially as Edinburgh has so much to offer.'

'Except that is maybe not quite what she was wanting,' said Emily. 'Probably more interested in seeing the ancient home of the Yesnabys.'

She disappeared upstairs and returned a few moments later, triumphantly turning the pages of Erland's well-worn address book. 'Found it at last, under a heap of old magazines I must have moved off the desk. Thank goodness. I got the address almost right, so we can get in touch with her. I'll write and let her know our change of plans. Sven can post it in Kirkwall. Meanwhile, let's just pray she isn't already on her way.'

With the problem of Alice Yesnaby taken care of as

much as was possible in the circumstances, the next on the list was Mary Faro. The suggestion that she might enjoy a short holiday, a pleasant change of scene, in Edinburgh, was met with a shudder of disapproval. While declining the offer more or less politely, she said later to Faro that much as she loved him and her dear family, and she was so happy to have had the chance to see Rose again, she did not like Edinburgh, which was putting it mildly.

Faro found it extraordinary that after nearly seventy years since the loss of his policeman father in an accident involving a runaway cab on the Mound, she still held the city responsible for his death.

Guessing her son's thoughts, she leant up and stroked his face. 'I know you understand, but it isn't just Edinburgh any more, either.' A deep sigh, a sad look. 'Dearest Jeremy, don't you realise, with all that intuition of yours, that your mother is just a wee bit too old to make long journeys any more?'

'Nonsense, Ma,' was the reply. 'You are as fit as a woman half your age.'

But even saying the words and ignoring the shake of her head, he knew what his mother had said was true. It was a long journey from Kirkwall to Leith, where Jack would be waiting for them, but it was often a tricky crossing over rough seas, the straits between Orkney and the mainland of Scotland were notorious. Seasickness was frequent, the feeling that death would be too good was bad enough for the young, but the consequences for a woman well over ninety might be fatal.

She was saying, 'I will be quite happy with Millie here, we will take care of everything and when Emily comes back maybe she will have decided what she wants to do.' She thought for a moment. 'It's a difficult time for her. I know she loved Erland, a fine man he was, and she grieves for him, but I think with all those years between them . . . the one thing I disapproved of when she married him was that he was old enough to be her father.' She looked at Faro. 'Aye, nearer your age than hers. And this is most often what happens: she's been left a widow. She's still young.'

'Not as young as you were, Ma.'

Mary sighed. 'She should marry again. It was different for me. I never had a man waiting to propose – even if I had wanted another man, which I never did, after your dear father. There could never have existed any man to take his place for me.' She gave him a sly smile and added: 'Not like yon nice John Randall.' She laughed. 'Anyone with eyes in their head can see that he dotes on our Emily. They would be happy together, and as Magnus thinks the world of him too, it would save Yesnaby's future.'

Faro laughed. 'You are quite a matchmaker, aren't you?'

She regarded him narrowly. 'Haven't had much success with you. You should marry Imogen.'

'And I would, believe me, if she would have me. It's not from lack of asking, I can assure you.'

When Randall called in later to check that Emily was sleeping well and was invited to stay for supper, it was clear to everyone – except Emily – that the doctor was really the patient and suffering from a dose of unrequited love. As Faro wryly observed to Rose, he seemed more than a little put out that this visit to Edinburgh was also in the nature of an experiment for Emily and Magnus, the prelude to a permanent stay once Magnus continued his education at a public school there.

It also seemed that romance was in the air at Hopescarth, as Millie reported to Emily that her friend, from Skailholm inn, said Sven might be courting. He had been observed visiting a young lady who had booked in on her way to Shetland from the mainland, according to Frank's register.

There were always rumours floating about regarding this handsome, unattached young Norwegian, his movements a source of constant interest and speculation, a gift to the gossips of Hopescarth. However, the possibility of an unseen rival for Sven's affections during her absence from Yesnaby gave her a feeling of disquiet and dread. But forever resourceful, if this was merely a passing infatuation, then she had the power to remove him from the scene of temptation.

She had an idea. 'I'm sure it isn't serious,' she reported to Rose. 'As a matter of fact, he has said that he would love to come to Edinburgh with us.' This wasn't quite what he had said, having merely hinted in general conversation when she had told him of their plans that he would like to see the city one day.

Rose was eager to support her sister, even though she considered that Emily's romantic notions of a future with Sven were ill-advised, so after speaking to Faro and putting the idea down as a thank you from Emily for all Sven's help, Faro agreed but not altogether enthusiastically, she thought, his accompanying wry glance hinting that he was more than aware of Emily's real reason. His only comment: 'It's your home, you can invite anyone you wish.'

He was present when she suggested to Sven that he would be most welcome to accompany them to Edinburgh, if he wished.

Sven's face brightened immediately. 'I would love that. I have longed ever since I came over here to see something of Scotland. He told me so much.' (It was always 'he' when he spoke of Erland as one might refer to a deity, Faro thought.) 'I read all the books in his library, and the history of Edinburgh is so exciting.' He sighed, 'It seems like a miracle that I am going to see it at last. I can hardly believe my good fortune, and I cannot thank you enough,' he added, with that gracious slightly foreign bow to Rose.

Emily was delighted and hugged her sister. This was one anxiety removed from their departure, Sven taken care of, but much still to do before they left. Tickets were to be bought and Jack informed when to meet the ship, while Mary helped with the washing and ironing of clothes to be packed. Although their visit was to be just two weeks there was still much needed, said Emily. Unlike Rose and Faro, she was not a seasoned traveller and had yet to learn the advantages of travelling light. She had moments of panic, only to be reassured that if she lacked anything, although the two sisters could never have worn items from each other's wardrobe – one small and curvaceous, the other tall and thin – there were many shops on Princes Street, and Rose would make sure that she enjoyed that experience.

Another problem was that boys of Magnus's age were constantly outgrowing their clothes and Emily thought about the unreliable weather and the vagaries of playing outside on Arthur's Seat, as well as his books and games that needed to be sorted out and packed.

Emily need not have feared. As always, there was a helping hand waiting in readiness. Watching her, Sven smiled. They were not to worry; he would act as their porter.

'You are so kind. Thank goodness you are coming with us. What would we do without you?' She was rewarded by Sven's most irresistible smile.

'It will be my pleasure, as always.'

With only two days remaining and all preparations safely under way, Emily decided that they should go into Kirkwall. Magnus was definitely needing a new suit in case, as she hoped, he had an interview at Fettes College. 'He grows at such a rate these days, and shirts get so short in the sleeves,' she said.

Magnus wasn't too pleased. He found going to outfitters one of the most boring things in life, but better the devils he knew in Kirkwall than wasting precious holiday time trailing round strange Edinburgh shops.

Meg was delighted at the prospect of another Kirkwall visit and particularly wanted something nice to take back to Sister Agnes at her school, the convent run by the Little Sisters of the Poor. English and history were her best subjects and it seemed that Meg was a favourite pupil by all accounts, while Rose and Jack were very happy with her progress.

For Faro, going into Kirkwall was a final opportunity to look in at the police station, and although he doubted it, to discover if there was any advance on whether the remains of L. Minton washed overboard from the royal yacht had been sighted.

Taking Rose aside to tell her of his intention, he added: 'We both know now that there's no longer the remotest chance of us finding any clues to solving the mystery of Mr Smith's murder.'

Rose nodded. 'Only the royal yacht might have the answer to that one. They must know perfectly well who this passenger was, preferring to travel incognito. Probably someone famous and very rich who had paid a small fortune for the privilege.'

'As well as his life,' Faro added grimly. And with a welcome change of subject: 'Let's make a day of it. I'll take you all to lunch.'

'A great idea, Pa. Having lunch out is always such a treat for the children, and for Gran.'

Faro laughed. He knew that Mary, despite being highly critical of the food being served in restaurants and horrified at what she considered unnecessary expense, would enjoy it. Magnus wanted to take Meg on a proper tour of the cathedral, whose name he so proudly bore, and show her where the saint's skull was buried. Meg decided that would be a splendid topic for school's inevitable 'My holiday this year' summer essay.

Rose was not greatly interested in shopping with, as she told Emily, the prospect of all Edinburgh's Princes Street at hand. She was eager to know if there had been any developments in the police station's records, and had decided to go with Faro.

He was less enthusiastic than she had hoped and did not think that a good idea. Asked why not, he replied that he could not see the sergeant welcoming the attentions of the very attractive Mrs Macmerry in her real-life role as a lady investigator. Policemen were probably even more conservative on the islands about what they considered a woman's proper role in a man's life.

Hurt by her father's rejection and his apparent lack of sympathy for women's present role in society, as an active suffragette annoyed and outraged by yet another display of man's injustice, she decided to be of more use walking with Gran, revisiting the places she had known in childhood, pretending that was the reason, rather than giving the old lady a helping arm up the steep hill to the cottage where they once lived and maybe seeing some of her old neighbours.

She had been surprised that for once Gran had been eager to join them on their excursion until Emily supplied a possible reason: if she and Magnus left Yesnaby House and went to live in Edinburgh, Gran would be content to return to Kirkwall and the tiny cottage where she had lived most of her life.

Sven set them down by the cathedral. With the future of the motor car still undecided there were interested contacts here in Kirkwall to be pursued, he said, declining the invitation to lunch. There were also still matters to be attended to in Hopescarth and back at the house. He would return for them at, say, four o'clock, if that would give them enough time.

'He is so good,' Emily said, repeating it as she did so often: 'What would I do without him?' However, her eyes narrowed slightly watching him drive off again. At the back of her mind, the thought intruded about how much time he would be spending on the motor car business and whether he had plenty of time, several hours in fact, for an assignation with this woman Millie had told her about.

After an hour's interval fortified by an excellent lunch, activities resumed and with shopping and other matters accomplished, the two children would have been quite happy to go back on the motor bus, but there were parcels to carry and so it was, that as the clock struck four, all feeling somewhat exhausted, they waited in the square, but it was half an hour later before Sven appeared.

He was full of apologies and looked anxious. On the drive back, Sven's preoccupation went unnoticed by his passengers, except for Faro, who had been hoping for some last-minute revelations at the police station. There had been none; a waste of time. As he and Rose were to discuss later on the ship going to Leith, their interest in the strange behaviour of the royal yacht anchoring so secretly away from Kirkwall, the cover-up of the man overboard whose body was still afloat somewhere in those wild seas around the islands, crowned by the mysterious identity of Mr Smith, who they believed had been murdered, were all mysteries destined to remain unsolved.

Rose could sympathise. She understood perfectly that Faro did not enjoy being defeated, his whole life story as a detective had been to find that final clue and bring the criminal to justice. This was a situation that ended the visit to Yesnaby for both of them on a sour note.

There was worse to come, and an even more sour note to end their visit.

CHAPTER FIFTEEN

Faro had been engrossed in his own thoughts on the drive back. Now, he learnt the reason for Sven's preoccupation.

He had bad news to impart.

In their absence, there had been a sinister attack on Yesnaby House.

As the party disembarked at the house, Sven assisted the ladies and whispered to Faro: 'Sir, I don't know how to tell Mrs Yesnaby.' He took a deep breath. 'While you were in Kirkwall, the garden has been attacked by vandals. It was when I came back to check some things for her that I looked out of the window and saw the damage.' He shuddered. 'I could hardly believe my eyes.'

Emily had to be warned immediately. She was horrified, especially as Sven was very distressed by the scene, his immediate thought being for Erland's precious orchids.

'It can't be local people. It must be plant poachers who

he warned us about. Sven says these orchids are valuable and very rare.'

Faro and Rose had followed them down into the garden. Faro was considering the scene before them.

The earth was disturbed but no orchids had been taken. They were untouched, unharmed. Most damaged was the rockery around the area of the ancient wall, all that remained of the original house, the mermaid stone almost obliterated by time's passing centuries above Erland's favourite place in the garden, a sunny sheltered spot.

Faro said: 'I don't think this is the work of a criminal gang, Emily, rest assured. There would have been more damage. This is the work of one person, taking advantage of the time that we were all in Kirkwall.'

'Yes,' Rose agreed. 'Nobody at home, not even Millie.' She knew but did not add that she suspected they knew what they were looking for.

'But who would want to dig up our garden? It's monstrous and wicked,' said Emily.

Mary wasn't willing to tackle those steep steps. She regarded the damage from the top and shouted down: 'I don't know what this world is coming to, people with nothing better to do than to break into gardens and make such a mess of them. The islands were never like this in my young day, everyone fighting to survive, that was more than enough to keep them busy, minding their own business.'

Sven was frowning, silently contemplating the devastation. Faro turned to him. 'Have you any theories?'

'I think this is the work of the archaeologists. They have

decided to extend their activities, waiting for their chance when we were all away.'

'If they knew so much about it, they would have surely waited a few days longer,' Faro suggested and Sven made no comment. After a moment's thought he added: 'By what you are saying, do you think they are searching for something they believe is hidden here?'

'Yes, sir, I do indeed,' Sven said quickly. 'It is what they have always been searching for, for years now: the Maid of Norway's dowry, of course.'

'That's just a story,' said Magnus scornfully. He and Meg had joined them and she was perched on the stone seat, smiling a little, unable to understand why grown-ups could make such a fuss about soil scattered about in a garden. Dogs did that all the time in Edinburgh, burying bones.

Magnus was regarding Sven sternly. 'Everyone knows that the ship carrying her treasures, her jewellery and money chests were lost. According to the few records of the time, after she died they carried her ashore and buried her – somewhere on the islands, no one knows where, lots of claims through the ages – but the treasure, her dowry, wasn't buried with her. The ship set sail for Norway, but they never got there. They just vanished, probably caught in a storm and sunk, or taken by pirates.' He shrugged. 'That's the theory, anyway.'

That was quite a speech for a ten-year old, Faro decided, and very knowledgeable about local history, he thought, giving the lad an admiring glance. Sven's tightened lips showed disapproval; he did not like being contradicted by a mere child and said coldly, 'It could have been someone who believed the story. They probably heard that Mrs Yesnaby was off on holiday and decided to take this opportunity.'

'What do you think, Pa?' Emily asked gently.

He looked at Sven and said: 'I think it is extremely unlikely that whoever did this got the day wrong.'

Emily sighed. 'I can't believe it was the archaeologists either; they have hardly been seen this summer. They've moved off to another more promising dig on South Ronaldsay. And I don't think we can include those divers still hoping, since some coins appeared down the coast, that they might have stumbled on that wrecked galleon from the Spanish Armada.'

Regarding the scene tearfully, she repeated: 'It is so awful. It must have been someone local, but who could have hated us enough to do this? Everyone loved Erland and knew how he treasured his garden. It's-it's like . . . sacrilege, somehow.'

Rose had said little. 'It looks as if a hurricane has swept across,' said Emily pointing to the ancient high wall. 'That has always protected the sunken garden from the weather and it has escaped almost every storm since Erland's great-grandfather landscaped it.'

There had been no storm that day; it was calm and bright.

After examining the scene carefully, Faro had returned to the house. He now came back down the steps to the garden and said: 'I've had a look at the ground on the outside. Whoever did this would have needed a ladder to climb the wall since there is no access to the garden except by those steep steps' – he pointed – 'or from the house.'

Emily sighed sadly. 'But Sven says there was no evidence of a break-in, apart from a half-open window.' She shook her head. 'My fault, I'm afraid, I'm a bit careless about security.'

'Which window was that?' Faro asked sharply.

'On the side of the house, the wall below Erland's study.'

'Oh, I know the one you mean and it is eight feet from the ground, so once again a tall ladder would have been needed as well as a very small, thin burglar. No normal-sized man could have got in that way.' He paused scratched his head and continued: 'As in all crimes, great or small, there has to be a motive. Any ideas, Rose?'

She shrugged and he continued: 'No clues of any kind inside and no evidence outside, no ladder marks against the wall. As for Sven's theory about the archaeologists, they cannot be blamed for this piece of vandalism.'

Faro continued to walk round the garden, silent and preoccupied. Rose asked: 'What's wrong, Pa? Care to share it?'

He smiled. 'Just something odd that I haven't worked out yet.' He gave her a hard look. 'Come, now, let me have your thoughts.'

She shook her head and he went on: 'You have been here before. Did Erland ever tell you anything?'

A sharp glance. 'What kind of "anything" had you in mind, Pa?'

He shrugged. 'All I can say is that from the first moment I stepped into this garden, I have felt . . . something. I don't pretend to be like you, Rose, I'm not psychic, but each time I have been down here I have had that same feeling, that this is a place of mystery. If I was psychic, I would say that it is haunted. No, that is the wrong word, haunting hints at ghosts and horrors.'

He stretched out his arms. 'Not that, this is a feeling of sanctity. I'm not much of a churchgoer, as you know, but sometimes I get the same feeling in ancient cathedrals, like a benign presence.' He gave her a shrewd glance. 'And I am sure you know what I mean, you must have felt it too.'

Evading his eyes, she didn't answer. A promise made must be kept.

He continued with a sigh. 'I'm trying to fathom what they were up to, whoever invaded this garden while we were out. Is it Huw Scarth's pot of gold? Is anyone daft enough to believe that old story?' He shook his head. 'I wish they'd had detectives then, someone as smart as Sherlock Holmes or even my very clever daughter would have sorted them out.'

She smiled. 'Flattery will get you nowhere, dear Pa.'

He frowned. 'But you know something, dammit! I have felt it in my bones every time we have stood here together.' He paused and added sternly: 'The time has come to share it, if we have any hopes of solving this particular riddle. Huw Scarth's pot of gold is nonsense,' he thumped his fists together, 'but it has something to do with the Maid of Norway's dowry, I'm certain of that.'

She was defeated and she knew it, sure that Erland would have forgiven her. She sighed. 'They are searching for where they believe it is hidden.'

'And that is?' he demanded impatiently.

'Buried with her, in her grave.'

They were alone now. The others had returned to the house, lured away by Mary's magic shout from the top of the steps: 'I've made some tea.'

Faro stared at her, pointed to the stone seat and she nodded. 'Yes, that was put there to protect her bones, to stop them being disturbed. She died on the ship and they buried her here. It was probably meant as a temporary grave with the mermaid stone to mark it, but in those troubled times, no one came.' Again she sighed, feeling guilty. 'Erland showed me, made me promise not to tell anyone. The secret has been passed down to the eldest Yesnaby, father to son, generation by generation. A sacred trust. They are its guardians and Magnus will be told when he is older . . .' She paused. 'And from the way he went for Sven so knowledgeably, I think he might know already.'

Faro drew a deep breath. 'And so I was right about that cathedral feeling. I seemed to know there was something.' She looked at him, smiled and took his arm. 'I guess I must have got that from you.'

He went over and touched the seat and whispered. 'Rest easy, little princess.'

They were walking back and at the foot of the steps he paused. 'I've never told you, but shortly after we arrived, I had a strange dream – more a kind of nightmare. I was in a funeral procession and they were burying a child. But it wasn't now, it was, oh, hundreds of years ago. It was so vivid, even the rain, the people chanting, and weeping as they carried the coffin. I normally forget dreams, but this one has haunted me; I still remember every detail as if it was last night.'

He smiled at her. 'There was even a dog running along with them, a big brute, some kind of hound.'

Rose was silent, then he saw that she was crying. 'My darling, what's wrong, what have I said?'

'Only that I had exactly the same dream, when I first came to Yesnaby, ten years ago. And I remember it too; I have never forgotten a single detail.'

His eyes widened. 'That is extraordinary. The same dream we both shared.' His arm tightened around her. 'Strange, strange. I just know it wasn't like me at all. It was as if someone else had taken me over.' He shivered. 'Quite extraordinary.'

'Tea is getting cold, look sharp, you two!' Mary called from above.

Still with his arm around her, they climbed the steps. They were used to solving mysteries, and mysteries needed logic. But for this strange dream, there was no logic on offer. They had both entered the past, in a happening beyond their understanding, but Rose could have told him something even more extraordinary about another creature who had shared it with them.

That big brute of a hound in Faro's dream.

That was Thane.

There were voices from the open kitchen door above them. Sven appeared with Flett, about to descend the steps into the garden.

Faro and Rose stood aside to let them pass and the policeman shook his head.

'Shocking business, sir,' he said to Faro and Sven added: 'I called upon him to inspect the scene.'

'Perhaps you would like to accompany us, sir?' Flett

said to Faro, obviously aware of the legendary detective's exploits as he added: 'You might have some ideas of what this was all about.'

'If you think I can help.'

'Much obliged, sir.'

Faro took Rose's arm and said, 'Carry on,' ignoring the policeman's look of surprise that a young, well-bred woman should wish to be included in such sordid goings-on.

Standing by the stone seat, touching the soil debris with his foot as if moving it might reveal some vital clue, his notebook at the ready, Flett coughed, straightened his shoulders in a businesslike manner and said to Sven: 'I am right in supposing that it was you who discovered that the garden had been attacked by vandals?' Sven said yes and they had to listen to the details all over again. At the end, Flett closed his notebook. 'We will need to have a statement from you, so that official enquiries usual in such matters can be pursued.'

Sven readily agreed and Flett asked carefully: 'Then have you any suspicions, as a local man, who might have been responsible?' As Sven's theory of the archaeologists had been firmly set aside by Emily, he said nothing and merely shook his head.

Flett pursed his lips thoughtfully. 'Mm. What I am asking is if you are aware of any folk who might have a grudge against Mrs Yesnaby?'

Sven stood tall at that and said indignantly, 'None at all. I can assure you of that. Mrs Yesnaby has just lost her husband, as you well know, and all of Hopescarth and Skailholm have been united in expressing their sympathy and condolences.' He shook his head. 'The Yesnabys are held in the highest regard and the community will be more than willing to assist you in your enquiries and see the criminal arrested and punished.'

Flett's frown deepened. He looked at Faro and Rose as if they might provide inspiration.

Faro shrugged. Although impressed by Flett's extensive questioning, he was bored and a little tired. 'We are at a loss.' To which Rose added, 'We can't help you, Flett, we were just here for Mr Erland's funeral, hardly time to get to know anyone or speculate on possible villains.'

The policeman regarded her in mild disapproval. What was this young woman doing? Who did she think she was, anyway, giving her opinion on men's matters of criminal procedure?

They returned to the house where Mary offered Flett refreshment of tea and scones, which he eyed eagerly but on second thoughts declined.

'I gather you will be leaving for Edinburgh within the next two days,' he said to Emily. 'I hope we will have made an arrest by then.'

'I hope so too,' Mary interrupted. 'I'll be living here on my own and I don't fancy that much, with a criminal lurking about.'

Flett smiled at her, he hoped reassuringly. 'No need for you to worry, Mrs Faro. We will be keeping in close contact. Rest assured you will be well guarded.'

'That's good of you,' Mary sighed.

'And I will look in every morning.'

'It's the nights that really worry me,' Mary muttered as

he departed, leaving them all baffled, annoyed and a little scared by what had seemed such pointless vandalism. There were arguments and speculations but not one with a logical reason. The most baffling and sinister was still how had the vandal or vandals got into the garden without entering by the house?

There was evidence that the house had been entered in traces of soil leading to the front door, but these were quite simply explained. Sven had carried them in on his boots on his way out after inspecting the damage.

Faro said to Rose, 'Curious, but from the soil, one or two faint footprints suggest there might have been more than one person involved.'

This possibility for speculation was cut short abruptly.

It seemed that surprises were not over for the day. The doorbell rang shrilly through the house and Emily, with Mary at her heels, opened the door to a young woman who smiled shyly.

'You must be Emily?' She held out her hand. 'I hope I've come to the right place.'

Alice Yesnaby had arrived.

CHAPTER SIXTEEN

Emily's feelings of wild panic were quickly suppressed. What she had most dreaded was happening this instant, those awful visions had come to life.

'Alice Yesnaby! You are most welcome. Do come in, my dear.'

Stepping across the threshold, Alice hugged her. She was trembling, obviously exhausted.

'I've had a dreadful time. I thought I would never get here. It's really quite remote, isn't it?' Emily glanced down at her down-at-heel boots sadly in need of a polish. 'It's a long way up the drive, from the motor bus stop, isn't it?' she added, following Emily and Mary, the latter rendered momentarily speechless, into the kitchen to be presented to the family who received this newcomer in jaw-dropping surprise.

The surprise they expected but least wanted. Only Magnus and Meg were unaffected by the arrival of this newcomer. They shook hands politely, Magnus giving his slight bow and a curtsey from Meg, which Alice obviously found very appealing.

She gave them both a hug to Magnus's embarrassment. 'Oh, what two darling children,' she exclaimed. 'Brother and sister, two young Yesnabys and so lovely.'

Emily explained hastily that only Magnus had that role. He was an only son, and Meg, who was trying to hide behind him, was her sister's daughter, she added pointing to Rose.

Not one whit put out, Alice said: 'But they are alike; it must be the Yesnaby family resemblance, of course.'

She was wrong but no one cared to contradict her, they had too many other problems. Only Meg, flattered and delighted at looking like her beloved cousin, decided that she rather liked this new lady.

As smiles were exchanged and the newcomer made welcome, the same thought running through all their minds was almost audible: what on earth are we going to do with her?

An attempt at normality was restored by means of Mary's ready poultice for all emergencies: the swift application of a seat at the table, a fresh pot of tea and well-buttered scones.

Alice beamed at them. 'Thank you, thank you so much, you are so kind. I am so hungry.'

As she tackled another scone and gulped down a second cup of tea, Rose tried not to stare. They should at least have suggested she wash her hands first. As for Emily, Alice wasn't quite what she had expected. To start with she was young, very young to be travelling alone. Not more than seventeen or eighteen, and very pretty, although her appearance was somewhat grubby to say the least, travel-stained and dishevelled, her hair – bonnetless – in dire need of washing.

All these were Emily's thoughts as well as Rose's as she sat opposite and they both listened to Alice's garbled account of what had led to this most inappropriate of arrivals.

Conscious of their eyes upon her, Alice stopped eating for a moment, paused to take a deep breath. 'Didn't you get my letter?'

Emily shook her head and Alice cried, 'But that is terrible. I posted it a week ago.' She pushed the plate aside. 'After I got yours' – she gulped – 'about poor Cousin Erland, I knew I had to come, although I had missed the funeral.' And a beseeching look at Emily. 'As you probably know, he always wanted me to see Yesnaby, our family home for generations.' She shook her head. 'I knew I had to come, he would have wanted that.' Another pause. 'I'm a teacher as I expect you know, so I am on holiday.'

She looked at their expressionless faces. 'Oh, this is really too awful. Without that letter, you can't have been expecting me. Oh dear, how awful, to come at such a time,' she added tearfully.

Emily stretched out her hand and made reassuring noises, while Mary clearing the table said: 'If you had delayed your visit a bit longer you would have found the house empty.'

Alice gave her a look of horror. 'Empty?' she whispered.

'Aye, empty. Except for me, that is. Emily and Magnus are off to Edinburgh to stay with Rose in a couple of days,' Mary added cheerfully in a determined fashion that made the situation quite clear, ignoring Emily's reproachful glance at this somewhat tactless remark.

Emily did some quick-thinking. She smiled and said rather lamely, 'Of course you are most welcome to stay, as

200

long as you like. Mrs Faro will take care of you,' she said looking at her grandmother severely.

The rejoinder was received with the vaguest of nods that not in anyone's eyes could have suggested eagerness to oblige. Alice looked at the old woman and didn't seem impressed either. She gave a stifled sob.

'Oh no, you are so kind,' she repeated. 'But I couldn't possibly. If-if it isn't too inconvenient and you can give me a bed for the night, I will leave immediately.'

Emily was conscience-stricken. She couldn't allow this poor girl, having travelled all that distance from Aberdeen – and by her appearance very much in need of hospitality, such as a bath and a warm bed, to start with – to set off home again the very next day.

She had a bright idea. 'You obviously didn't get my last letter, but why don't you come with us to Edinburgh? We are sailing to Leith.' Alice was giving it some thought and Emily added enthusiastically: 'Do you know Edinburgh?'

A shake of the head. 'I have never been there. It is rather a long way from where I live in Aberdeen – not in the city itself, I have hardly ever been there either. We are out in the country. My father had a small croft before he died,' she ended sadly.

Emily leant across the table and put her hand on Alice's. 'Then you certainly must come to Edinburgh,' she said with a glance at Rose, who was making a mental note of the number of beds now needed in Solomon's Tower and how very surprised Jack was going to be at this invasion from Orkney.

She could almost hear his comment: 'Haven't seen anything like it since the Vikings left.'

Emily was on her feet ready to show Alice to a bedroom. 'You must be tired; perhaps you would like to rest?' There would be no meal that evening, the hearty lunch provided by Faro had taken care of that necessity. 'We'll send a tray up to your room and I believe there might be some hot water for a bath, if you wish.' Erland had been proud of their up-to-date water-heating installation. 'Have you some luggage?'

Magnus was on his feet. 'I will carry it upstairs, Ma. Which room is Miss Alice to have?'

Emily hadn't had time to think about that, but Mary, who had disappeared for a moment, now reappeared and said: 'I've prepared a bed in the room across the corridor from yours.'

That used to be a dressing room and Emily gave her grandmother a grateful thanks.

'Your luggage?'

Again, a stifled sob from Alice. 'As I was trying to tell you, I lost everything. I had a disaster on the ferry. The crossing was a bit rough and although I am a good sailor, the elderly lady who had been sitting next to me was feeling very ill and I decided she would feel much better with some fresh air. So I took her on to the deck.' She shuddered. 'Just in time, she needed both my hands for support but as she leant over the rail to be very sick, the ship gave a horrid violent lurch and my-my valise containing tickets, money – everything,' she sobbed, dashing a hand across her eyes, 'slid down into the sea and drifted away and there was nothing I could do.' She sighed. 'It was terrible, terrible but we were shortly to land and at least I had the small trunk I travel with.' An agonised glance, a groan and taking a grubby handkerchief from her cloak pocket, she dabbed her eyes.

Clutching it in her hands, she whispered: 'I know what happened was my fault. I was late and nearly missed the boat and when we landed my trunk was not in the hold. As far as I know, it is still in Aberdeen.' Eyes widening in a despairing sigh, she added: 'They have promised that it will arrive in Kirkwall tomorrow. But what was I to do? I was absolutely desperate. I had no money, nothing.' She shook her head. 'The motor bus driver was very understanding and kindly let me travel to Hopescarth without a ticket.'

Sven, who had listened silently to this tale of disaster, stepped forward and gave a little bow. 'Do not worry, Miss Yesnaby. I will take care of this for you. I will go to the ferry office tomorrow and retrieve your luggage.'

Alice looked across at him and clasped her hands. 'Oh thank you, thank you.' She smiled gratefully, a lingering glance, perhaps for the first time seeing this was a very handsome young man who had come to her rescue.

Rose looked sharply at Emily, whose relieved expression concealed a sharp stab of despair at Sven's eagerness to help. The thought that entered Emily's mind unbidden at his returning smile to this damsel in distress indicated clearly that this was a very attractive girl whom he was not displeased would be coming with them to Edinburgh.

Following Emily and Alice upstairs, Rose said: 'I'll run you a bath.'

'Oh, thank you. I'm so grateful,' Alice replied, removing her travel-stained cloak to reveal a gown also rather dirty and creased. Aware of their glances, she said: 'My best clothes are with my luggage.'

Emily said tactfully. 'We will find something for you until Sven collects it.'

Alice smiled. 'Sven? Is that his name?'

'Yes. He's Norwegian.'

A gentle nod. 'I guessed he was foreign.' She said this in a way that hinted that she approved.

Emily ignored that and considering the tall slender girl critically, opened her wardrobe. 'You can have something of mine to wear meantime.'

'You have some beautiful clothes.'

Emily sighed. She would not be wearing any of the lovely bright colours that Erland had chosen for her until the widow's six months of mourning dress was ended. It was often usual after that to wear dark colours for the rest of the year, but she thought he would forgive her for returning to the turquoise and rose pink that he had loved.

She opened a drawer and took out a selection of underwear. 'There will be something here you will need.'

Alice gave a cry of delight as she handled a petticoat, touching the lace bodice. Rose was very conscious about hands and nails in particular and manicured her own frequently. She would have liked to do the same for Alice's, whose were sadly neglected. Gran had always been such a stickler for soap and water and clean hands inspected before meals. The old adage about cleanliness being next to godliness could well have been reversed in Mary Faro's book. She wondered if Gran was also offended by Sven's dirty fingernails, hands engrained from frequent gardening with his precious orchids.

An hour later, an almost unrecognisable Alice emerged from the bathing ritual. 'It's like the transformation scene

204

in Cinderella, isn't it, Mam?' said Meg, as Alice rather self-consciously came into the kitchen and smiled at them.

'Well, now!' Mary gasped.

It was well indeed, a beauty had strode into their midst. A beauty with long pale-gold hair. Emily's dress, though a little large did not disguise her slender curves.

She took a seat at the table with them, said thank you over and over until her gratitude became something of an embarrassment to Emily. After all, she was kin to Erland; a girl who had made a miserable long journey deserved the best they could do for her and she wanted to know all about Yesnaby. The house was so magnificent and, oh, how she wished she could have enjoyed all this, with time to spare. If only she had made that visit, as Cousin Erland had wanted so badly, before – now it was too late. Just a day or two and then they would go to Edinburgh. Of course, she was grateful . . .

Listening to her, watching her as she spoke, Faro and Rose were impressed. Discussing her on their daily walk the next morning, she was refined, well bred, and obviously well educated, quite unlike a humble country lass. She didn't sound like a crofter's bairn, with not even a hint of the local accent which, Faro remembered from his visits to Balmoral in the late Queen's reign, was utterly baffling and often like a foreign language.

They stood on the clifftop before returning. It was a beautiful cloudless day, with visibility to the far horizons, the sea path travelled by the Vikings long ago.

Rose sighed. 'Not many more days like this, Pa.' Taking his arm she said: 'I wonder if we will ever come back.'

'You might, Rose. Indeed, I hope you will.'

She looked at him. A lurking sadness in his words making her remember he had passed the age when a man could hopefully see his future in decades.

'You must come, Pa. Bring Imogen, she would love it.'

He shrugged, smiled. 'Maybe.' They headed back up the drive where their moments of peace were ended by the woeful scene in the kitchen.

Alice was crying. Standing beside her looking awkward as men do sometimes when women are upset, Sven was saying: 'Please, Miss Alice, do not upset yourself.'

She looked up as Faro and Rose came in. 'My trunk – it isn't at the ferry. It hasn't turned up. No one knows what has happened to it. All my things lost—' she wailed. 'What am I to do? I have nothing – nothing.'

Emily, putting a comforting arm around her shoulders, said gently. 'It isn't the end of the world and there are lots of shops when we get to Edinburgh.'

'Not without any money. Oh, this is awful, awful. Not only clothes – everything.'

Emily exchanged a helpless look with Rose. Surely not everything – she had only intended a brief visit to Yesnaby.

Sven said. 'I will go again, this afternoon. They said I could try later when the next ferry arrives. It will probably be on that one,' he added encouragingly. 'Perhaps, Miss Alice would like to come into Kirkwall with me.'

'What a good idea, you would like that I am sure,' said Emily, and Rose looked at her. Why treat her like a spoilt child, with her lost luggage the end of the world rather than an irritating incident encountered by most travellers at some time?

206

She was smiling now, putting on a brave face and saying yes, she would like to see Kirkwall.

Sven eyeing her, bowed and said to Emily, 'It may be cold in the motor car, perhaps a warm blanket, Mrs Yesnaby?'

Watching them leave, Faro had retreated upstairs to the telescope while Rose and Mary went to help Emily resume her packing.

'What do you think of her?' Rose asked.

Emily smiled indulgently. 'She's very young, you know, and obviously hasn't been away from home much in her short life.'

'Her parents must be quite well off?'

'Aye, an only one. I've thought about that,' Mary put in. 'No doubt skimped themselves and scraped for years to get her educated and find a good husband.'

'I can't imagine that she will have much trouble finding one.'

Mary chuckled. 'With her looks, she'll be fighting them off. Did you see the way young Sven looked at her, wanting to take her into Kirkwall in the motor car? No offer to take the two bairns this time. Well, well.'

Rose looked quickly at Emily, and saw by her expression that it was far from well for her. Aware of her sister's confidences regarding Erland's protégé, she wondered how long it had been going on and how deep it was. She felt concerned that the situation was identical to John Randall's passion for Emily, and as Faro would have put it, poetically and ironically, 'There are those who kiss and those who are kissed'.

It was early afternoon when the two returned from Kirkwall. Still no luggage at the ferry office. Sven shook his head. 'They fear it is not going to arrive and Miss Alice was asked to sign a claim for lost luggage.'

Alice seemed more resigned than angry. There were no tears or wailing this time, just a sigh and a shrug. 'It could have been worse, if I had come here and found the house empty.' A faint smile. 'But you have all been wonderfully kind. I dare say it will turn up and I am sorry to have made such a fuss after all you have been through.'

'So she has grown up a few years in a few hours,' Rose said to Faro, leaving him after lunch to return upstairs to find a distraught Emily pulling out drawers, scattering their contents.

'Never mind about Alice. This is serious, Rose. It's the Yesnaby Jewel, our family heirloom. It's not where it should be. I'm sure I saw it – here!' She pointed to an empty jewel case and sat down heavily on the dressing-table stool. She put her hand to her face. 'Rose, it was Erland's, his most treasured possession, to be worn on state occasions, but fortunately for me they never happened. I would never have worn it, in fact I thought it was quite hideous.'

Rose knew that was right. She had encountered the Yesnaby Jewel on her visit ten years ago and there was quite a story, which she preferred to forget.

Emily was saying, 'Gold. Very large and heavy, golden oval-shaped pendant. In its centre a crowned mermaid, her tail studded with precious stones, sapphires and diamonds, and the mirror she held trimmed with pearls.'

Rose nodded. The pendant was an exact copy of the mermaid stone in the ruined wall of the original house.

Emily continued: 'It is supposed to be at least two hundred years old, handed down to the eldest son and heir.'

She sighed sadly. 'I can't imagine Magnus or his wife will like it, either, or whoever else inherits it after we are gone.'

Rose said nothing as she remembered Erland's words. The jewel had a very precious secret. Inside was a lock of pale-gold hair, taken from the tresses of the Maid of Norway before they laid her beneath the mermaid stone in the garden. This was also the secret passed on to the next in line. Not usually to a woman, unless there was no son as heir, Erland had said. Women talk too much.

Emily wasn't talking this time, she was frantic and moaned that she had searched everywhere.

'Were you going to take it to Edinburgh?' Rose asked.

'Yes, the thought had crossed my mind to take it to a jeweller in Edinburgh. That's how I found it was missing. As far as I know that had never been done; it has never left the house before and this seemed a good opportunity to have it valued.'

'There was no provision for something so priceless, such as a bank strongbox?'

'No,' Emily said sharply. 'Erland never even thought of such a thing. The jewel was the soul of the house. It would have been like giving away its heart, handing it to an alien source. He really believed in it and felt the house of Yesnaby would be cursed and fall without it. We were the guardians.'

Rose shared this information with Faro, whose logical mind rejected it as superstitious nonsense although he was careful to treat Emily's anxiety with gentleness and tact. He said reassuringly, 'The house won't be completely empty, Gran will be here. It's probably just mislaid. It'll turn up and she will look after it.'

This new situation regarding the missing jewel alarmed Mary. Taking into account the break-in, who knew what sinister forces were at work. 'Perhaps that was what they were looking for,' she grumbled.

'Hardly, the garden was the last place they would search, Ma.'

Packing went ahead, trunks were stored ready to be transported to the ferry in hired transport, the motor car to remain in the garage awaiting Emily's instruction on her return, now almost decidedly its subsequent sale.

With preparations almost complete, Sven's main concern was for the care in his absence of what he now regarded as his orchids. After being on beck and call for help with their luggage requirements, he spent hours in the sunken garden ensuring that his orchids would take no harm during his week-long absence.

Emily, gazing down from the window, noticed that Alice, who told her she passionately loved all flowers, was now also spending a lot of time in the garden, and obviously sharing Sven's devotion to orchids, which she said she had only ever seen before in books.

Rose was another candid observer of the two fair heads together, laughing and talking, undeniably a very handsome young couple, and she felt her sister's despair.

Once finding Rose at her side as she looked out of the high window, Emily said acidly: 'Do you know, I am beginning to think it was a great mistake inviting him to come with us to Edinburgh. We should be leaving him here to take care of his damned orchids.'

Rose was sorry for her, realising that the unseen young

woman, who according to the gossips he had been visiting in Skailholm, was no competition for the one on hand, the quite beautiful girl who had arrived on the doorstep of Yesnaby. It seemed unlikely that he ever gave a passing thought to Emily and their very brief idyll – a few kisses – which she believed meant that he loved her and saw in them a future for them both.

Time moved apace, soon days became hours and on the eve of their early-morning departure, Emily rushed downstairs with a shout of triumph. 'I've got it!'

The Yesnaby Jewel was found.

Emily was enraptured but completely mystified. 'It wasn't in its case. It was away at the back of the drawer. I was sure I had looked there, everywhere in my frantic search. But no matter how,' she added, clutching it to her heart.

Later she said to Rose, 'I have an idea what happened. The only logical reason, unless I am going mad, was that Magnus had been showing it to Meg, and knowing it was a naughty thing to do – he's forbidden to poke about in my dressing table – perhaps he heard someone coming and didn't have time to replace it in its case.'

She sighed. 'I've just asked him and, of course, he denies it completely.' She shook her head. 'He was quite upset when I accused him and I know he never tells lies. But it is still very weird, it doesn't make sense, does it? I mean, how we can miss something we search for when it is just under our noses all the time.'

Rose reassured her about that. With a meticulous index system recording even the smallest details in her professional life, she could be – according to Jack – alarmingly careless when it came to looking after her personal possessions.

Emily bit her lip and said gloomily, 'I am glad I am not the only one. Perhaps it runs in the family.'

Rose, however, decided to have a word with Meg. When she mentioned the Yesnaby Jewel, Meg's eyes brightened.

'Have you seen it?' Rose asked. 'Has Magnus ever shown it to you?'

Meg shook her head. 'Of course not, but I would love to have seen it. He said it was very precious and that as Aunty Emily was very upset about losing it, he decided that we should search for it. I thought that was a great idea, and Aunty would be delighted if we could find it for her. Trouble was we had no idea where to begin, just knowing it must be somewhere, but that could be anywhere, this is just such a great big house.

'I was sure that the most likely place was still Aunty's bedroom so when you were all busy downstairs, we crept in and searched everywhere, especially under the bed, but all we found there were dust mice that had escaped Millie's cleaning.' She laughed. 'Don't tell Grandma, or poor Millie will get into trouble.'

'Did you look in the dressing-table drawers?'

Meg gave a shocked exclamation. 'Of course not. Magnus said that was not allowed. They were very private.'

Rose believed Meg, her story sounded right and she was not a child who ever told lies: the nuns at her school were very explicit about making hell very real and scary.

The only other person who seemed likely to have lifted it and then put it back again was Millie, who might be short in many things but was the soul of honesty. Could she

212

have been driven by curiosity while dusting her mistress's dressing table but had been interrupted?

Discussing it with Faro and considering the secrecy surrounding this ancient relic, they concluded that it was unlikely that Millie had ever heard of the Yesnaby Jewel.

Faro shook his head. 'Just one more mystery we are unlikely to solve.'

Rose sighed. 'Another one to add to our list. It's growing, isn't it?'

Faro laughed. 'We must all accept that mislaying things in the house happens to everyone. Perhaps, as Emily now accepts, most likely she had taken it out of its case at some time, meant to replace it and forgot.'

Even as he said it, and despite the fact that Emily seemed notoriously careless about leaving windows open and losing material objects, he thought this an unlikely theory. 'I am taking it to Edinburgh with me,' she said. 'I'm not letting it out of my sight again, curse or no curse. I still believe it should be valued.'

Mary had watched over their preparations. There was no joyful holiday ahead for her, only the sad parting from her beloved Jeremy. Well aware when he took her in his arms that this might be their last farewell on this earth, he knew that she who never cried was fighting back tears.

'For the present,' he whispered. 'I'll be thinking of you and I'll come again soon, I promise.'

She looked up at him, and although most days she did not feel her age, it was strange to have a son of seventy.

She smiled wanly: 'Come again, lad, and bring Imogen.'

The hour of departure had arrived, the end of the sad

213

occasion of Erland's funeral with its ironic consolation of bringing the whole family together under one roof again. For Faro this had been an unexpected reunion with his mother and his two daughters, especially Rose, someone to share his delight in solving mysteries.

There were no glowing successes to report this time, however, rather they were leaving two dismal failures behind them. The secret visit of the royal yacht, with the mysterious passenger, Mr Minton, who had fallen overboard and, as far as they knew, whose body would now be in the deep sea somewhere between Shetland and Scandinavia.

More baffling still, the murder of the mysterious Mr Smith, with its solving and bringing to justice the person or persons involved now the business of Orkney police, who they were unlikely ever to meet or hear from again. Unless his murder and the revelation of his secret identity were sensational enough for the scandal columns of the Sunday newspapers.

Such were the thoughts of Faro and Rose as they went down to take a last look at Erland's garden with its secret. It was a cold, blustery day with rain that fell like teardrops on the stone seat.

Emily leant over the wall high above them. 'Time to go.'

Faro took Rose's hand and they climbed the steps together.

They both smiled, a little sadly.

'Farewell, Yesnaby.'

CHAPTER SEVENTEEN

Edinburgh

They had arrived at last. The end of a smooth voyage across the legendary stormy firth, but they had been favoured since it had fewer rolls and lurches than the ferry to Stromness.

Nevertheless, there were sighs of relief when Leith's busy harbour came in sight, from all except Magnus, disappointed that there had been so little excitement and he had hoped, he whispered to Meg, that they might have had a more eventful time than playing cards to pass the journey.

Meg didn't mind, although it had seemed a long time since they left Kirkwall, and her excitement grew at the thought of seeing Thane again.

As the ship docked, Rose anxiously regarded the quayside. There was no sign of Jack. She said nothing to the others but his absence bothered her. When they stepped ashore, a man came forward, bowed and said: 'Mrs Macmerry? Chief Inspector sends his apologies, he is unable to meet you but there are motor cars at your disposal.' He pointed. 'If you will permit me to escort you home.'

Rose murmured 'Typical' to her father who grinned: 'A policeman's life, my dear,' as they trooped behind the messenger who summoned a porter to bring their luggage. There was an unexpected problem. Too much luggage for the space required for seven passengers.

As Jack's messenger sighed, saying there had been a mistake, Rose wished she had her bicycle, waiting at home for her return.

Some decision had to be reached and Sven stepped forward, eyed the forlorn trunks lying on the quayside and bowed.

'I will take some of these in a hiring cab and meet you at the house.'

Sighs of relief all round and Emily's thanks plus her usual murmur, 'He is so good. He thinks of everything,' as he handed them into the two cars and saw that they were comfortably seated with rugs for the journey.

He gave a brief salute and said, 'Do not worry.' Nevertheless they drove off watching him with anxious eyes, remembering Alice's woeful tale of lost luggage and her bitter disappointment that it had not arrived before they left Orkney. In borrowed robes ill-fitting her slender frame, she still managed to look like a fairy-tale princess, Rose thought, and she had seen Emily's look of despair as the sailors on the quay had stopped to gaze at Alice, holding on to Sven as they descended the gangway.

At Faro's side, Rose glanced back at Emily in the motor

car with the two children. Although Sven was never hers except in her imagination, she wondered if her sister realised that she had lost him the moment Alice Yesnaby walked in the door.

Heading through the little town, Magnus, who had prepared his history in advance, pointed out that this was where Mary Queen of Scots set foot in Scotland on her return from France. On to Leith Walk, the long road ending in the centre of Edinburgh. Over the North Bridge with its view to the castle perched high on its volcanic rock above Princes Street. Tall church spires, a sharp turn left and down the High Street and the shadow of the extinct volcano that had shaped Salisbury Crags, past the Palace of Holyroodhouse and through the Queen's Park. To bid them welcome, a fine sunny day with a few cumulus clouds floating over the magnificent lion's head of Arthur's Seat, towering above them as they approached.

'We're home!' And there was Solomon's Tower, nestling as it had for centuries past at the base of Samson's Ribs.

Alice was as excited as the two children, exclaiming with delight. This was new territory for Emily, and Rose watched her father's face, haunted by memories, both good and bitter, from days with his doctor stepson, on hand to help him solve murders. Young Vince, who had travelled far beyond Edinburgh to become Dr Vincent Beaumarcher Laurie, a physician to the King's household.

Before the front door was opened by Sadie Brook, from behind the house the huge deerhound rushed to greet them.

'Thane, Thane!' For it was to Meg's side he ran and the others watched as the small girl embraced the great dog,

Magnus a little unsure and cautious after a frightening encounter with a gamekeeper's Labrador, while Faro shivered, remembering that weird nightmare about the Maid of Norway, then telling himself that it was nonsense, that all hounds looked alike.

'Thane!' Now it was Rose's turn and by the time they were inside the Tower, everyone had received a polite welcome, including the newcomers.

Smells of baking drifted from the kitchen and Sadie had them sitting down to a meal, which told Faro that Mrs Brook's niece had been well trained and left Rose in no doubt that Jack was well-cared-for in her absence. Going over the domestic details of what would be required for the guests, Rose apologised for the extra work involved but her fears were swept aside by the smiling housekeeper.

'Glad to have you home again, and Meg too. She is looking so well; the holiday cured that nasty cold. Mr Jack told me about bedrooms for your extra visitors and we've opened some of the spare rooms upstairs.'

'They haven't been used for years, not since I came to live here. I've hardly ever set foot in them. Are they all right?'

'A little dusty, but most had beds. Some very ancient ones and new mattresses were needed, but Mr Jack gave me leave to call in the services of that shop in George Street. He said you wouldn't mind me using your bicycle. It's been a great help.'

'I'm glad of that. Motor cars are great but not nearly as negotiable in traffic.'

Following her up the spiral staircase, Rose sighed with relief as she opened doors on trimly furnished rooms with comfortable-looking beds adorned by white covers, and the sight of billowy pillows made her realise that she was very tired after the voyage. She wondered how the others were faring, particularly her father.

Thanking Sadie for her excellent work, she added: 'They will be glad we have a bathroom. I hope we have enough towels to go round.'

Sadie nodded. 'All taken care of, Mrs Rose, nothing for you to worry about.' And with the evening meal over she showed the newcomers to their rooms, some of which overlooked Arthur's Seat.

There were decisions to be made according to the length of the visit and Meg, who had followed them, whispered: 'Aunty Emily was so kind to us, she must have our best bedroom, with the four-poster bed.'

Rose had never liked that particular room. Her stepbrother, Vince, had inherited Solomon's Tower from Sir Hedley Marsh, its previous eccentric owner, who had used the great bed to house his vast horde of cats, and for Rose, somehow the smell still lingered.

Meg, however, had always wanted to sleep in the four-poster. 'It's big enough to share with Aunty. And Magnus can have the daybed in what was once the dressing room. Grandpa can have my room, it's snug and cosy.'

As for Alice and Sven, their rooms had been skilfully adapted at short notice for a temporary stay. Apologising to Sven, who had just arrived, Sadie said he would have the nanny's room next to the nursery, now to be Alice's room at the top of the tower. He did not seem to mind, although Emily did but couldn't see any excuse or any valid reason for objecting to this proximity to Alice without making a great fuss.

Their luggage now spread out tidily in the hall, Sven said: 'It is all there. I made a careful check at the dock office, just in case Miss Yesnaby's had turned up and been forwarded from Kirkwall.'

A sharp intake of breath from Alice. 'Don't tell me – I can't bear it, I was still hoping.'

He shook his head sadly: 'There is no trace so far, but don't give up hope,' he added cheerfully.

'Hope, after all this time,' she exclaimed, 'and I am still in borrowed clothes. All my best dresses lost,' she moaned.

Emily put a hand on her arm. 'Never mind, we will go shopping on Princes Street tomorrow.'

'As I told you, Emily, I have no money to buy clothes or shoes. I had everything new especially for the visit to Yesnaby. Oh dear, this is awful.'

There was silence all round, sympathetic murmurs but a certain weariness at the continued saga of Alice's lost luggage. In fact, they all thought Emily's offer was exceedingly generous, considering that Alice needed clothes only for a few days in Edinburgh before returning home to Aberdeen.

Rose told her there were no plans for formal visits. With that she had to be content, sighing and saying of course she had other clothes at home but not nearly as nice as her best ones, which had been lost.

Jack had come in while all this was being discussed. After fond greetings to Rose and Meg, he turned to Alice and the dread subject was renewed. 'If it turns up, we will forward it on to you, so don't worry,' he added consolingly.

As this was a special occasion, it was to be celebrated not in the kitchen, normally the hub of the house, but in what had once been the great hall of the Tower with its ancient tapestries of harrowing scenes from Greek mythology mercifully faded and almost obliterated by time. Impossible to heat in winter, the stone walls let in icy draughts and it was only in summer the great hall could be comfortably used, supplemented even on the warmest day by a log fire in the huge medieval fireplace, built originally, Jack suggested, to roast an ox to be consumed at the massive oak refectory table.

Rose apologised that there was no drawing room. 'They didn't go in for such niceties when this tower was built, more for defence and keeping the reivers and the English at bay. Presumably, they had music of a sort as entertainment,' she added, pointing to the minstrels' gallery above, 'but Jack and I live in the kitchen, and what guests we have, we also entertain there.'

She smiled at them. 'But this is something special, this is a family occasion. It's so delightful, so marvellous to have all the family together.'

Faro agreed but sighed, his thoughts with Imogen, sad that she should have missed not only historic Yesnaby House but also this restored pele tower that she would have loved.

Seated round the table, what followed was not in the ancient tradition of the banquet suggested by their surroundings, but considering that they had just arrived and were very hungry, Sadie had worked wonders with a delicious beef and vegetable stew and mashed potatoes, followed by an apple dumpling.

When at last the log fire fell to ashes, they retreated to the kitchen. It had turned chilly, and cool draughts seeping through the stone walls had also brought the tapestries' gruesome depictions uncannily to life. Whilst there was still daylight Meg had taken Magnus out to explore the wonders of Arthur's Seat, accompanied by Thane. Interested in his reaction to the newcomers, their pats on his head politely received, Rose was amused and glad that Magnus seemed to warrant his particular attention. A great deal of tail-wagging indicated approval, accompanied by an expression that seemed to her and to Meg the equivalent of a human smile.

As they sat around the kitchen table to exchange ideas with Emily, whose visit would be a short one before Magnus's tutor arrived at Yesnaby, she had decided to explore the possibilities of schools in Edinburgh, taking him with her when interviews could be arranged.

Sven would, of course, be returning to Yesnaby with them. He acknowledged this information gratefully, saying again how honoured he was to have been included in Mrs Yesnaby's holiday.

Emily laughed. 'You know perfectly well we couldn't do without you, Sven. As a general factotum, you are irreplaceable.'

Looking across at Alice, Rose asked: 'What are your plans? You may stay as long as you like.'

Alice smiled politely. 'Thank you, if you can put up with me just for a day or two.' The absence of appropriate clothes obviously worrying her, Emily and Rose could see that she was tired after the long journey and suggested she might like to go to bed. She seemed grateful and Sadie showed her to her room. A little later Emily and Rose saw the two children safely bedded down, although it looked as if there was to be an extra sleeper.

Meg said: 'Thane always sleeps in my room, Aunty.'

He had followed them up the spiral staircase. 'He looks as if he wants to stay.'

Rose frowned but Emily could not resist Meg's look of appeal. 'Then let him.' She laughed. 'It's a big enough room for all of us. Maybe Sadie could fetch his rug.'

Downstairs, Jack was busy sorting out papers, frowning over bills no doubt, thought Rose. He looked up and grinned as she followed her father out, heading for Salisbury Crags.

Jack laughed. 'An evening stroll? No, thanks.' And blowing Rose a kiss, he added: 'Don't get lost, love, there might be wolves.'

It was an old joke between them as there hadn't been a wolf on Arthur's Seat for more than a hundred years, Rose said, linking arms with Faro. Tonight she felt they were both too tired for the Radical Road, Faro's favourite walk on the Crags with its magnificent view over the city. Instead she stopped by her favourite seat on the garden wall.

'Moonrise on Arthur's Seat,' she sighed. 'The loveliest moment of the day watching it creep over, at this time of year it's like a great big orange. Don't you miss these moments on your travels, Pa?'

Faro sighed. 'Sometimes. I've seen that same moon rise over so many different countries in the past years.'

Rose laughed. 'And I'm still amazed that it looks exactly the same in Arizona as it does in Edinburgh.'

'And in Ireland. We have Imogen's word for it.'

'You miss her, Pa.'

'Always, even here where she has never played any part in my life. If she got any of my letters, I am hoping she'll come here or that we can arrange to meet somewhere in Scotland, depending on her lecture dates.' And taking Rose's hand, he said, 'Meanwhile, I am more than content being with my two lassies again – and their bairns. I am glad fate spared me to enjoy being a grandfather.' He paused. 'And glad you found happiness again with your Jack. He's a fine man, I couldn't have wished better for you.'

'Poor Emily, and what has fate in store for her, I wonder?' Rose said, aware that she was testing the ground.

He thought for a moment. 'Aye, she's young enough and a rich widow, with Yesnaby an added attraction. The good doctor seems wild about her; that would be a good move.'

'Pity she doesn't feel the same.'

'Pity she's wasting her time on Sven.'

Rose's eyes opened in amazement and he grinned, 'I guessed, saw it right away.' And wagging a finger at her, 'Because your old policeman father has retired doesn't mean he has also retired his observation and deduction. I don't think she ever had much hope there, but now what we are seeing is inevitable, that young attracts very young.'

'You mean Sven and Alice?'

'I do. Thick as thieves those two. Surely you've noticed, and Emily must be blind if she hasn't.'

Rose sighed. 'Oh, I think she has all right, maybe it's the Nelson touch. What do you think of Alice?'

Faro frowned. 'I haven't made my mind up there. All that beauty, all that innocent appeal.'

It was turning too chilly to stay seated. The hour knew its warm day was over, the trees drooping their heavy-leafed heads into sleep, and as they walked back, he added: 'She just seems too good to be true.'

Sven had joined them in the kitchen again after making certain that everyone's luggage was stored in their appropriate bedrooms. He took his place across the table from Alice, at Emily's side, to be rewarded by what perhaps only Rose noticed was a rather proprietorial smile.

Jack looked up eagerly as Faro and Rose sat down. Flourishing one of his papers, he said, 'Here is one bit of useful information, one thing you will be surprised to hear, a fragment of our mystery on the royal yacht solved.'

Eager faces were turned to him as he said: 'I wanted a few more details so I made enquiries through what we, in the police here, call the usual sources and it turns out that the passenger lost overboard on the ship's list, Lindsay Minton, was not a man, but a woman.'

Gasps of astonishment greeted this piece of news, although it was becoming fashionable and quite common for girls to be given a male name, especially when there was no son to be heir.

'That's amazing,' Rose said. 'What else – what could they tell you about her?'

'They are not at liberty to give details, other than that she had not come from London with the yacht, but had boarded it when it reached Norway on what was to be the homeward voyage.'

'How awful,' Emily said.

'It is, indeed, but presumably her kin have now been informed.'

'Poor souls. They will be horrified.'

Jack nodded. 'Especially as her body has not turned up yet or been washed ashore, as far as we know.'

They were speculating on this extraordinary revelation when there was a slight cough from Sven, who had been listening intently.

'If you will permit me, I think I can shed some light on that mystery.'

CHAPTER EIGHTEEN

All heads turned towards Sven and he smiled at them, leaning his elbows on the table. 'Remember the night when we thought there was a man overboard on the yacht? I was out gathering in my lobster creels as usual, the last of them not far from the shore, when I saw a woman's head in the water. I was somewhat shaken. For a moment, I thought I was seeing this selkie, that Archie Toft raves about. Nevertheless, I was curious so I went close and saw that this was a human woman and that she was in considerable distress.

'Her foot had caught in one of my fishing nets. I got her into the boat, I had no idea who she was, presumably a local girl, except that she was not dressed for swimming.'

He coughed again and looked embarrassed. 'She was almost naked, clad only in a thin nightgown. I apologised for the net and when I asked her if she was from Hopescarth, she began to cry. She was terrified and pointed to the yacht. She began to cry and implored me not to take her back there as she had jumped into the sea to escape from some man.'

'What happened to her after that?' Faro demanded sharply.

Sven closed his eyes as if it distressed him to remember. 'She was in a very bad way, crying and completely terrified of whatever had happened to her on the yacht. It sounded as if she had been . . . indecently assaulted by some man, a fellow passenger and she jumped overboard to escape him.'

'Why didn't you bring her to us?' Emily asked.

He looked at her. 'It was very late, all of you would be in bed. I didn't want to disturb you or alarm everyone. You could do nothing and the girl was in considerable distress, shivering and in a state of collapse. I had never imagined myself in such a situation before. I did not know what to do so I decided to take her to the cottage, get her out of that wet nightgown clinging to her, wrap her in something dry and warm.'

'You could have taken her to Dr Randall. Doctors are used to being woken in the middle of the night,' Rose reminded him.

'True, that was my first thought, except that his surgery was miles from where I landed and even had she been capable of it, she could not walk that distance in her bare feet and she was too heavy for me to carry.'

They considered his tall slender frame and Emily asked: 'What was her story, then?'

He looked at Emily as if seeing her for the first time. He shook his head. 'A quite extraordinary story. I couldn't believe it then, and I still wonder about it.'

'Why didn't you tell us about her?'

'Because she begged me not to let anyone know, to let him – this man who had been pursuing her – believe she had drowned.'

'What was she doing on the royal yacht?' Rose asked.

'She said her mother was from Ireland, a lady-in-waiting to Queen Maud. There was some connection with your Queen Victoria, and her mother hoped to marry a German baron she'd met at Trondheim. That was where this young woman encountered the gentleman who wished to meet you, Mr Faro. He was very keen to marry her, but she decided she wanted to go back to Ireland, to her family there. She was given a place on the yacht when it arrived in Norway a few weeks ago and there he was again. He was relentless in his pursuit of her, and it ended on the deck when he had drunk too much and . . . raped her.' He paused and looked at the women anxiously, as if the word might offend them. 'That was when she jumped overboard.'

He paused for breath and Faro asked: 'Why didn't you tell us this story when Mr Smith came to Kirkwall?'

Sven said: 'I could not, because she said he was there. As she had not been washed up, he would not believe she drowned and as the yacht was under his orders, he guessed she had swum ashore and would try to get to Kirkwall and escape back to Ireland.' He paused for breath. 'And so I made a promise to look after her.'

'And how were you to do that?' Faro asked.

'She was a helpless, very sweet girl and I was sorry for her predicament.' He smiled at the memory and Rose glancing quickly at Emily saw her expression harden. 'She could hardly wear my clothes, so I went to a second-hand shop in Kirkwall and bought her a dress and a cloak, just something to keep her warm.' He shrugged. 'Then there was another problem. I could not keep her in my cottage since the lady who cleans and does my laundry would discover her, so I had to put her into the hotel.'

Which made sense of Millie's reported gossip that the Norwegian was a cross-dresser, queer too, but that he might be courting a lass he visited in the hotel, as he continued: 'I had enough in my savings for a ticket to the mainland and then she could make her way across to Ireland.'

'How was she to do this? Get to Ireland without money?' Emily asked sharply.

He shrugged. 'She said there were people in Glasgow, friends of her mother, very rich noble people who she thought would help her.'

There was a slight pause as the listeners tried to digest this extraordinary story.

Then Emily said, 'Poor woman. How awful. Where is she now?'

Again, Sven shrugged. 'I haven't the least idea. Safely home again, I hope. Two days before we left,' he took a deep breath and looked at them, 'that business I had in Kirkwall, the day when I didn't wait for Magnus and Meg' – there was a collective shiver as they remembered the terror of the sea cave – 'I had to go to the bank, draw out my savings, go to the shipping office.'

Jack leant across the table and said sharply: 'You surely realise that the authorities should have been told, that they were looking for a floating corpse when the lady was still alive.'

'I am afraid that slipped my mind. Only her safety, getting away, seemed important.'

Jack gave an exclamation of annoyance. 'Then Orkney police must be told immediately and you will be required to sign a statement that she is still alive.'

'I shall do so gladly when I return.'

'They might want it sooner than that.'

Faro had been very quiet, now he asked: 'What about Mr Smith and his accident, falling into the sea in Kirkwall? Did that happen before your Miss Minton left?'

Sven sighed. 'Yes. And that was terrible. He was not convinced that she had drowned. He had rightly guessed that she had swum ashore and that someone was hiding her. So he came to Kirkwall to look for her.' He paused and looked at Faro. 'I expect he was desperate and thought you might know something, that having been a policeman, sir, you might be able to advise him, give him help in tracing her whereabouts—'

That threw some light on the strange interview with Mr Smith as Sven went on: 'He saw her in the hotel – it was the evening he had agreed to see you, sir. She was terrified because the ship was due to leave that night and he threatened to have bad things happen to her mother if she would not come back to the yacht with him, so she agreed to meet him near the quay.'

He paused and frowned. 'She tried to reason with him but he went on . . . er, making improper advances. He would not let go. She struggled free and ran away. He followed. Another struggle and he fell into the water. I had promised to meet her with some money. Then she told me what had happened. She was terrified.'

He paused and Faro asked: 'What did she tell you about Mr Smith?'

'Very little. Just that he was a millionaire and very powerful in Europe, his real name was known the world over and he had many influential friends.'

Faro and Jack exchanged glances. This account of Miss Minton's encounter with Mr Smith and his accidental fall into the sea did not fit with the recovery of his body. All his valuables, his gold watch and signet ring were intact, but his wallet was empty with no papers to identify him and no money. They both had the same thought, a certainty.

Someone had helped this girl to kill him. They looked at Sven.

'What was she like?' Emily asked. 'How old was she?'

He smiled. 'Young, I am not very good at guessing ladies' ages but I would say not as old as you.' Emily managed to conceal that made her wince. 'Not much older than Miss Alice, in her twenties, and not so pretty,' he added shyly.

Sven had left them a lot to think about, especially Faro and Jack, who were the main ones concerned. Jack, now aware of the reason why Mr Smith had failed to turn up for supper, while both he and Faro guessed that he had been murdered. They could inform the Orkney authorities, but how were they to trace Miss Lindsay Minton, the prime suspect, who was probably in southern Ireland by now?

And then there was the royal yacht anchored at Yesnaby. They would not want Mr Smith's murder and his real identity to be linked to them. The King would not be pleased at all, especially if Mr Smith was the alias of the millionaire he had rented it to.

They could watch the newspapers' report on some person of note and see if the date coincided.

What should they do meanwhile? Both felt that as policemen they should pass on this information, which they did not doubt would be hastily filed away by higher authorities preferring to regard the incident as an unfortunate accident and Mr Smith's unfortunate demise as regrettable.

Jack shuddered. 'I'm glad it's none of our business. Let them sort it out. If we are called, and I sincerely hope not, then Sven here will have to give evidence.' He had decided there was much to be admired in this young man who had the makings of an excellent policeman: the soul of discretion, albeit with a lamentable weakness for rescuing damsels in distress.

'We could do with a lot more like him in the force.' To which statement Faro reminded him: 'Let's not forget that he was also an accessory to Mr Smith's murder.'

CHAPTER NINETEEN

After Sven's astonishing revelations, they settled down to have a holiday to enjoy. There were no problems; the weather stayed fine for Meg to show Magnus her favourite places on Arthur's Seat, accompanied always by Thane; Jack went to work as usual, and with no calls as yet on her professional life as a lady investigator, Rose took up the reins of domesticity again, happy to go shopping in Princes Street with her sister and have long walks with Faro when he was not engaged in making copious notes, mainly, she guessed, recording the Yesnaby visit and his encounter with the late Mr Smith.

Once a policeman, she thought, always a policeman, when they put their investigative heads together to see what they could make of the murder of Mr Smith, and they continued to be haunted by the unsolved mysteries from Orkney that refused to be banished, despite their resolve to let sleeping or dead bodies lie – and that included the story Miss Minton had told Sven. Perhaps that was not quite all the truth, and they decided that Sven must have been severely infatuated to have dug deep into his savings to assist her escape.

Having shopped with Magnus and made enquiries about the possibility of Fettes for his further education, Emily had a new anxiety. Sven was spending a little too much time with Alice, to her dismay proving the rumour that he was attractive to young girls. The remark he had made about Miss Minton not being as old as Emily still stung, and she was being forced to recognise the end of her fantasy future with Sven.

She had tried in vain to get to know Alice, who when she was not with Sven seemed content to sit in a corner and read a book or a magazine for hours on end. She declined shopping expeditions, which Emily dismissed as embarrassment at having no money. She went for walks as far as Duddingston Loch with Sven but had no interest in any of the family activities. A difficult guest to entertain, questioned about her life in Aberdeen, the response was a shrug. No, she hadn't any siblings, she was an only child. Her crofter father had died when she was very small and she had no memory of him. There were just the two of them all these years living alone, her mother had also been a schoolteacher who had married beneath her, and was abandoned by her family.

Emily shook her head and said to Rose: 'I don't know what to do with her. What has happened to all that animation she had when she arrived in Yesnaby? Edinburgh has no attractions for her, she's just bored, and restless too.' She shrugged. 'I can't explain it, it is as though she's just waiting for something to happen.'

* * *

With a family of different ages and different interests, a routine had been set by Rose and Sadie. The day began at seven when Sadie came downstairs and prepared breakfast, a large pot of porridge. Jack and Rose then appeared and Jack departed promptly at eight. Sven and the two children were next, then Emily, seizing the chance of that vast poster bed to herself, took the luxury of what she called a long lie. As for Alice, she didn't like porridge – strange they thought for a crofter's daughter – and sometimes did not appear until midday.

Faro was the earliest riser, having reverted to his early life as an Edinburgh policeman with a brisk walk before breakfast, as he put it: 'before the air was breathed'. Each morning he would set off for the Radical Road on Salisbury Crags. Built in 1822 as work for the unemployed weavers, it provided a magnificent view over the often still sleeping city.

Whatever went on in the rest of the world, or with other people who lived in the area, Arthur's Seat was unchanging and obeyed no human law, governed only by the passing seasons. That offered a curious kind of comfort, even on the bad days that life had thrown in Faro's way.

The only firm rule was that whatever they did during the day, all met together in the kitchen for supper prepared by Sadie, and notice was to be given to her if there was any change to this plan.

As the days slipped by and the weather held, there was a picnic to Portobello, very fashionable and popular as Edinburgh's beach resort. This event was hugely enjoyed by the two children, armed with buckets and spades and the promise of ice cream. It made Rose decide that their family holiday was proving a great success, and it was to be made even greater by the arrival of another visitor

One afternoon, Rose opened the door to be greeted by an elegant lady, tall and slender, whose beauty was undimmed since their last meeting fifteen years ago. She had bright auburn hair and green eyes, and as she smiled, she reached out her arms and Rose hugged her delightedly.

Imogen Crowe had arrived

Here she was, following Rose into the kitchen dressed in the height of fashion that Emily had seen only in Jenners' windows in Princes Street.

As they embraced, Imogen laughed. Yes, she had kept it a secret. She wanted to surprise Faro, who at that point walked in from the garden. And surprise him she certainly did – although, he remarked later, a shock might have been nearer the mark.

Seated at the table, holding hands together, she said that having this conference in York next week, she could take the train there from Edinburgh. Sure now, wasn't Faro always going on about her not being part of the family and this was the great chance to meet up with them. So here she was and them sitting there grinning like apes, delighted to see her.

A great fuss was made by all, and Rose said that as Alice was about to leave there would be a bedroom for Imogen. That was not quite what Faro had in mind.

'She will share my room,' he said firmly and no one batted an eyelid.

As soon as they were alone, no easy matter to achieve in that now overcrowded household, walking on the hill,

Imogen took his arm and told him she was quite enraptured by his lovely family.

He put an arm around her waist. 'It could be yours too, Imo darling. You know that. You just have to say the word I've been waiting to hear for years now.' She swept him a fond glance and sighed.

'I may be doing just that, Faro darlin'. I'm sorely tempted. Now that I am free to travel in your country, maybe it would be a good place to settle down. Edinburgh is all you have said it would be, if we could find a place of our own . . . The Tower is grand, very imposing and historic, but I would want something a little more modern,' she sighed, 'like one of those fine houses in the New Town.'

Their walk was interrupted by Meg and Magnus with Thane, who caught up with them, closely followed by Sven and Alice. Introductions made, they returned to the Tower, and Imogen whispered: 'Do I detect romance in the air? Those two have the very makings of childhood sweethearts.'

Faro couldn't have agreed more as she went on: 'And that other pair, Alice and that young fellow, Sven, don't you think there's something there? They have the look of sweethearts.'

Faro laughed. 'What a matchmaker you are, Imo, worse than my mother.'

'How is she?'

'Very well and, I have to say, she will be furious at not coming with us after all and meeting you.'

Imogen laughed. 'She has hopes of me making an honest man of you, Faro.' And her attention drawn again to the couples heading towards the Tower: 'Tell me about that girl.' So Faro explained the Yesnaby connection and how she had kept in touch with Erland.

Imogen sighed. 'She's a beauty, right enough. I'm sure I've met someone like her but I can't think where.' She shrugged. 'Maybe all lovely young girls look alike when you get to my age.'

Faro laughed. 'And you look about twenty-five.'

'Flattery will get you nowhere, Faro.'

'I know, my dear, but I keep hoping.'

She found Rose and Emily in the guest bedroom and as she arranged her hair in the dressing-table mirror, they were very complimentary about her dress and the small amount of luggage she carried.

She laughed. 'With engagements all over the place, you soon learn the trick of travelling light.'

As she stood up, Emily said: 'You have such a tiny waist.'

'And a big bosom and a bustle. It's what the designers call the fashionable S shape for ladies. Doubtless invented by men!' And touching her waist, 'The answer to this is a very tight corset.'

Both Rose and Emily groaned and she smiled. 'Don't do it, if you don't have to. I can tell you it's beastly and uncomfortable, but I only wear it for those special occasions when I am expected to appear not only as an authoress, but as the picture of fashion. You two are fine as you are.'

Then to Emily, pointing to the necklaces hanging by the window, 'You have some nice pieces there. But what is that large pendant?' She didn't add what she was thinking, that it was too ornate and rather ugly to go with any fashionable dress.

As Emily told her that this was the Yesnaby Jewel, a family heirloom, very old and priceless, Imogen exclaimed, 'Shouldn't it be in a safe somewhere, isn't it risky just hanging there?'

'After I mislaid it in Yesnaby and found it again, I wasn't going to let it out of my sight so I decided to bring it to Edinburgh and have it valued.' She shrugged. 'I'm a bit careless about possessions like jewellery, I'm afraid. Never have much call for them in Yesnaby.'

Jewellery was also on Faro's mind just then. Not the Yesnaby Jewel but a ring for his love. Neither engagement, nor wedding ring, alas, which he would have preferred and, given time, he hoped might come to pass, but a more modest precious stone.

He knew exactly where to find what he was looking for. Not far distant there was an old Jew who kept such a shop. Faro had known Mr Jacob for years and knew that he could be trusted on such matters.

He made his way down to the Pleasance. The shop was still there and so was an older Mr Jacob, who greeted Faro warmly. They had done business together through the years, both of a personal nature and for the police.

As the trays of rings were set before him, Mr Jacob was interested in how long Faro was to be staying and where he was living at present.

When Faro said Solomon's Tower and that he had come down with his family from Yesnaby in Orkney where his mother still lived, the old man's eyes widened.

'Now that is a coincidence, Mr Faro. Only yesterday I had a lady from Orkney with a piece she wished to have valued. It was very large, very old and I could see even at first glance that it was also very valuable. I needed no eyeglass to see that the jewels were real. I asked where she had come by such a piece and she said it was a family heirloom and she wished to know what it was worth.

Faro smiled. So Emily had already been in with the Yesnaby Jewel, as Mr Jacobs continued, 'I shook my head and said it was priceless. She was clearly upset by this and asked was it worth a thousand pounds. I said much more than that.

'She thought for a moment and said would I buy it, give her a thousand pounds for it. I had to tell her that I did not keep that amount of money in my shop and not even my bank account could rise to such a sum. Besides, I doubted if any of my customers would wish to buy it. She wasn't very pleased, said she needed the money now, picked it up and stormed out of the shop.' He sighed. 'I was sorry to have disappointed her, such a lovely young woman in financial difficulties.'

Faro returned to the Tower, baffled and extremely concerned about Emily who, Rose said, had gone with Imogen on a picnic to Portobello where the children had seen a notice that there was to be a sandcastle competition that they were eager to enter.

Shocked as Faro told her of his visit to Mr Jacob, she exclaimed, 'This is dreadful, Pa. We had no idea Emily was in such dire financial straits. I understood that Erland hadn't left her as much as she thought there would be, but needing a thousand pounds straight away and she's never even hinted at it! What on earth can she need all that money for? It's a fortune, more than most folk can ever hope for in a whole lifetime.'

She shook her head. 'I can't understand it. She has always told me everything and she could be sure that we would help. But a thousand pounds!' She sighed. 'We certainly couldn't raise that kind of money. Oh, poor Emily, trying to sell the Yesnaby Jewel. I know she doesn't care about it – you can see how careless she is, never even locking it away, says who would want to steal it – but if Mr Jacob told her it is priceless . . . And it should go to Magnus.

'I don't know what has come over her, really I don't, Pa. This changes everything. She is welcome to stay with us, of course, but she certainly won't be able to send Magnus to Fettes. And she has already been there, she was so sure about it.'

A thought came to Rose. 'If she was so desperate, I wonder if she has tried any of the big city jewellers, like Hamilton & Inches.' She rushed upstairs to the bedroom but the jewel was still hanging there. She gave a sigh of relief as she returned.

'Mr Jacob must have got the shock of his life too. A customer wanting a thousand pounds.'

'Oh, he was very impressed by our Emily,' Faro said. 'Called her a lovely young woman.'

Rose shook her head. 'Sounds as if he needs new spectacles. Let's keep this to ourselves, Pa. I'll tell Jack, though.'

Emily returned from Portobello in a merry mood, unaware of their brooding glances. Only the children were rather sour, having failed to win a prize with their sandcastle.

'It was won by a lad from Bath Street, but these local ones can do lots of practise at castle building,' said Meg.

'We did get a highly commended, so that was something,' said Magnus. 'And some sweets,' Meg added and Magnus was placated by an offer from Sven to take him rowing on Duddingston Loch, having been agitating for this since they arrived. He was not allowed to take a boat out at home; the waves were too dangerous and unpredictable, but the smooth waters of the loch were irresistible.

Emily was pleased to see that he and Sven had become friends and the Norwegian lad often went out with the children, happy to be with them rather than seek Alice's company.

It was a fine evening, so Meg went along, disappointed to be told by Sven after a close inspection, that the boat would only hold two safely.

'I'll stay with Thane. I have my sketchbook so I'll draw the church while I wait.'

Not until distant cries and shouts carried on the still evening air did she realise that she was alone. Thane was no longer lying peacefully at her side.

She ran back to the loch and could see the boat in the distance. It was wobbling a bit, but she couldn't see either Magnus or Sven. After yelling for them both and getting no replies, she shouted for Thane, but he had deserted her too, so she began to run for home, for help.

She panicked. There was something wrong.

There was indeed. They had been halfway across the loch when Sven had suggested that as Magnus wasn't managing to steer very well, they should change sides. Standing up,

243

Magnus grabbed hold of Sven, lost his balance and fell into the water. Sven thrust out an oar for him to grip, missed him and hit his head. Knocked out momentarily by the blow, Magnus opened his eyes and realised he was drowning, his feet trapped in the long weeds in the loch.

But he wasn't alone, he was being dragged by one arm towards the nearest bank on the far side of the loch. Thane had come to his rescue. When they reached dry land, Thane still panting looked at him anxiously. Magnus put his arms round his neck.

'He saved my life,' is what he told Emily when he and Thane arrived at the Tower having crossed the Musselburgh railway line at Samson's Ribs. A sorry drenched sight of dripping water, they were met on the road by the parents, alerted by Meg, and rushed indoors to be dried off and Magnus wrapped in a blanket. A very wet Thane regarded all this attention enigmatically.

'I never saw him go,' said Meg. 'He must have covered that distance in seconds, heard Magnus before I did. I didn't know he could swim.'

'All dogs can swim.' But Rose already had her own theories about Thane's remarkable rescue mission. He had saved Magnus's life as he had often saved her own in the past.

But where was Sven?

He walked in at that moment white-faced and anxious as questions were hurled at him, his answers cool and collected as was his way. Why didn't he try and rescue Magnus?

'The boat had developed a leak and I had to steer it into

the shallows and wade ashore. The boat was wrecked; it was very old and I shouldn't have taken it out. Of course, I went to look for Magnus but I guessed he had swum ashore and would be home by then. I realise I am to blame for all this and I am very sorry. Now if you will please excuse me,' and with that he gave a little bow, and departed up to his room.

The next day, all went about their business as usual. The ladies went into town to look at the art gallery and have afternoon tea, leaving Faro to his deliberations, Emily having observed that he seemed to have a lot on his mind – she was right about that. Meanwhile, the children, with Magnus none the worse for his experience, drifted off with Thane on their endless exploration of Arthur's Seat.

When they gathered in the kitchen at supper time, Sven arrived with some surprising news.

Alice had gone.

They were aghast. She had never mentioned this to anyone, never said a word.

'I am as surprised as you are, Mrs Rose. She asked me if I would go with her into town, she wanted to make some enquiries at the railway station. I said I would go with her and noticed she was carrying a small valise. I decided she must intend shopping. However, when we reached the station she asked me to wait until she went into the ticket office. She came out and said, "Goodbye, Sven, there is my train now over on the Aberdeen platform."

'"Did you intend this?" I asked, and she said, "No, I was going to let Emily know and go tomorrow, but when I saw this train was leaving in five minutes, I decided I would go now." She wanted to go home again and she was very homesick in Edinburgh. But I was to give you her apologies and she would write when she got back to Aberdeen.'

Somehow Emily was not taken aback by this news, aware that she was secretly glad that Alice was now away from Sven. That was a great relief.

She would not be missed, since she never really wanted to be in Edinburgh with them.

Emily said: 'We should have let her remain in Yesnaby.'

And it was from Yesnaby they heard the next day. Letters forwarded by Mary.

'Here's one from Alice, I recognise her writing.' As Emily tore it open, Faro said: 'That's remarkably quick.'

While they were pondering about the speed of the mail, Emily was reading: 'Sorry to hear about Erland, but I will not now be making the visit.' Taking a deep breath, she continued: 'It is a very long way. I know I should have come a while ago while I was still fit but I am sorely troubled with rheumatism in my old age, seventy next birthday—'

Emily threw down the letter, looked up at them, at their astonished faces as realisation dawned.

'Seventy next birthday.'

Who, then, was Alice?

CHAPTER TWENTY

They went to the first mention of Alice and her arrival in Yesnaby. Who beside Erland knew of her existence?

John Randall knew and so did Theo Garth. Erland was known as a generous man, so why did she not get a mention in his will, he had wondered, as the only Yesnaby apart from his son and heir Magnus, who after Emily inherited everything.

Doubtless there were others who also knew about her.

They turned to Sven, who had stood listening, very pale and unhappy. Emily guessed that this had been a shock to him, especially if he had been in love with her, as they had all suspected, and she had merely dumped him at the railway station. Emily felt torn between relief that she was rid of this young, pretty rival and sorrow for his distress. She said: 'You knew Erland very well. You were always close to him. Did he ever talk about Alice?'

He looked miserable. 'I knew of her existence, yes, and

that he was looking forward to meeting her this summer. He talked of her just . . . just before.' He looked imploringly at Emily. She reached out and touched his arm.

'Did you get the idea that they were about the same age?'

Sven merely looked bewildered, shaking his head again and Emily said: 'I had always imagined they were contemporary, that's why I got such a shock when I opened the door and saw her.'

Sven put both his hands on the table, leant against it. He looked ill, exhausted. 'If you will excuse me, I am not feeling well.' Turning to leave them, he bowed and added: 'Perhaps something I ate,' although they all knew that wasn't the real reason.

'Poor devil,' said Jack. 'It's been a great shock to him.'

'And to all of us,' said Emily sadly.

'He keeps to himself, but he must have had a future together in mind,' Rose added, looking at her sister, aware that the words must hurt her, but she must face up to the fact that, from Sven's reactions as a rejected lover, she was wasting her time.

Still considering Rose's words, Faro was deep in thought. 'Her existence was not a secret. Randall and Garth knew of her, so there were maybe others in Hopescarth that Erland had talked to about her.'

'I don't think that was very likely,' Emily said sharply. 'He wasn't the kind of man who would sit down and chat to strangers in the local pub. He never went to Skailholm, didn't drink all that much and preferred to do it at home.'

Jack was also thinking hard. 'So we can cross out local gossip, which got to this girl and gave her the idea.' He looked across at the two children playing 'Snap!' rather noisily, uninterested in yet another grown-up drama.

Emily said: 'She wasn't a local girl, that's for sure. Everyone knew everyone and she wasn't the kind of girl who, once seen, would be forgotten,' she added bitterly. 'Now I realise why she was always so vague and didn't want to talk about her background. I thought she was just bored!'

'I think the answer is in Aberdeen,' said Imogen. 'Maybe she worked for the real Alice, a nurse or something.' And turning to Faro, 'Why don't we go and find out? We can take the train to Aberdeen, and the local one the rest of the way.'

'If this Kirkentilly she talked about really exists.'

'We can soon find that out,' said Jack, an enthusiastic collector of maps and railway timetables. He had local maps of most Scottish cities and triumphantly pointed to Kirkentilly a few miles west of Aberdeen near Banchory.

It was the only sensible solution, a crime to be investigated, if she was defrauding the real Alice by this impersonation. It remained to decide who would go.

Emily said: 'Pa and Rose, of course. They are our detectives, our crime-solvers.'

Faro politely suggested Imogen, since it had been her idea, but she said no, she would stay with Emily and make the most of the novelty of being with Meg and Magnus, who seemed to enjoy her company.

She had sounded a little wistful and said to Faro, 'I should have had bairns of my own, if I hadn't been too busy with a career. Everyone I knew in Carasheen was amazed, seeing that they produce them yearly, dear God, in multiple numbers.'

She watched him changing his shirt. 'Maybe if we had met earlier, got married when we first met in that border town long ago, when you were on a case and I was writing. Maybe you don't remember.'

'I must remind you I have an excellent memory and I remember every painful minute of our first encounter. Flaming red hair and a temper to match.' He looked at her in amazement.

'Holy Jesus, I thought, handsome devil of a man and the rudest I've ever met. Sure now, and you didn't like me much then.'

'It was mutual, I thought. But we've made up for it.'

'And how!' she laughed as he said, 'Come here,' and he took her in his arms.

They must leave as soon as possible and Jack consulted the timetable for the next suitable train, wishing he could accompany them but having no new excuse to provide for interfering with his daily schedule.

'Sven will help to look after us,' Emily said. She took some soup up to his room but he declined, saying he felt really dreadful, feverish, as if he was sickening for something. He said that she should stay away, and keep the children away from him, in case he had something infectious.

She came downstairs and reported it to Imogen: 'Poor Sven, I think this is emotional rather than physical.'

Imogen laughed. 'Sure now, but men with a cold in the head go back to being babies again.'

They had forgotten it was a local holiday weekend and the Aberdeen train was crowded. Faro and Rose were lucky to get seats in adjacent compartments but with no possibility of mulling over their speculations. Racing across the platform at Aberdeen, with minutes to spare they caught the local train that set them down at Kirkentilly.

'I hope she got the telegram Jack promised to send her,' Faro said anxiously as they hurried down the solitary village street. It was not an imposing address Emily had written down for them. Tiny houses, grey and shabby, tightly crammed together with front doors leading straight out on to the road. Gardenless, if any existed then they must be at the back, and it didn't look as if the elderly woman who opened the door to them was well off, either.

'Yes,' she smiled. In answer to their question, she was indeed Alice Yesnaby, and certainly more in keeping with the middle-aged relative Emily had conjured up from those cards to Erland through the years.

Invited in, they had decided not to frighten or cause her undue worries, if they could manage to get the vital information they needed without disclosing the real reason for their visit. They had agreed on their story, that they were in the area seeing a friend in Banchory and Emily had asked if they would look in on her. She had written a card, which Rose handed to her.

As the two women talked, commiserating about Erland's sudden demise with Rose answering anxious questions regarding Emily's future, this gave Faro opportunity to take in the surroundings. A room neat and clean, shabby with age but well-cared-for with embroidered texts, crocheted cushions and a few books.

Alice Yesnaby was eager to make them welcome and repeated over and over how glad she was to see them both, what a great pleasure to meet Erland's sister-in-law and Emily's father even in such sad circumstances. As she moved about the room, setting it to rights, straightening a cushion here and there, they saw that she was lame and walking with a stick, but although in obvious pain she insisted they have a cup of tea.

Rose gave her a hand with taking down the china cups from the sideboard shelf and received a grateful smile. 'I have some scones, they are quite good from the shop. I used to make my own,' she added sadly.

The conversation was still general and polite as befitted relatives meeting for the first time, although Faro and Rose both hoped for an opportunity when they could get to the point of their visit regarding the bogus Alice. Accepting a second cup of tea, Rose could not help glancing nervously at the loudly ticking clock and Faro had anxious thoughts regarding that local train back, the only one in the day if they were not to spend the night here.

When Alice said: 'I lost both my parents when I was young. I used to teach in the village school here until the rheumatism got the better of me,' she added ruefully. 'I had no relatives that I knew of except Erland, and that was why I always wanted to meet him.'

'Have you always lived on your own?' Rose asked.

'Always. I enjoy my own company, I like walking and there are lots of books to read—'

'Have you never had a companion, or needed a nurse or a maid?' Faro interrupted.

Alice smiled. 'I've always been healthy, hardly ever seen a doctor. As for a maid, why would I need a maid?' She stopped, something in their faces disturbed her. 'Why are you asking all these questions, is there something wrong?'

Faro and Rose exchanged a glance. It was time to tell her the truth.

Rose said: 'A young woman turned up at Yesnaby pretending to be one of the family. She was pretending to be you, Alice.'

Alice's hand went to her mouth. 'What a wicked thing to do. I haven't anything to steal, no money, nothing like that. So why should this person want to be me, an old woman?'

'That's what we are here to find out,' Faro said grimly.

'We thought you might have some idea who she was,' Rose added. Producing her sketchbook, she showed Alice a quick drawing she had made on one of their outings at Yesnaby. 'This is pencil, but she had long pale-blonde hair and hazel eyes.'

Alice studied the drawing. 'She is very bonny, I can see that, but I've never seen anyone who looks like her around here.'

Remembering that Alice had been a schoolteacher, Rose added: 'She was very well educated, could she have been one of your pupils?'

Alice shook her head. 'I'd have remembered that face. Refined-looking, if you know what I mean. Upper class, certainly not a village lass.'

Rose looked at the clock. 'Ten minutes to the station, Pa.'

They stood up and thanked Alice for the tea, said they had been glad to meet her. It was mutual and she apologised for not being able to help them. 'I'd like to know, will you write me a wee note when you find her?'

They promised to do so, although both felt that explanations – if ever they did find her – might need more than a wee note.

As they boarded the train, Faro said wearily: 'Bit of a wasted journey, Rose. We are no nearer to finding out the truth: who she was, and more important, why this imposture.'

Sharing seats with strangers in the railway carriage packed with returning holidaymakers, Faro was very thoughtful. They decided to walk home from Waverley Station and he said: 'It's being well educated that bothers me most.'

Rose sighed. 'Is this to be yet another of our unsolved mysteries, Pa? We are certainly accumulating them at regular intervals.'

Faro shook his head. Approaching Solomon's Tower, they stood aside on the road as a hiring car swept past them from Duddingston direction.

What were they to tell Sven? That they were no further forward, that their visit to Alice Yesnaby had been a waste, not only of time, but for Faro, one of the precious remaining days with his daughters in Edinburgh.

A surprise awaited him.

They were indeed further forward. It was Imogen who provided the missing clue.

CHAPTER TWENTY-ONE

In the course of conversation, Emily had told Imogen about the mysterious visit of the royal yacht anchored offshore nearby Yesnaby House, and remembering Faro had mentioned that Imogen had once been a guest, she asked what it was like being entertained by royalty.

Imogen smiled. 'Sure now, and it was a great experience, not to be missed. Once in a lifetime, I thought, when the invitation came to a party on the *Victoria and Albert III* cruising off the west coast and to be harboured overnight in County Cork.

'That was two years ago and fortunately we were both home at the time. Faro wasn't invited, which was just as well,' she added slyly, 'seeing as I got along very well with HM. He is a great flirt, and he seemed to like me' – she sounded surprised – 'with all those lovely women around, yet he had somehow singled me out for his special attention.'

Emily smiled. It did not surprise her in the least, seeing

that Imogen Crowe, already a famous authoress, and with her lovely Irish accent, also combined beauty with brains. No wonder he had decided that she should have a free pardon for her imprisonment as an Irish terrorist. Her uncle, a member of the Irish Republican Army, a fanatical patriot who was also her guardian, had brought her from Carasheen to London with him, where he planned to assassinate Queen Victoria. The plan failed, he took his own life but the police put her in prison as an accessory. She was fifteen, an orphan, and when at last she was freed on lack of evidence, she was sent back to Ireland but forbidden re-entry to the United Kingdom.

'I had the greatest time on that yacht. HM suggested I might come along on one of their cruises sometime. Fat chance of that, I thought, knowing exactly what that wicked man had in mind, and I had better things to do than join the long queue of his mistresses. But I was flattered to be invited and I made a lot of influential contacts for it was only months after that I got my free pardon.'

She stopped suddenly, her eyes widened and she snapped her fingers in the air. 'Holy Jesus! I've got it, Emily – at last!'

Emily stared at her. What on earth was she on about?

'That Alice, I knew I wasn't wrong that I had met her before, but for the life of me, I couldn't think where. I meet so many lovely young girls like her all over the world. But now, I've got it: it was in Cork on the King's yacht.' And drumming her fingers on the table, she went on, 'Let me think, it's all coming back now. She was on the cruise, a lady's maid to someone or other, and she helped me when I got my lace gown torn in the dancing – I thought it was done for. I was mad because I bought it in Paris and it was wildly expensive, but she had noticed it and said she was used to this sort of thing, she'd fix it. It happened to the ladies all the time and those men dancing the reels didn't know their own strength, great strong brutes.'

And this triggered off Emily's memory. Sven's damsel in distress had come from Cork. She had been on the royal yacht.

'What was her name? Can you remember?'

Imogen frowned, shook her head. 'Lily . . . Lil . . . No, no. I'm usually good at names. It wasn't that. Something similar – Lindy?'

That fitted. Emily whispered: 'Lindsay. Lindsay Minton.'

Imogen looked at Emily wide-eyed. 'She must have guessed that I recognised her. Now I know why she always seemed to be avoiding me, although I made little of it. I didn't realise that was the reason, I thought she was just naturally a bit shy and standoffish with all of us.'

At this point Faro and Rose arrived home, weary from their seemingly pointless trip to Aberdeen. Greeting them, Imogen was quick to tell them what she and Emily had just discovered. So Alice Yesnaby was Lindsay Minton, the girl who jumped overboard and who Sven had rescued and helped to return to Ireland.

They looked at each other in horror, as the thought struck home.

Rose said: 'If Lindsay became Alice, then Sven must have known.'

Faro nodded grimly. 'They must have been in this together. But there must have been a reason, some kind of plan, a motive.'

Rose frowned. What could have been strong enough? And they remembered meaningless incidents that now had a deadly reason as Rose recalled Emily saying: 'She sits in the house all day as if she is waiting for something to happen.'

Now they knew what that something had been.

'The vandalised garden at Yesnaby,' said Rose. 'I remember Alice's filthy fingernails. Of course, she had been with Sven and they had been searching for something.'

Emily had said nothing but seemed in a state of shock, there was so much she could not take in or did not want to believe of these revelations. She whispered: 'The Maid of Norway's dowry?'

'Perhaps,' said Faro and snapped his fingers. 'No! We're missing the real reason, something more tangible than an old legend.'

Emily said: 'The Yesnaby Jewel.' And Faro remembered his visit to Mr Jacob just days ago and the old jeweller telling him about the enquirer who had wanted a thousand pounds for it. His description of that 'lovely young woman' certainly didn't fit Emily. But it fitted Alice/Lindsay exactly.

He looked at his daughter. 'Tell me, have you taken the jewel to be valued yet?'

Emily sighed. 'No, I've still got to do that before we go back to Yesnaby.'

'You were never in financial difficulties and asked Mr Jacob, the old jeweller in the Pleasance here, to buy it for a thousand pounds?'

Emily gave a shocked exclamation. 'Of course not. I've never met this Mr Jacob. Where on earth did you get that idea that I would ever sell the jewel? Fancy you believing such a lie!'

There was a sudden stillness.

Faro and Rose exchanged a look and without another word, they rushed upstairs. Followed by Emily into her bedroom where she unlocked a drawer in the dressing table. And the jewel was there, in its case.

Sighing wearily she closed the drawer. 'I took your advice, although I'm so used to seeing it I would never notice if it wasn't hanging among the rest of my necklaces.'

They were astonished that she took so little care of it. 'Really, Em,' Rose said, 'going out all day with the children and leaving the door unlocked.'

The Tower was like that: they used the kitchen door so that Thane had easy access. It could be bolted from the inside and they reckoned that he was a sufficient deterrent to keep any intruder at bay. However, neither Rose nor Jack could decide where the key was, and indeed, if they had ever seen one.

'We never lock doors in Yesnaby. Oh, don't tell me we might have had a burglary here, when I was out,' groaned Emily.

No, but it was a simple matter for the bogus Alice to take the jewel and try to raise a thousand pounds. Faro said: 'When you were out, certainly. But not a burglar.'

'I don't understand, Pa. What do you mean?'

'I mean, Em, someone from inside.'

Emily looked shocked and bewildered. 'But that isn't possible, not one of us.'

Faro let that sink in and said slowly, 'Tell me, where is Sven?'

'He's gone, left just before you arrived.'

'Gone where?' Faro demanded.

'Back to Orkney. He took a hiring cab from Duddingston. Going for a ship at Leith. Said it's been on his conscience, not telling the authorities about Miss Minton in case they are still looking for her. And this business about Alice, poor Sven, he just can't understand it.'

Faro and Rose gave her a hard look, not entirely without sympathy, and Rose said: 'That's a pity, Em, because the rest of us can.'

Emily merely shook her head. 'Poor Sven, he told me not to worry, that he would come back.' She was still refusing to recognise the truth about Sven, still willing to be blinkered when the obvious was striking everyone else.

But Emily had a secret. What they didn't know – or perhaps could not understand – was that they were making a terrible mistake. Sven was coming back for her. He was going to marry her. He loved her, he said, and had always loved her.

When the children were told that Sven had left, Magnus nodded. 'He tried to kill me, you know, that night on the loch. He deliberately hit me with the oar. I tried to tell you but you wouldn't listen, Ma. You insisted that it was an accident, that Sven would never do that. You said he was fond of me.' He looked at her for a reassuring comment, but there was none. With a shrug he added: 'Maybe he was sorry, because he has been very nice to me ever since.'

'Yes,' Meg said solemnly. 'I've noticed that he has been especially nice to Magnus but he gives Thane a wide berth.

He's scared of him, and I don't think Thane has ever liked him, right from when you first came.'

'How can you tell that?' Emily demanded.

Meg shrugged. 'I just know.'

As they all remembered the wrecked boat and Sven's surprise at finding Magnus, rescued by Thane and safely back at the Tower, Emily put her hand to her mouth, an agonised cry: 'I can't believe that. Not Sven – oh no!'

The two children were watching them eagerly. They never quite understood what grown-ups were going on about but this looked interesting, especially as they had seen him leave and he had been very brusque with Meg when she asked him if he was going somewhere exciting and could they go with him.

'Are you going on the train?' Magnus asked.

Sven had growled. 'None of your business.'

'When are you coming back?' Meg asked, and he had almost pushed her aside as he rushed out.

'Will Sven be coming back to Yesnaby with us?' Magnus asked Emily, rather hoping the answer would be 'no'. Instead his mother regarded him tearfully and Imogen, Grandfather's lady – now one of his favourite people – stepped in and said: 'Would you two like me to read the next chapter of the story I am writing about two Irish children who go for a holiday in a haunted castle in the middle of a loch in Kerry?'

'Yes, please!'

'Upstairs to your room, then.'

As the children dashed out, Faro put a delaying hand on her arm. 'I didn't know you wrote children's stories.'

She smiled at him sweetly. 'Neither did I, but this conversation is rather unsuitable for children, don't you think?'

'Thanks,' said Rose. 'You're a gem.'

As the door closed, Faro thumped his hands on the table. 'Listen, all of you. This speculation isn't getting us anywhere.' And to Emily in particular, 'We must face facts. Sven has gone, he's a thief and a liar—'

'But where is Alice?' Rose interrupted.

'I think I know the answer to that.' Faro had been very thoughtful, his expression grave. He gave her a long, slow look.

'Alice is dead.'

CHAPTER TWENTY-TWO

'Alice dead! You can't mean that, Pa,' said Emily.

Faro turned to her. 'I do mean that. Alice is dead and Sven has killed her, and made his escape before her body is found.'

A numbed silence greeted this shattering thought.

At last Rose said: 'Presuming you are right, Pa. How and why?'

'Let's deal with why first. They were in it together. This Miss Minton he rescued, and maybe that was where he got the whole idea of passing her off as Alice Yesnaby. But she was no longer of any use to him. She had served his purpose and the failure to raise a thousand pounds made him realise that she knew too much. She was getting nervous and might betray him—'

And Rose remembered those hours she sat, restless, bored and Emily saying it was as if she was waiting for something to happen. As Faro went on: 'He knew he had to get rid of her and get the jewel himself.'

'Always the jewel,' cried Emily. 'Then why is it still upstairs, why didn't he take it with him. That doesn't make any sense.'

'You locked it away, remember. And we were due back. What if we walked in? That was him in the hiring car we met on the road.'

Rose looked at Emily's stricken, bewildered face as she whispered so that the others didn't hear, 'They are wrong about Sven. He loves me. He's promised to come back for me. We're getting married.'

Rose stared at her in astonishment. Poor Em, she still wants to believe that there has been a terrible mistake, that he is an innocent victim, this protégé of Erland's who had been such a friend to the family, remembering grateful smiles and those repeated words: whatever could we do without him? Now that was finished and done with and she still couldn't take in that this young man she had set her heart on was in fact a ruthless killer.

'I can't take any more of this,' Emily said out loud. 'You are all wrong,' and she ran out to the garden and left them.

Watching her, Faro said grimly, 'We can presume the girl didn't know what was coming to her. Look outside – Arthur's Seat is made for murder, with eminently suitable places where corpses could be tucked away and lie hidden for years.'

'And he had plenty of opportunities on those evening walks they took together, to find a perfect hiding place,' Rose said with a shudder, gazing out of the window across the vast expanse of the extinct volcano on the slope of which Edinburgh's residential south side had taken shape.

Faro looked over her shoulder. 'I would hazard a guess that one of the many secret caves that the children took him with them to explore was marked down as Alice's future tomb.' He looked out of the window at the darkening sky. There would be no moon tonight.

Jack came home. Faro and Rose took him aside and related the day's dire revelations. He listened carefully, said that he found it unbelievable. Not only that Sven was a thief and a liar, but a killer. 'You'd be hard-pressed to see a more open, honest-looking face.'

Faro murmured: '"Oh what may man within him hide/ Though angel on the outward side."'

'I beg your pardon?' Jack stared at him in amazement. 'What's that all about?'

'Shakespeare,' Faro replied. 'In simple words: murderers usually look no different to a man or woman you would walk past in Princes Street any day of the week.'

Giving his son-in-law a wry glance, he didn't add that in fifty years with the Edinburgh City Police, he had yet to encounter a murderer bearing the brand of Cain across his forehead.

'I hope you've got it wrong about Alice,' Jack said, 'seems a bit of a wild speculation to me.' He shrugged. 'Better begin your search in the morning. I'd like the children kept out of this.'

'We need Meg's help, Jack.'

He looked at her sharply. He hated the thought of anything remotely unpleasant touching his little daughter. But Rose was right: Meg knew Arthur's Seat.

'So be it.'

It was doubtful if any slept well that night and Rose guessed by her sister's red-rimmed eyes what those hours of darkness had been for her.

Sadie was the only one not involved in this grim drama. She was her usual brisk, cheerful self, although it was obvious from the family's silence and their unsmiling expressions over their breakfast porridge that something was amiss. She hoped it was not her cooking.

Jack prepared to leave for the Central Office. 'I wish I could come with you, only to prove that you are wrong. I can't wish you luck, I can only hope that there is another explanation.'

The early morning mist that so often hid Arthur's Seat had given place to bright sunshine, radiant over an innocent landscape and out of keeping with the grim task ahead.

Meg and Magnus were thrilled to have Grandpa with them on what was to be just a pleasant walk, for him to see the caves. He had told Magnus on one of their picnics, how when he was a little lad playing with some other children they had discovered fourteen tiny coffins buried in a cave. The identities of the tiny dressed dolls, who or why they had been put there, was a mystery yet to be solved and perhaps one of the reasons that had made him a detective.

Watching the two children racing ahead brought him the ominous feeling that, so many years later, he was in for a grimmer discovery, a dead girl in one of those caves.

Emily was in a state of shock, silent and withdrawn among her tortured thoughts, and Imogen, saying she would stay with her, handed Faro a glove that Alice had worn.

Rose eyed it scornfully. 'Thane isn't a bloodhound.'

'No, but he's a hunter. Knows a lot more than we humans do about tracking down prey and I suspect he will know what we are looking for,' Faro added grimly.

Without the least idea of what was involved and having been informed that Grandpa would enjoy this nostalgic tour, Meg was delighted to take the lead. It was rough-going in places and Faro, feeling the effects of the steep climb, decided that his intuition had been wrong when at last they came downhill again towards Samson's Ribs and were just above Duddingston Loch.

Meg said: 'I left this one until last.'

Magnus said: 'It's my favourite and very well hidden because some of Bonnie Prince Charlie's army camped on Arthur's Seat when he had Edinburgh under siege.'

'And down there,' Meg pointed, 'is the house in Causewayside where the Prince and his officers stayed while they were planning the campaign.'

The cave was certainly well hidden and as they went nearer, Meg moved the overhanging vegetation aside and said indignantly, 'That's not right. It's hard enough to find but someone has been here and put a lot of stones in the entrance.'

Thane and the glove had not been needed. The grim possibility was now almost a certainty, as Meg said: 'I wonder who could have been here? It's been my secret and I've never told anyone about it.'

'Except Sven, remember,' said Magnus. 'He was always so interested in Edinburgh history.'

'But he was one of us and he promised not to tell,' Meg continued indignantly while Magnus looked at the grown-ups, with a question unasked. He was a jump or two ahead of them. He knew that Sven was a bad man who had tried to kill him. He had his own terrifying experience of the young man the grown-ups thought so wonderful.

Faro thanked Meg, who said: 'I hope you enjoyed it, Grandpa. The caves are such fun.' She thought he looked rather tired and took his hand as they scrambled down, back home to be offered cups of tea and newly-baked scones by Sadie.

Such normality seemed strange to Rose and Faro, their appetites dulled. Emily and Imogen had to be told. Imogen listened unsurprised as Faro said: 'We need to get Jack.'

Emily said: 'You don't know for certain that there's . . . there's anyone in the cave. It could be a landslide.' They looked at her pityingly, still trying to find excuses, reluctant to believe what lay behind those stones.

Sadie was sent off on Rose's bicycle to the Central Office. Jack had been out but would get Faro's note to 'come at once' when he returned. Rose groaned, knowing only too well what that meant. 'We might be in for a long wait,' she said as they sat around the table and tried to pretend that this was just another ordinary day.

Faro was strangely quiet, thoughtful. Rose looked at him, realising that he had some plan regarding Sven in mind.

Imogen took them aside. 'Emily can't stay here, it is too cruel for her. I'll think of a good excuse. We might take the children to Portobello again. What do you think?' They looked at her gratefully. Emily's misery was heart-rending; torn between angry denial and defence of Sven, it was a relief when she left with them.

An hour later, Jack rushed in. 'That note. What's happened?' His first thought was the children, and in particular, Meg.

Faro told him about the cave and what they believed that it contained. He listened grimly. 'Right. I hope you're wrong, but off we go.'

Rose said, 'I'm coming too.' The two men looked at her and shook their heads. 'I've seen more dead bodies than either of you. Remember I lived in Arizona for ten years. Fought off Apaches and cattle rustlers.'

'No,' Faro said firmly and Jack added: 'This is no picnic, Rose. Imogen and Emily and the children will be back soon. Meg will want to know where you've gone.'

It was a lame excuse, but Rose had to abide by it, however reluctantly.

Faro and Jack were very silent on their way up the hill and removing the stones, they found what they were dreading. A still figure at the back of the cave, with long fair hair falling over her face. Bruise marks on her neck indicated that she had been strangled – Sven's work – and beside her the valise he said she had been carrying to the railway station. A pathetic collection of the few possessions she had acquired through Emily.

Jack said he would notify the police station and have the body removed. An inquest and a search for the killer would follow.

'Can I ask you a favour?' said Faro. 'She hasn't been dead long and I have a plan to save you searching for her killer. Its success lies in the fact that Sven has not the slightest idea that we have discovered Alice's identity, thanks to Imogen's memory about meeting her on the royal yacht.'

'A stroke of luck that was.'

'Indeed, but he thinks he has got away with it. However, one important factor remains. The vital link: the Yesnaby Jewel and the reason for all this. He didn't take it with him – Emily still has it and we can be fairly sure, according to her, that he will come back for it. Before Saturday when he believes she is going back to Orkney.'

Jack had listened, frowning. 'And so I am to conceal a murder?'

'Only to capture the murderer.'

Jack sighed. 'You sound very sure and you're very persuasive.'

'You'll do it?'

'It's very irregular. Totally against all the rules.'

'For one policeman from another?'

They both grinned and Jack said: 'If you are wrong, my job might be in peril. Whatever happens, we would do well to be watchful in Solomon's Tower.'

He had alerted the authorities in Kirkwall, although they thought that Sven's plan to go there was merely a lie to fool Emily. 'If he had got hold of the jewel he would be on his way to London or God only knows where, somewhere far away where he could cash in the priceless jewel for a lot more than a thousand pounds. As it's still here, that's a different story.

'But for his plan to succeed, there's a time limit. And that is what we are banking on.'

What an end to the holiday, an extraordinary holiday it had turned out to be. And what lay ahead in the remaining days?

* * *

It was the discovery of Alice's body that finally jolted Emily back to reality, from her fantasy world that had allowed herself to be gulled by a ruthless killer.

'And who knows,' said Rose, who had long since run out of patience, 'you might be next. You still have the jewel and he promised you that he would come back.'

'For me,' Emily whispered and shook her head. 'To get married, spend the rest of our lives together, that's what he said. And I believed him, believed that he had always loved me. Oh God, it's so awful.'

Rose said to Faro: 'I wonder when his audacious plan began, when he lured Lindsay Minton into playing the part of Alice Yesnaby?'

Faro thought about that. 'If we presume he has always been after the jewel, then it was triggered off by this impending visit from Erland's relative, who none of them had ever met, their sole communication Christmas cards through the years.'

He sighed. 'Have no doubt that we are dealing with a very clever fellow and not one afraid to take a gamble on high odds. Let's imagine that the moment he rescued the Minton girl—'

'You think that was the truth?'

'Yes, with maybe a few exaggerations for our benefit.'

'Did he immediately think she could be Alice, and put the plan to her when they were sleeping together at the hotel?' Rose said.

'She was probably besotted with him, ready to do anything. And if persuasion failed, if she declined, then he might remind her that he had helped her get rid of the obnoxious Mr Smith by hitting him over the head, robbing

271

him and pushing him into the sea at Kirkwall.' Faro shrugged. 'A little none too gentle blackmail and aware that she was in a tight situation, his final persuasion was no doubt that he had a plan by which they could get a thousand pounds and set up the rest of their lives together. Criminal, of course, but to a woman in love . . .'

He paused and they avoided thinking of Emily as Rose said, 'So we have the set-up: Alice appears at Yesnaby but we are leaving for Edinburgh so Emily suggests, as she has come a long distance and wouldn't want to stay there alone, she should join us. She tells Sven and part two of the plan is in operation. Emily is taking the jewel to Edinburgh and, always careless about its safety, he has this brilliant notion that Alice should steal it and get a jeweller to buy it for that thousand pounds.'

Faro shook his head. 'But as with the best laid plans o' mice and men, it doesn't work out that way. What neither realise until Mr Jacobs tells her is that the jewel is priceless. What can anyone do with a priceless jewel? They must reach a collector, a very rich man or an entrepreneur, possibly in London or New York, since it is not negotiable in the marketplace.

'I think it was somewhere about this time that Sven ran out of patience. The end of the Edinburgh holiday was in sight, Emily and the jewel would be returning to Yesnaby, but most dangerous of all, his accomplice was losing her nerve, terrified every day that Imogen might remember that they had met on the royal yacht. He is scared and there is only one solution: persuade Emily of his undying affection and kill off the bogus Alice.'

Rose said: 'Maybe he always intended to get rid of her, once he had the money to move on to other pastures.'

'One thing he still doesn't know is that Imogen has recognised her, told us and that we have put the pieces together. And that is to our advantage.'

Emily came in and slumped down at the table beside them. Faro looked at her with compassion. She said: 'I owe you all an apology. I just hope you find him. All those lies he told me and, fool that I was, I believed him. Always ready to help, so calm, so smiling.' She shook her head. 'Do you know, I have only once, in the two years he has been with us, seen him lose his temper. A terrible, frightening rage. We all get angry sometimes, but this was scary because it was so unlike him.'

'When was that?' Faro asked.

'After the reading of Erland's will. I felt sorry for him because he obviously felt cheated that he should have been left more than a small yearly pension. He expected a lot more than that. I tried to say something consoling and he just glared at me and said: "After all I have been."'

Reporting this scene to Jack, he merely nodded and Rose asked: 'Tell me, what was it you had against Erland?'

He gave her a surprised look. 'What do you mean? I had nothing against him.'

'But you knew something about him. I could tell when you went silent and thoughtful.'

Jack sighed. 'Oh, I might as well tell you, but for God's sake don't tell Emily. She's got enough to bear and this is something I wouldn't want her to know – ever. When you were visiting them, the year Magnus was born, one of our older officers was from Orkney and I happened to mention that you were related to the Yesnabys. "Oh, is she?" he said. "We once handled a paternity case, a woman from Norway claimed Erland Yesnaby was her son's father. No proof, of course, letters and that sort of thing, and the lad would have been grown up by then." So it was dropped, but I gather Erland had a soft heart or a bad conscience and sent her some money, which was probably the reason for her claim. She wanted more, to keep her mouth shut.'

Rose's eyes widened. 'If Sven was Erland's son, it explains why he was so furious that he had been more or less cut out of the will. He must have hated Erland for not acknowledging him.'

'And it is still the most popular motive for murder.' He thought for a moment and added firmly: 'You know, he might even have murdered him, I've never thought of that before, but as a passionate gardener he probably had access to a number of unidentifiable poisons. So easy, too. And Dr Randall was taken aback that this strong, healthy man should have gone into his garden for an afternoon nap and taken a heart attack. It would never have occurred to him that there was anything suspicious when he signed the death certificate.'

'The only way to prove it would be to exhume poor Erland.'

'We can't do that to Emily, she's had more than enough. Or to John Randall, the scandal would probably end his career.'

'The possibility that Sven killed Erland – I'm just thinking—'

'I know what you're thinking – so am I – that he tried to kill Magnus, the son and heir, drown him on Duddingston Loch, and before that, leave him in the sea cave.'

Rose's eyes widened in horror as she remembered. 'And that left only Emily.'

'Killing her would be risky. So how about marrying her, instead? No problem there. She loves – loved – him, and then he could arrange to do something that's quite usual with second marriages: get the will changed so that if Magnus died without issue – a ten-year-old boy – then Yesnaby would come to him.'

Rose said: 'I wouldn't give much for Magnus's survival without Thane having been there to keep him from drowning.'

CHAPTER TWENTY-THREE

The family gathered – Emily absent, still too shocked to take part in the discussion that followed – and when Jack told them that Sven was probably Erland's son, he added, 'She must never know.'

Faro said, 'I think we have Sven's motive for all this at last: traditionally the most compelling reason for murder. If Jack can be persuaded to keep silent on the discovery of the girl's body for the moment, I have a plan. But for it to succeed, it is vital that Sven does not see policemen swarming over Arthur's Seat.'

Jack wasn't keen on the idea but Faro was certain that he was lurking about Edinburgh in cheap lodgings, lying low, awaiting the right moment to strike. Jack had confirmed this by studying the list of ships' passengers sailing from Leith to Kirkwall. Sven Johannson wasn't among them and it was unlikely he would have not given his right name, since he had no reason to be fearful.

There was a time limit. Sven had to appear before the end of the week to claim Emily and the jewel, before she and Magnus returned to Orkney.

They were eager to know how Faro intended to trap Sven. And horrified that he intended using himself as bait.

'You can't do that, Pa,' Rose protested.

He looked at her. 'I can. And I know what I'm doing. It won't be the first time I've trapped a killer.'

She wanted to say: but you were young then. Now you're an old man. Sven is young, strong, less than half your age. but she knew he would never listen. And Imogen could have added, he never did.

The plan was when Sven came back, with some excuse about not going to Orkney, after all, he would have thought of something to convince Emily – he had been thinking about her, wanting her so much, just to be near her – to go back to Yesnaby together.

'You have a gun?' Faro asked Rose. She nodded and he said: 'Keep it at hand, just in case.'

She said: 'You're mad trying something like this.'

'Am I? He wants the jewel. The plan is that I will have it – or so he believes. I'll need Emily's help, if she hasn't changed her mind about him, and Jack's to set the trap.'

Rose groaned. 'Oh, Pa, please, please don't. There must be some other way.'

'Then name it, but be sharp about it.'

'At least take Thane with you.'

'He comes with me. We both like the Radical Road in the early morning. Don't look like that, Rose. It's a perfectly simple plan. Told that I have the jewel he follows me on to

277

the Crags. Remember, he has no idea that we know the truth about him. As far as he is concerned he is going to meet me, and with a fresh pack of lies, get that jewel. What he doesn't realise or remember is that there is only one exit to the park from the Crags, down the hill, and that's where Jack and the police will be waiting to arrest him for the murder of Lindsay Minton. Now, I have to talk to Emily. The success of it all depends on her.'

He was glad to see that she was looking stronger, more resolute. She was his daughter and he believed she could be relied upon to find an inner strength, assuring him that she wanted this man who had tried to drown her son, put behind bars. He didn't tell her that murder was a hanging matter.

'If I am to catch him, your help is crucial. There is a time limit. He believes you are sailing for Kirkwall on Friday, the day after tomorrow. He has to come for you . . .' He paused seeing her wince at the memory, in the death of a dreamt-of future.

'Solomon's Tower is perfect for watching anyone approaching by the road, so when we spot him, you and Imogen and Rose must do your best to keep him occupied and give me time to start off for the Crags. Just act normal. Once you tell him that I have the jewel, he'll set off after me.'

He sounded so confident they gave up trying to dissuade him. A terrifying plan and Rose thought it was insane, that it could never work, and what was finding a killer, solving those mysteries that had beset them in Orkney, compared with throwing away his life?

She begged Imogen to intervene. But Imogen merely shrugged sadly. 'He is Faro. You cannot change that. God knows I've tried.'

The trap was set. All that remained were those endless hours of waiting. In vain it seemed, with a mere twenty-four before Emily and Magnus were booked on the ship sailing for Kirkwall.

Sven knew that but would he come? What if he had changed his mind, thought of a different way to get the jewel? If Faro's plan failed and he had made up his mind to follow them to Orkney, once Jack told the police about the body in the cave, it would be another murder investigation with himself in charge of a hunt for the killer.

As for Faro and Rose, they would be out of it, on their separate ways again, Faro travelling with Imogen, and Rose as a lady investigator, two detectives with their mysteries solved but without that most important conclusion, their personal capture of the killer.

The hours grew short, their tensions increased and it was vital now to take turns watching the road from the upstairs window. At the first sighting, Faro would be out of the door, across the garden and up the hill to the Radical Road.

Reaching the door, Sven would find it bolted, providing more delay for Faro. Emily would make excuses, apologise saying that there had been high winds and it was constantly blowing open, that it needed fixing.

Hearts beating fast, and even better than they had hoped, he appeared on the road early that morning while the children were still abed. Rose and Emily sighed. That was a relief, their presence might have caused complications and Sadie had been sent home for the weekend.

As footsteps approached, Emily was preparing to delay unbolting the door. All seemed right, all going to plan.

Except for the fog. The early-morning fog, a wisp of it drifting down from Arthur's Seat, their unseen enemy no one had taken into account.

Imogen and Rose saw it creeping across to Faro as he covered the distance to Salisbury Crags, while downstairs Emily had opened the door, let Sven in, giving excuses for the delay.

He sat down and was offered tea. The kettle was on the boil and his eyes narrowed when Imogen and Rose appeared. This was not what he had wanted; he had hoped to find Emily on her own. He was biting his lip, his patience fraying.

Ten minutes passed, plenty of time for what they hoped would pass as normal conversation, for Faro to be on the Crags before Imogen and Rose excused themselves to resume their packing upstairs, leaving Emily alone with him.

The door had hardly closed when with a few preliminary questions about her travel arrangements, he asked if she had managed to get the jewel valued.

Playing for time, her heart beating wildly, Emily pretended not to hear. He came round the table, stood over her and said: 'I hope you have kept it safe.'

'Oh yes.'

'Where is it now? Locked away upstairs, still?'

'Oh no, it's with my father.'

'Your father!'

'Yes. I haven't had a chance to do anything about it, too busy. So Pa said he would take it into some reputable jeweller to be valued before I go.'

'And where is your father now?' he demanded sharply.

'Oh, he's on his way into Edinburgh with it. Seeing the jewellers first thing. Left just before you arrived. You just missed him.'

There was no sentiment now, no pretence of affection. He looked at her coldly. 'Which way did he go?'

'By the Radical Road. He prefers taking that way, it's a shortcut.'

He was no longer listening. The door was open and he had gone, swallowed by what was now the fog's white shroud. Rose and Imogen ran downstairs. Emily was trembling, clutching the table. They regarded her anxiously: 'Did he hurt you?'

'No, no. This is just reaction. I was so scared that he would guess.'

Rose felt rather sick. 'Now everything depends on Pa. Damn that fog – we never bargained for that. If I was a Catholic I'd say a prayer and get out my rosary.'

Imogen said: 'I'm one, Rose. And I know all the words.'

Faro was shivering, in what was now a fine drizzle. Seated on a boulder, he had lit a pipe to calm his nerves while he waited, unable to see through the mist. At last, echoing footsteps as a tall figure stumbled forward.

Sven was out of breath, he had been running fast to catch up. Faro stood up, shouted a greeting and, preparing to keep up the pretence of a chance meeting as long as possible, he started walking briskly. But Sven was having none of that, and seized his arm.

'I am not here for a pleasant stroll, Mr Faro.' He held out his hand. 'I am here for the jewel. Emily wants it back. I am to take it back to her. She has changed her mind.'

'Is that so? Well, I have changed mine. And I haven't got the jewel. I forgot to pick it up.' Sven glared at him angrily, thwarted, fists clenched menacingly.

Faro smiled. 'Tell me, where is Alice?'

'Alice? I have no idea. Emily must have told you, she left me.'

'I think it is the other way round, that you left her.'

Sven paused. 'I don't understand.'

'Oh, I think you do. You left her for dead, in that cave on Arthur's Seat.'

Sven froze. Was Alice still alive? If so, then she had probably revealed all. He panicked and Faro saw it in his face. Now was the time to get him moving towards those steps and the waiting police.

But he didn't. Not without the jewel, and as far as he knew, Faro had it and was lying. He leapt at him and in one strong movement threw him to the ground. Thane saw it happening. His menacing growl was the last thing Faro heard, as Sven's fist thundered into him and he rolled to the edge of the cliff, face down, frantically clinging on to thin air.

He yelled and Sven hit him again. As the world turned black and slipped away, his last thought: so this is what it is to die.

* * *

Rose heard that last cry echoing faintly through the shroud of mist. As soon as Sven started off, she had said: 'I'm going after them.'

They tried to hold her back, implored her not to go, said it was madness, but she wouldn't listen: 'We are both mad, Pa and me, it runs in the family.'

And without another word she dashed out. Sven could run fast, but she could cover the distance on the road, reach the Crags before him on her bicycle. With no idea what she might do, except be at Faro's side with her derringer, she pedalled downhill fast through the mist and across to the Radical Road, and when it became too steep, too uneven, she threw it aside. There were noises ahead and she began to run, stumbling through the mist that enveloped her. Like a shroud of death, she thought grimly, for that was when she heard the faint cry.

On she ran, gun in hand. But there was no one ahead of her. Only silence. Until a faint corner of the mist lifted to let her see what she most dreaded. Twenty feet away, on the steep edge of the cliff, a figure lay, spreadeagled, still and unmoving.

She screamed: 'Pa!'

Thane was sitting beside him and it touched a memory, one of those popular sentimental paintings of a sick – or dead – child, watched over by the faithful dog.

Reaching them, Thane gazed up at her as she dropped on her knees beside her father. He was so still, so white, touching his face she knew this was how dead people looked.

Rapid footsteps approaching. Sven – and she took the

gun from her pocket, levelled it. He'd pay for this. She was a good shot and it wouldn't be the first time she had put a bullet through the heart of an evil man.

'Rose!' Through the mist, Jack and a uniformed policeman.

'He's dead,' she whispered, her eyes streaming.

Jack pushed her aside, knelt down, turned him over gently and took the pulse in his neck.

Looking up at her, he sighed. 'Not dead, Rose, not yet. And for God's sake put that gun away before you kill someone.'

A slight movement, a mere flicker as Faro's eyes opened. Bewildered, he saw Rose and Jack. Why was he still alive? He remembered fighting with Sven and being knocked out. He should be lying on the road far below, dead, his neck broken.

He tried to sit up, Jack's arm supporting him. 'Take it easy. God, you look done in. Are you hurt?' He shook his head. 'Damned near the edge, another few inches – tried to push you over, did he? You were great, you know, I never believed this mad plan would work.'

'Did you get him?' Faro asked weakly.

Jack grinned. 'Gave himself up, you might say. Came running down where we were waiting, yelling and looking over his shoulder as if the hounds of hell were at his heels.' Pausing, he gazed along the deserted cliff path. The mist had risen. He shook his head. 'Something had scared the wits out of him.'

They began slowly heading towards the Tower, Rose pushing her bicycle and Thane trotting along at her side, with Faro between Jack and the policeman, wondering if he would ever make it that far. Where Sven had hit him, his head was throbbing, bruised as if he'd done a few rounds in the boxing ring of his younger days. His legs felt like straw, and he was suddenly very, very tired. He covered the last hundred yards in a daze.

When the door opened he fell into the arms waiting for him, and insisting that he was unhurt, was settled down with a very large whisky – nobody had the temerity to offer tea.

Later they wanted to know what happened. And he found he couldn't remember apart from Sven striking him. Falling, falling, thinking so this was what dying was about, then. It was all a blank, like the fog that had enshrouded him.

'No damage done,' he assured them.

'Quite amazing, isn't it?' they exclaimed.

'Except for that huge tear across the back of your jacket,' Imogen said ruefully. 'That's done for. You'll never wear that again. You were needing a new one, anyway.'

A pity, it was his favourite Harris tweed and he hated buying new clothes. Later, chiding Rose for having followed him that day, she said: 'I wasn't much help after all, was I? Didn't he protect you?' she added with a reproachful glance at Thane, who turned his head, looked at Faro with what seemed the nearest equivalent to a human wink.

And so it was over. The holiday ended as Rose and Jack waved them goodbye with promises to the two children that they would meet again soon. Emily had been pleased that John Randall would be waiting for them at Kirkwall and his message touched all their minds with a single unspoken thought: 'Wouldn't it be nice?'

Faro and Imogen needed little persuasion to stay until Imogen's talk at York, and on one of their walks she said solemnly, 'I said a prayer for you, Faro, and I gave a promise that if you survived, I would marry you. That's if you still want me.' His answer needed no words as he took her in his arms.

The past was something to push to the back of one's mind, forget and get back to normal. He still wondered about that huge tear across the back of his tweed jacket. As if a mighty crane had hauled him bodily back on to the cliff.

Rose might have an answer, once he had worked it out logically for himself.